HELL

The Possession and Exorcism of Cassie Stevens

TOM LEWIS

Tom Lewis

ISBN: 978-1-72-684594-6

FORWARD

When we speak of demons, it's with regard to incorporeal entities known as spirits. Spirits are unique in that, while they are able to interact with matter, as is often witnessed in hauntings and poltergeist activity, spirits do not consist of matter, nor are they bound by physical laws that regulate matter.

A demon, or evil spirit, if you will, is a particular subspecies of spirit that is forever locked in a perpetual state of hatred and rage – a hatred of life; a hatred of humanity; a hatred of creation; a hatred of beauty – in a sense, they bear a hatred of all things that make existence pleasurable. Hatred, you might say, is the essence of the demon.

No one can list with any degree of certainty the precise sequence of events that lead a particular individual to become the target of a demonic attack. Yet in the clarity of hindsight, we're often able to isolate factors that certainly contributed to such a state. Or, more precisely, factors that opened a person to vulnerability for such an attack. The case of Cassie Stevens presents us with one such example.

When considering the tragic events that occurred at the garment mill on the night of November 21, when viewed in the clarity of hindsight, their inevitability seems certain. And of Cassie Stevens' presence at the site of those events being a contributing factor to the fire that claimed thirty-six lives, there remains little doubt among Church officials. The speed, persistence, and tenacity of that fire, despite the heavy rainfall that night, support a finding of its supernatural origin.

While opinions differed as to the nature of Cassie's affliction, the consent among Church and civil authorities was unanimous that the phenomena first began to manifest itself on October 31.

That was the night Cassie Stevens died.

And, as was the conclusion of the Ecclesiastical inquiry into the matter, that was also the night something followed her back from the other side of death.

That something was a demon.

— From "Into the Periphery" by Rev. Sean McCready. Reprinted with permission.

CHAPTER ONE
Abandon All Hope

"Through me the way to the suffering city;
Through me the way into eternal pain;
Through me the way among the people lost...

Abandon All Hope, Ye Who Enter Here."

— *Inferno* by Dante

****

October 31

A fierce storm raged across the sky. Lightning flashed in blinding streaks and thunder echoed through the hills. It was the night of All Hallows Eve — the night that once celebrated death — and a lone car sped down a lonely forest road beneath its dark shawl. The storm that swept in that night wasn't like most storms to rattle the New England Coast. This storm brought something grim and ominous, and it would soon descend on the four teens in that car.

Sixteen year old Cassie Stevens watched from the backseat as rain pelted the windshield in thick splatters. It could almost be hypnotic, she thought, the way the wipers slapped away the water. Or even calming...

That is, it could be calming for anyone else...

But it couldn't be for Cassie. She hadn't experienced calm in three months.

Not since the night *It* entered her.

Her friend Trish sat beside her in the backseat and upfront was Silvia in the passenger seat. Seth was driving, like he usually did when they hit the raves. They were all her age.

Seth was a special breed of asshole, who raged for the pure sake of rage. Like the girls, his hair was dyed black as his soul. But while the girls dressed more goth, his style was punk, with long black jackets, torn jeans, worn out concert shirts, and boots.

The rave had been at the usual spot — an abandoned garment mill twenty miles outside their small coastal town of Capetown, Maine. They had arrived shortly after sundown and were hammered and stoned within the first half hour. That was something Seth was good for — he always had pills.

He also knew the rites — the dark ones they practiced on those moonless nights amongst the graves.

"Can you turn it down?" Cassie shouted over the punk rock music that pounded from the stereo. It had been blasting the entire drive and her head was throbbing.

Seth shot her a smirk in the rearview mirror, then cranked it up. Cassie glared for a moment, then settled back in her seat. She glanced out the window to her right. Dark silhouettes of trees swept past, masked by thick splatters of rain. She breathed on the window to fog it up, then wrote "Seth needs to die" with her finger.

This wasn't Cassie's thought, but she still felt it in her mind. Like she had so many other thoughts over the past three months.

"Hey," Seth hollered back. "Can one of you beer me?"

"Turn that shit down first," Trish hollered back.

"Beer me, or we crash." And like an asshole, he took both hands off the steering wheel.

Instantly the car lurched to the right, splashing into mud on the soft shoulder. Seth grabbed the wheel and corrected back onto the road...

And headlights were coming right at them.

The impact came within seconds. There was the jarring crunch as metal crushed in on itself; the feeling of time slowing; of being thrown and battered; of slamming into windows and doors; of metal bending and glass shattering...

And then they were still. The car lay on its side in silence. There was no more music or engine sounds, only the patter of rain.

Cassie had faded impressions of light and darkness.

Like flickering images of a slide show, these impressions assaulted her — the rain pouring in through the shattered windows, peppering her face with wet pellets. The feeling of being trapped and unable to move. Unable to speak or cry for help. Unable to breathe...

She had a vague awareness that she was dying. Out here in the rain. On this night. In this car. This was how she would die.

This is how her mom would find her...

A sudden lucidity struck her, and it was the first she had felt in months. The voices and thoughts that had filled her mind were gone, and her mind was free. She was free to feel, and think, and just be. And an anguished knot curled in her stomach over things she had done the past three months. Of the way she had gone off on her mom earlier that night. She would never have a chance to apologize. All she could do was whisper it softly in her mind.

I'm sorry, Mom. I'm so, so sorry...

Then it all stopped — the remorse and reflections — all of it replaced with a sudden, terrifying realization:

Something was in the car with them.

From the corner of her eye, she had glimpsed a dark shape that appeared like a shadow. It had vanished as she turned in its direction, but it wasn't gone. She felt its presence remain — something unseen, and unheard, yet unmistakably felt. Like a whisper from the darkness of an empty room, or the putrid wretchedness of a bloated corpse, its presence filled the cramped space with a sickening aura. And that aura was of unmitigated hatred and horror.

It was watching her.

She had feared this moment would come. Ever since that night of the Harvest Moon, when they had gathered beneath its ghostly pall on that remote estate, she had known a reckoning would come. And now it had. She was dying, and this thing had come to exact its terrible toll. And no words could describe her terror at that realization.

She was lost, and death would soon open its gates to an eternity of horror.

They were always watching, she realized — every thought and deed; those things she thought were known only to herself — nothing had been hidden. They had been there in her darkest moments, lurking unseen in shadowed corners of infinite torment and despair. Always there. Always watching. And always waiting.

We are Legion; for we are many.

And now, as she sank into that abyss of endless darkness, *It watched.*

And waited.

CHAPTER TWO
Cassie

The Cassie Stevens who died on that bitter Halloween night was almost unrecognizable from the shy young girl of just a few years earlier.

Cassie was only six when her family moved to the quiet seaport town of Capetown, Maine. Her father, Rick, had just been hired to teach physical education at St. Matthew's High School, so they left the dry heat of Arizona for the weathered shores of New England.

Capetown was quintessential New England with its Colonial-style wood-paneled houses and shops, and streets lined with elms. It was built on a peninsula that faced the mainland on its west side across a narrow sound. To its north were thickly wooded hills, and on its southern edge was the tip of the peninsula, where its historic lighthouse stood proudly against the rugged shore.

Cassie was smaller than most girls her age and had

grown self-conscious about it from years of teasing. Her hair was soft and sandy colored like her mom's, and she usually kept it up in a baseball cap. Her blue eyes and freckled nose were from her dad.

She had three addictions growing up — video games, comics, and writing. And writing probably topped the others. She ate it up and loved trying to imitate the styles of her favorite authors. And while writing short stories was fun, what she really liked writing was poetry.

Rick coached Pee Wee league baseball at a town park during the summers, and Cassie often tagged along to work on her poems in the bleachers. Her mom, Alison, rarely attended the games and spent the time with other school moms or working on the ceramics business she had started from home. The result was Cassie growing up with a closer bond to her dad.

After the games, her dad would take the team out for pizza at a parlor near the wharf, and it gave Cassie a chance to get to know the boys as friends. They often challenged her to the video games that lined the parlor's back wall, and she usually kicked their butts. But it was all in fun. She was coach's daughter, so they looked out for her.

It would make their shun of her a few years later that much more painful.

****

It was during the summer after third grade that Cassie met the boy who would impact so much of her life. She was in the bleachers that sunny afternoon when she spotted a new boy playing shortstop. He was her age, had blond hair, and looked like a "surfer boy," as she later described him to a friend. He was Justin Mahoney.

After the game, Rick walked Justin and his dad over to meet Cassie. "Nice to meet you," his dad said with a smile as they shook hands. But Cassie's attention was on Justin's green eyes. They gave her butterflies.

"Hey," Justin said with a friendly nod.

"Hi," she said back. Or at least she hoped she said something and didn't just stare like an idiot.

Justin's family had moved to town less than a month earlier, and Rick asked if she would mind showing Justin around.

"Okay." She noticed her palms were sweating.

When she got home that night after the postgame pizza, she ran upstairs and took a long appraisal of herself in her mirror. She thought she looked cute. Maybe a little tomboyish with the baseball cap. She tossed it on her bed. Now what to do with her hair that fell past her shoulders?

"Does my hair look okay?" she asked her parents in the living room a few minutes later. It was down at the moment.

"Sure, honey. Your hair looks fine," Alison said.

"What if I got bangs?" Cassie asked, motioning with her fingers just above her brow line.

"There's nothing wrong with your hair the way it is," Alison said.

Cassie frowned. She was hoping to hear that it looked good. She turned to her dad, who had been watching from the couch beside her mom.

"Dad?"

He smiled. "I think your hair looks pretty just the way it is."

That was the answer she was looking for. She grabbed him in a hug, then raced back upstairs. Once she was gone, Alison turned to Rick.

"What on earth was that about?"

Rick just smiled. "I think she has her first crush."

Rick was right, although Cassie would never admit it. She woke up early the next morning and removed the front basket from her bike and everything else on it that looked dumb. Then she biked over to Justin's, and they pedaled off through town.

Their first stop was the pizza parlor near the wharf. Justin was a game geek too, so they played several rounds of video games before heading off.

Next came a sandwich shop, where they bought some sodas, then pedaled off down Main Street. They passed the old Mayflower Theater, a book store, a record store, and a collection of cafes and coffee houses. They finally reached the lighthouse on the bluff at the tip of the peninsula, and she led him down a trail to the tide pools on the rocky shore below it.

On their way back, they stopped by the pet shop, where Cassie showed him the German Shepard pup she was getting. It was part of a deal she made with her parents if she aced her classes. Which she did.

Justin came with Cassie and Rick when they picked up the pup later that week. She'd already named him

Rex. They took him back to her house, where Alison finally got to meet Justin.

Rick grilled hamburgers out back while Cassie gave Justin a tour of her house. It was a two-story Colonial house at the end of a cul-de-sac. There were three bedrooms upstairs and a living room, dining room, kitchen, and laundry room downstairs. Cassie's room overlooked their large backyard, which Rex was already exploring. A dense forest bordered the yard, and Cassie often spent afternoons exploring its trails.

Over the coming years, Cassie and Justin hung out a lot. A favorite ritual was dollar movie nights at the Mayflower Theater. Mayflower was an old bijou along Main Street. It had a single screen that often showed classics (John Wayne was Justin's favorite). It lacked the frills of the multiplex across town, but you couldn't beat dollar movie nights.

Another ritual was going to the comic book store each month when the new comics came out and taking them down to the bluff near the lighthouse to read.

There were also bike rides, and exploring, and hiking, and video games, and sneaking into the old lighthouse...

Cassie and Justin became close friends by the time they started high school.

And Cassie often wondered what it would be like to kiss him.

But the winds of change were already blowing into her young life, and she would soon lose that opportunity. Along with something much more tragic.

CHAPTER THREE
The "After"

With the start of high school came new faces, and one of those was Molly Daniels.

Molly was every freshman girl's worst nightmare. Already, at fourteen, Molly was captain of the freshman cheer squad, had legs that went on for days, and, as far as Cassie could tell, had been born with breasts.

Justin was quarterback for the freshman football team and had caught the attention of most of the freshman girls. One of them was Molly. She approached him at a party after one of the games, and the two were dating a week after that. They made that perfect homecoming couple.

Cassie was crushed when she found out. She stared at the short freckled girl in the mirror that night, and wondered why God couldn't have made her tall and blonde and hot like Molly. In this new world of changing hormones, comics and dollar nights just couldn't compete with tight sweaters and short skirts.

She still saw Justin around school after that, and things were always friendly as they said "hi" to each other in the hallway, but the closeness was gone. And she didn't really have anything to fill that void.

March 7th of that year would bring the next change in her life; and while losing her closeness with Justin was crushing, this next change was catastrophic. It would forever divide her life into two periods — the period before that day, which she called the "before"; and the period after that day, which she called the "after".

Cassie was in Mrs. Mitten's algebra class that morning, trying her best to pay attention and just stay awake. Mrs. Mitten had a talent for making an already confusing subject even more confusing. Luckily, Cassie had her dad to help her with her homework.

There was a knock at the classroom door, and the assistant principal entered. She strolled over to Mrs. Mitten, and the two spoke briefly. Mrs. Mitten glanced at Cassie several times while they spoke and finally motioned her over.

"Cassie, can you come here. Bring your books with you."

Cassie loaded her books in her backpack and approached the teacher. She couldn't think of anything she'd done wrong, so whatever this was, it had to be a mistake.

"Cassie. Your mom's here," Mrs. Mitten said

quietly so the other students couldn't hear. "Vicky will take you to see her."

Cassie followed Vicky to the school's office, where her mom sat waiting outside the door. She didn't look mad, but she did look worried. Or was it scared?

"Mom?"

Vicky gave Alison a reassuring nod. "Everything's going to be okay, Alison." She then gave Cassie's shoulder a squeeze before heading inside the office.

Cassie looked at her mom. "What's going on?"

"Your father had a heart attack," Alison said as they pulled out of the school's parking lot.

For the longest moment, Cassie could only stare. She had heard the words, and knew their meaning, but her brain refused to connect them together.

Heart attack. Dad.

"He's going to be okay, right?" she finally asked, once her brain was again able to process thoughts.

"I hope so, sweetie," Alison said and gave Cassie's hand a comforting squeeze. "I hope so."

She's scared, Cassie thought. She could see it in her eyes. Cassie choked down a lump in her throat. Her mom didn't believe there was any hope. And a sudden numbness swallowed her up.

Her dad was going to die.

****

Rick Stevens never awoke from his coma. Cassie and her mom were at his bedside when he passed, and no gentle words could assuage Cassie's heartache as she held his hand in a final goodbye. If there was a level of anguish beyond devastated, that's where Cassie's heart was. There would be no more weekends at the park watching him coach baseball, or summer vacations, or trips to see Grandma, or picnics at the bluff. Even those evenings they had spent doing her homework — when she had grumbled, and complained, and thrown so many tantrums — she found herself longing for just one more.

But it would never happen. Death had seen to that. Death had taken him from her.

It was Cassie's first experience with death, and she hated it. She wanted to spit in its ugly face and tell it to fuck off. How could anything have so much power? In the blink of its cold, uncaring eye, it had wiped away a life.

It had wiped away her dad's life.

Rick was laid to rest a week later at the Faulkner Cemetery. Faulkner was the county's oldest cemetery, named after an early family of settlers in the region. It was built on the southern slope of Pioneer Hill, a lush forested hill overlooking the town and peninsula. A single narrow road, in desperate need of repair, ran along its southern border before winding down to the town. From there, on a clear day, you could see across the treetops to the lighthouse on the far side of town.

It was quiet, and peaceful, and gave her dad a nice view.

Over the coming months, Cassie spent many afternoons and evenings at her father's grave, drawing inspiration for her poems from the haunting surroundings. A deep melancholy had fallen over her, and this was increasingly reflected in the often morose and brooding tone of her poetry. Where they had once sang the happy themes of springtime, they now mourned the dark winter nights of pain and loss.

It was on one such night, as Cassie sat alone staring into the starlit sky, that she met the trio of goth teens who would shape the next stage of her life.

CHAPTER FOUR
Ye Shall Be as Gods

"...in the day ye eat thereof,
then your eyes shall be opened,
and ye shall be as gods..."

— *Genesis* 3:16

****

Cassie sat at her dad's grave that night, as she had on so many nights since his death, staring off into the infinity of space. She had thought she was alone, but she soon heard voices approaching. She ducked behind his gravestone and watched as three teens walked past on their way to a nearby grave.

There were two girls and one boy, all about Cassie's age, and even from this distance, she could see the dark theme in their appearance. The boy wore a concert shirt, dark jeans, and a long black jacket. The girls wore black skirts, and all three had black dyed hair.

But it wasn't only their appearances that were dark; it was the way in which they blended with these haunted surroundings. They were as at home among the dead, as athletes were on a game field. This was their sanctum.

Soon, the sweet smell of pot drifted to Cassie. She had never tried it but knew the smell from beneath the school bleachers where the stoners hung out.

As they passed around the joint, Cassie saw the taller girl arranging sticks on the ground between them. She then placed candles in a circle around the sticks and lit the candles.

"You know, if you're gonna sit there and watch us, you might as well come out." It was the boy who said this, and Cassie's stomach dropped. She'd been spotted. All three goths looked her way.

"You're not fooling anyone," said the tall girl, clearly annoyed at the intrusion. "You just look like an idiot."

Cassie rose and stepped out from behind the gravestone. She considered running for a moment, but then the shorter girl spoke.

"It's okay. We won't bite," she said, "unless you're into that kind of thing." She shot Cassie a grin.

"So you coming, or going?" the boy asked.

Cassie decided to come, trying her best not to appear as nervous as she felt.

"What's your name?" the shorter girl asked as Cassie walked up.

"Cassie."

"Here. Sit by me," she said, patting the grass beside her. "I'm Silvia. That's Trish, and that's Seth."

Cassie sat down and nodded shyly to each of them. "Hey."

"So I'm guessing that grave over there belongs to someone close," Seth said with a nod toward the grave she had just come from. "Was it daddy?"

"Yeah."

"And I'll bet that's got you all bitter and pissed off. Like, 'How could death take him from me? Blah, blah, blah.' Am I right?"

Cassie hesitated a moment, then nodded. "Yeah. Pretty much."

It was then that his eyes locked onto hers and they held on like a vice. Something dark and knowing lived behind those eyes — something that terrified and yet intrigued with a strange thrall. He had answers to the questions that plagued her.

"How would you like to find out," he said.

****

From the moment she first met the goths, Cassie felt a strange unease stir within her like a warning. She could see they were dark, and that alone wouldn't have raised concerns, but it was their degree of darkness and fixation with death that roused those initial fears. Yet it was their knowledge of death that also lured her to them. She could tell they had answers to the questions that plagued her: What was death, and what came after it? What happened at the moment of death? What had her dad seen as death tore him into its terrible clutch?

Was death something to fear?

Cassie sensed she was stepping down a dangerous path, but she convinced herself that she was only going to peek into their mysterious new world and could always escape unscathed back into the safety of her old world at any time.

It was a lie.

At her deepest core, she always knew she was closing a door behind her and saying goodbye to her world of bright sunshine and colors, and entering a cold world of mist and night. But the sunshine held no answers for her, and the night did. And so she went.

Cassie's induction into this new world was slow, but progressive. One by one, new canons were learned, and old moral tenets excised. And the whole time, Cassie continued to reassure herself that there was nothing to fear; she was simply gaining knowledge. And knowledge had to be good.

Over the coming months, the changes came in incremental steps, with each step built upon the previous one so seamlessly and effortlessly that Cassie barely noticed the changes as they occurred. But those around her noticed.

By this time Cassie was a sophomore and had distanced herself from most of her old friends. Seth, Trish, and Silvia attended a public school across town (when they felt like attending), so Cassie spent most of her time at school alone or in the library reading a list of books Seth had suggested. She had dyed her hair black, despite her mom's protests, and her clothing had taken a darker tone as well.

Alison blamed herself for the problems Cassie seemed to be having. Without Rick's income, Alison was forced to take a job bartending at a pub down by the wharf. She worked long hours till late in the night, so she had almost no time to spend with Cassie. But by that point it wouldn't have made a difference. The changes had already burrowed deep roots within Cassie.

What Alison and Cassie's classmates saw were only the exterior surface-level changes. The dark hair and clothing, the truancy and drugs. What they had no way of knowing were the profound interior changes that had occurred. In the year since Rick's death, Cassie's life had become a danse macabre with darkness. And *Death*.

Death came to have a peculiar allure to Cassie that she was only now discovering. It wasn't something to fear, but rather to be explored. It promised answers to timeless secrets, and paths to reach beyond its walls. *I am only secret*, she once felt it whisper to her on a dark moonless night as they lay amongst the ancient graves in the older portion of the cemetery. *Fear me not, for I am not threat.*

The goths also introduced Cassie to drugs at their gatherings, as a way to expand her mind, "to see the world unfiltered," as they described it. There was so much to explore beyond the physical world and its limitations. Theirs would be the secrets of eternity.

Over the remainder of her sophomore year, Cassie and the goths would gather together at the cemetery late at night and recite chants from ancient occult texts Seth had found. Afterward, as dawn approached, Cassie would stagger home in a drunken daze, barely slipping inside before her mom awakened. Her grades and attendance had taken a sharp downturn, but that no longer mattered to Cassie — what she was learning out there amongst the graves was so much more important. It was eternal.

Cassie, Trish, and Silvia gravitated toward Seth as the unofficial leader of their little clan. Despite being an asshole at times, he possessed the easy charisma of a cult leader, and there was a magnetism to him that Cassie couldn't deny. And while Silvia and Trish were steeped in occult lore, their knowledge paled in comparison to Seth's. Seth was not only versed in modern occult practices, but he also knew the dark rites that had been practiced by the ancients who had once gathered on moonless nights when the veil between the worlds of the living and the dead was at its thinnest, to offer dark sacrifices to their grim gods. It was on nights such as these that Cassie and her friends gathered at the cemetery to conduct séances to reach beyond that veil.

Death was merely another doorway to be explored in Cassie's new world.

And on several nights during the summer preceding her junior year, Cassie sensed that doorway opening. But it would be on the night of the Harvest Moon that Cassie's final baptism into darkness would occur.

That was the night of the Black Mass.

CHAPTER FIVE
The Black Mass

The full Harvest Moon hung like an enormous orange light in the night sky, casting its eerie pall over the fields that sped past the car window.

Cassie and her goth friends had been driving for an hour, and according to the GPS on Trish's cell phone, they had another twenty minutes to go.

Seth had been secretive about their destination all night and didn't reveal it till they were well outside of Capetown. They would be attending a Black Mass being celebrated by a satanic coven in Oakwood County. And Seth was on a high.

Seth had heard rumors of it a month earlier and had traced every lead he knew to score them invites. He finally got them from a friend who played bass for a black metal band. This Black Mass would be the real deal, his friend assured him. It was the seventeenth century French version that had been a coveted secret among the French elite before its ban in the latter half of that century. And it certainly wasn't like the pussy bullshit that had sprung up in this country after the millennium — no, this shit was real, and not simply an homage to some metaphoric symbol of rebellion.

His friend also warned him that it was invite only, at a secret remote location, and anyone disclosing it might not live long enough to regret it.

These people had ways of finding out.

"Prepare to be freaked the fuck out," was how Seth had teased the night ahead to the girls as they drove off. And when the reveal came, they were. Cassie in particular.

Her first reaction was unease, as a small alarm prickled in her mind. But she shook it off. This night was to be about knowledge and expanding her mind to these hidden secrets. How could that be dangerous? And if things got too scary, she could always bail.

It was the same lie she had repeated to herself more times than she could remember.

Only secret. Not threat.

Silvia and Trish were down for it and didn't experience the unease Cassie felt. For Trish, it was a chance to expand her own mystic skills on a foundation of wisdom passed down over the centuries. For Silvia, it was more out of curiosity. She had heard talk of the Black Mass among her friends in the goth community, and it had piqued her interest.

Seth's motive was twofold — first was the purity of the rite itself. This was the real deal, unfiltered and uncensored. But a close second was the rush. He got off on shock and rebellion, and what better way to tell the world to fuck off than paying homage to Satan.

And so they went, into the night, and into the tragic chain of events that eventually led to Cassie's death.

"Turn left up here," Trish said, reading from the GPS on her cell phone. They were so far away from any cities or houses that all they saw were rolling hills and trees.

Seth turned off the gravel road they had been on for the past twenty minutes and onto a paved drive. They drove a short ways before they ran into a gate. Two large men in suits stood there. One of them approached the car, and Seth rolled down his window.

"This is private property," the man said, looking in the window at the four kids. "You're going to need to leave."

"*In nomine dei nostri,*" Seth gave as the password his buddy had told him to say.

"Let me see your invitations," said the man, and the hard look in his expression never changed.

Seth handed him the four engraved invitations and watched as he examined them. He handed them back and nodded to the other man to open the gate. "Stay on the drive, and follow it to the end," he instructed them.

The drive wound through an orchard of citrus trees and crossed a narrow bridge before opening into a clearing surrounding the main house. The road ended there.

The house was a large Tudor, built of gray stone with ivy curling up its sides, and in the orange glow of moonlight, it couldn't have looked more menacing.

Next to it was a large barn built of dark oak wood with a gravel lot out front. It was here that everyone was parking.

They parked the car and walked over to the barn. Two more men stood outside the door checking everyone's invitation and ID before they were allowed to enter.

Once inside, the barn was dark and lit only by black candles along the walls. They were handed dark, hooded robes and told to wear them over their clothes. They quickly slipped into the robes, then joined the other congregants toward the back of the barn. They were gathered in a half circle around a marble altar. The altar was about three feet tall, and draped in a burgundy-colored cloth with an inverted cross embroidered into it. Black candles stood at either end. And barely visible in the flickering candlelight was a goat's head mounted to the back wall behind the altar.

The room was mostly silent while everyone waited for the ceremony to begin. Cassie snuck glances at the other congregants. There were about forty of them, all in their hooded robes with their heads bowed in silent reverence.

The ceremony began promptly at the stroke of midnight. A door in the back opened, and a tall man with long black hair and priestly vestments strode over to the altar. He genuflected before the altar, kissed it, then positioned himself behind it to face the congregants.

A girl in a dark robe approached the altar. She removed her robe and let it slide to the floor from her naked body. The priest took her hand and helped her onto the altar, where she lay down on her back. He placed a silver chalice on her bare stomach and then, turning to the congregants, used his left hand to make a reversed *sign of the cross*, touching first his abdomen, then his forehead, then his right shoulder, and finally his left, all the while reciting the Latin invocation:

"In nomine magni dei nostri Satanas, introibo ad altare Domini Inferi."

"*Ave, Satanas*," came the response from the congregants, and Cassie made an effort to follow their lead. As she did, she felt that small alarm stir in her mind. She dismissed it again, but this time it left her feeling queasy.

With the invocation finished, the ceremony commenced. A small lamb was led over to the altar on a leash. Taking a serrated knife, the priest sliced across the lamb's throat. Cassie gasped in horror but somehow managed to keep it quiet. Nobody had warned her that animals would be killed, and nothing could have prepared her for that sight.

Silvia stood beside Cassie on her right. She sensed Cassie's revulsion and gave her hand a gentle squeeze to calm her. The lamb's sacrifice was to serve a higher purpose.

Turning back to the altar, Cassie saw the priest was

now filling his chalice with blood that gushed from the lamb's throat. When he was finished, he resumed his place behind the altar, while the lamb was left to die off to the side.

The priest then pricked his finger with the knife and squeezed it until several drops of blood dripped into the chalice. He then dipped his finger into the chalice and used the lamb's blood, mixed with his own, to trace symbols across the girl's bare breasts and abdomen.

When he was finished, he proceeded over to the girl's legs and spread them open. He pulled aside his vestments, revealing his naked body beneath it, and thrust himself into her.

A murmured chant arose among the congregants, and with each thrust of the priest's pelvis, the same Latin phrase was repeated over and over. Cassie listened to the words but was only able to pick out a few. The ones she caught were "*Ave*" and "*Satana.*" This continued, with the chants repeated in rhythmic timing to the copulation, until the priest and the girl reached their climax. Then a hush fell over the congregation.

The priest took the chalice and pressed it between the girl's legs, allowing her vaginal excretions to drain into it. He then resumed his position behind the altar and placed the chalice on the girl's abdomen.

One of the congregants carried to the altar a gold plate with a round white wafer of bread on it. Cassie recognized this as a Communion Host from the

Catholic Mass. It was something she had been taught was the manifestation of Christ's Body, under the appearance of bread.

This was wrong. Even though she no longer held to her Catholic beliefs, there was something insidious in profaning that wafer. And as she watched the priest dip the Host into the chalice, that silent alarm sounded again in her mind. It was only with difficulty that she was able to silence it this time.

The priest raised the desecrated Host above his head in a mock benediction, and the congregation murmured a response in Latin. Cassie was only able to pick out two words. "Versus Christus."

The priest lowered the desecrated Host and ate it. A congregant joined the priest at the altar, and the priest handed him the chalice. The congregant sipped from the chalice, then walked over to the front row of the congregation and handed the chalice to the person on the far right. That man sipped from it, then handed it to the congregant beside him.

As Cassie watched the chalice being passed from one congregant to the next, that alarm sounded for the fourth and final time, and a queasy feeling settled in her stomach. She felt that she was being asked to consent to something but was unclear what it was. When she made a feeble effort to resist it, it came back more forcefully.

The chalice finally made its way to her, and she now had to make a choice. She could give in to whatever consent was being demanded of her, or she could refuse...

And everybody would know.

She looked around at all those hooded figures. They had to know she was hesitating.

But why was she hesitating? She didn't have an answer for that.

Only secret. Not threat, her thoughts reminded her.

And with her eyes closed, she raised the chalice to her lips and consented to that demand.

The contents of the chalice were gruesome and bitter, and she forced herself to keep from gagging as it entered her mouth, and seeped down her throat.

From that moment on, her memories of the night were hazy, and her only clear memory was of a sudden onslaught of voices that whispered in her mind.

You belong...

Serve him...

All hail... his...

You belong...

His...

All hail... his... Satana...

Hail... Satana...

****

It was early morning by the time Cassie crawled in through her bedroom window and crashed down on her bed. She felt sick to the point of nausea in every way possible — physically, emotionally, and spiritually. It had been a mistake. The whole night had been a mistake. She had consented to something that the deepest, most honest part of her knew was abject evil, and there would be dire consequences to pay.

She leaned over the edge of her bed and vomited across the floor.

What she didn't know at the time, and wouldn't fully realize until she lay dying several months later, was the enormity of the terrifying and pervasive forces she allowed entry into herself that night.

CHAPTER SIX
The "Other"

Cassie awoke the morning after the Black Mass with a fever. She didn't go out at all that day, or the next day, which was Sunday, and it wasn't until Monday that she finally pried herself from her bedroom.

By then, the deep changes within her had already begun.

As she rode the bus to school that day, she noticed a change in the way things appeared. It was subtle, but appreciable, and the best way she could describe it was that things had lost their vibrancy. Where only days before there had been life and vibrancy in the world around her, things now appeared as if seen through a hazy net. Objects still appeared in detail, but they were dull and lifeless, like ashen drawings in a book. And maybe that was the best way she could describe it — *things felt dead.*

This change came to her hearing as well. As she

roamed the hallways at school, sounds came across as flat, with no distinction in their tone or resonance. The sound of a bird or automobile carried no difference in its qualities from spoken words, and music came across as merely a series of beats, without the emotional effect a pleasant melody had once carried.

The world had lost its *flavors*, is how she would later characterize it.

And then there was the déjà vu.

Over the coming weeks, Cassie experienced increasingly frequent occurrences of déjà vu. It might be something as simple as a face she saw in a crowd, or the fearful look in a dog's eye as it cowered from her path, or even the way the sun gleamed from a storefront window, and she could expect to have several such occurrences each day. And the effect was unnerving.

But the most significant of the changes — and the actual cause of them — was something Cassie called the "*Other.*" Beginning less than a week after the Black Mass, Cassie became aware of the constant presence of something with her. It was like having a second half to herself that could freely invade her mind and intrude on her thoughts; it left her sickened with the realization that her deepest, most personal thoughts had been fingered by a terrible filth.

And equally alarming was that it was planting its own thoughts in her mind.

"I'm feeling something in my head," she told her goth friends as they shared a joint in the cemetery one night. "Are you guys feeling anything?"

The others exchanged looks and shook their heads.

"No. Not really," Trish said. "What are you feeling?"

"It's like I keep having these thoughts, but they're not mine. Something's putting them there."

"What kind of thoughts?" Silvia asked.

Cassie shook her head. "Really messed-up ones. Like angry and disturbing, and really, really dark."

"I thought you liked dark," Seth said.

"Not like these."

Trish seemed to get it. "I think it's your Other. Do you feel it around you too?"

"Yeah. Like all the time. What does it want?"

"To show you things?"

Silvia nodded. "It's there to help you learn."

"Well, it's not," Cassie said. "And it's scaring the hell out of me. How do I get rid of it?"

Silvia and Trish looked at each, then back at Cassie. Trish shook her head. "You can't. You already invited it in."

"I didn't invite anything in."

"Yeah. You did. We all did."

"Then why don't you guys have it too?"

Trish shrugged. "Because it chose you."

"Why do you want to get rid of it?" Silvia asked.

"Because it's always there," Cassie said. "And its thoughts scare me."

"Maybe it's trying to enlighten you," Silvia offered.

"I don't care. I want it out."

As the weeks went by, these intrusions by the *Other* became even more frequent and pervasive. There were times when Cassie could no longer discern where her thoughts ended and this *Other's* began, and she felt herself being forced from control of her own mind and body. She was being made a captive within her own self, as this *Other* exerted an ever-increasing dominion over her.

She was angry most of the time now and lashed out at the smallest provocation, often for no reason at all. She had cussed out several teachers in front of the class and told one to fuck off when he sent her to detention. It became almost a sideshow for the other students and might have even been amusing for them, had it not been for the *Disturbances*.

Cassie's classmates, her mom, and teachers sensed something was profoundly wrong with Cassie, and it couldn't be dismissed as adolescent rebellion. It was something they came to refer to as the *Disturbances*. Whenever any of them were in her presence, a subtle intuition alerted them to danger. It was the primordial instinct our ancestors felt as stealthy predators stalked through the brush beyond the glow of their campfires. But it wasn't anything in particular they could point to in Cassie — she was petite in size and posed little threat to them physically. It was something internal to her — some part of her being that they sensed posed a threat not only to their bodies but to their souls. And a warning told them to avoid drawing attention to themselves. But for those unfortunates who ignored that warning, they came away from those encounters gripped by a profound sense of dread.

Whatever existed inside Cassie, it knew them now.

Another example of the *Disturbances* was something they referred to as the *Confusion*. This occurred mostly in class, although several instances also happened in the cafeteria. The *Confusion* would occur when someone was speaking and they would find themselves suddenly confounded and at a complete loss for words. It was significantly more severe than a lapse in their train of thought — the *Confusion* would momentarily sever any association between thoughts and their corresponding words and would leave the speaker staring helplessly into space without the ability to compose thoughts or sentences. All efforts to do so came out as randomly ordered words and sounds that were completely nonsensical.

The final example of the *Disturbances* was what is commonly known as "telekinesis." Several students reported seeing objects appear to move of their own volition. A pencil would fly from a desk, or a book fall from a shelf. One report even had a cafeteria tray fly from a table and across the cafeteria. Cassie's presence was the common factor in each occurrence.

As her descent into possession by this spirit (or *Other* as she called it) progressed, Cassie found herself increasingly acting under sudden irresistible compulsions. There would be the urge, whether it be for sex or drugs or angry outbursts, followed by the action, without any opportunity for deliberation. On one occasion when the urge struck, she had found a student studying in the school library during a break. She led him beneath the bleachers on the football field, ripped his clothes off in a frenzied haste, then mounted him right there on the dirt.

This boy had gone along quite willingly at first. It was a hookup with a cute, albeit weird, chick, so sure, why not? But as she rode him, with ever-aggressive sways of her pelvis, he happened to catch the look in her eyes — and it was pure animal ferocity that stared back at him. It scared the shit out of him. He pissed himself as he squirmed out from beneath her, then fled in only his drenched boxers and shirt. He understandably never told anyone what had happened.

The intensity and frequency of the *Disturbances* and compulsions coincided with the increased dominion the spirit exerted over Cassie. Within two months after the Black Mass, the self that was Cassie no longer had any meaningful control over her body or mind. What remained of that self was left to drown helplessly in a putrid cesspool of bile and wretchedness. It left her without any form of reprieve or the ability to recall any experiences of happiness or joy or love she might draw relief from. There existed only the memory that there had once been memories of those feelings, but without the ability to recall the memories or the feelings themselves.

Cassie was possessed, and a captive in her own body and mind.

****

Alison came home early from work on the evening of October 31st. Cassie's school had called to let her know that Cassie had been suspended for using drugs. Alison stormed up the stairs to Cassie's bedroom and found her door shut. This came as no surprise, since Cassie kept it shut most of the time lately. That was going to end. She knocked twice.

"Cassie?"

When there was no answer, she opened the door and stepped inside. Immediately she was hit by the cold. The room felt like ice, and she could actually see her breath.

She also noticed the stench. It was gut-wrenching, like rotten eggs, or meat left in the sun for weeks. Alison gagged and nearly vomited. She pulled her shirt collar over her nose, but it did nothing to mask that stench. She hurried from the room and into her own bedroom and grabbed a scarf. She wrapped it around her head so it covered her nose and mouth, then returned to Cassie's bedroom.

Alison began searching the bedroom for the source of that stench. First she searched the desk, then underneath the bed, then the closet, and finally the bathroom. She half expected to find a dead animal, but in the end she found nothing out of the ordinary; only the usual scattered mess of clothes and papers. Nothing that could be causing that smell.

As she walked back into the bedroom, she realized something. No matter where she stood in the room, the smell was equally strong. It didn't come from any area in particular; the room itself was the stench.

She stood there for a moment puzzled — the inexplicable cold and this stench that, despite the scarf, was still overwhelming — what was happening?

A vague sense of dread crept over her. Something was seriously wrong in this room — and with her daughter — something that couldn't be easily explained away.

She crossed over to Cassie's desk and began rummaging through it. She knew Cassie kept a journal, and she needed to find it. Maybe something in there could explain Cassie's increasingly aberrant behavior, and this... this *phenomena* with the room? Was that the word she was looking for?

Of course the journal wasn't in her desk. That would have been too obvious. So next she searched her closet. She rummaged through the clothes and shelves but again came up empty.

Think, Alison...

On a hunch, she headed over to the bed and lifted the mattress. There sat the journal, pressed between the mattress and springs.

She couldn't stay in the room to read it — not with that stench, and the cold was beginning to sting her arms. So she took the journal with her downstairs to the living room. She sat down on the couch and began reading. And what she read horrified her.

A good deal of the journal consisted of poems. Alison already knew Cassie loved to write poems and had happily read some of them to Alison and Rick in the past. A past that seemed so distant now. Those poems had been colorful and happy, but what Alison was reading now was not. Cassie's recent poems showed a morbid preoccupation with darkness and death.

And with something Cassie called the *Other*.

Alison checked her watch. She had just enough time to run to the store before Cassie got home. She grabbed her keys and hurried off.

****

Cassie arrived home that night while Alison was still out. It was already past eight, and Cassie was running late for meeting up with Seth and the girls. She rummaged through her closet, flinging through clothes draped across hangers and digging through piles strewn on her closet floor. Many of them hadn't been washed in weeks, but she couldn't care less — it's not like guys gave a shit what she was wearing; they only cared about what was beneath it.

"Drugs? You were doing drugs at school?"

Cassie took a quick glance at the doorway where her mom now stood. She hadn't even heard her come in.

"It's not a big deal," Cassie said and returned to sorting through her clothes.

"The hell it's not," Alison shot back. Then she realized Cassie was looking for something to wear.

"What're you doing?"

"Finding something to wear. Do you mind?"

"Yes. I do mind. You're not going out."

Cassie stopped, mid-toss of a torn concert T-shirt. "Say again?"

"I said you're not going out," Alison declared, realizing it was the first time she had asserted herself to Cassie in a long time. It was something she should have done a lot sooner.

Cassie shot her a grin. "News for you, Mom. Yes, I am."

"News for you, Cass. No, you're not. And you're not seeing Seth and those girls anymore."

Cassie's grin turned into a glare. "You can't tell me what to do."

Alison confidently folded her arms across her chest. "As long as you're living in this house, I sure as hell can."

Cassie's glare was now turning to hatred, and vicious thoughts pressed into her mind.

Fuck her, they told her. *What does she know. She's useless.*

"You can't stop me," Cassie snarled.

"Like hell, I can't," Alison shot back.

"Why? Because you're my mother? Little late for that, mommy dearest."

"That right there. That belligerence. That stops right now."

"Big word, Mom. You learn that at the bar, or while sponging off dad all those years."

Alison staggered back. That last blow had stung, but there was no way she was going to let Cassie see that.

"You're grounded, Cassie."

"*What?*"

"I said you're grounded. You're to come straight home from school, and you're not to hang around Seth and those girls anymore."

The rage inside Cassie was at a boiling point and ready to explode into violence. "Get out!" she shouted, and when Alison just stood there, Cassie hurled a handful of clothes at her.

"I said get out!"

The ferocity in Cassie's voice startled Alison, and she stepped back into the hallway. Cassie stormed over to the door and slammed it shut. Then locked it.

"I hate you!" Cassie shouted through the door, then kicked it. She stormed over to her closet, grabbed a handful of clothes, and heaved them on the floor. Then she plopped down on her bed and let her rage boil, as that voice in her head told her how wrongly Alison had treated her.

She has no right.

She's just jealous of you.

She can't stop you.

Just do it...

And the voice was right. How could her mom stop her if Cassie decided to sneak out? Call the cops? She didn't have the balls.

Fuck it, Cassie decided, rising to her feet and

heading over to her closet. She was going to sneak out anyway. If her mom found out, tough shit. What was she going to do, ground her twice? How's that one working out for you, Mom?

Cassie dug through her closet, pulling out the sluttiest, gothiest outfit she could find — a slit dark skirt, torn fishnets, and concert shirt. She quickly slipped into the clothes, then hurried into her adjoining bathroom where she lathered on makeup worthy of her goth-babe outfit.

When she finished, she stepped back from the mirror and gave herself a once-over appraisal.

She was going to rock this night.

She turned from the bathroom and crossed her bedroom to the window. She slid it open and climbed through, taking care to make as little noise as possible. Might as well postpone the fight with her mom as long as she could.

She crept across the narrow sloping roof to the edge and eased over it onto a trellis mounted to the side wall. She scrambled down it to the lawn out back, then hurried over to the corner. She peeked around it, and, seeing her mom was still inside, she raced off into the night.

Six hours later, Cassie Stevens would die in a car crash.

CHAPTER SEVEN
A Tale of Two Deaths

The oncoming car belonged to Maggie Dunne. She and her seven-year-old daughter, Katie, were returning from Maggie's parents' home in Boston when the rain hit. She had considered turning around at one point but decided to press on through the storm. Surely the roads would be empty at the late hour, and on this miserable night.

What she never expected to encounter was a car driven by reckless teens on a drug-and-alcohol binge.

It was a decision she never forgave herself for.

Mere seconds passed from the time she rounded the bend till the moment of impact. It was barely enough time for her to lay on the horn and glimpse her daughter sleeping peacefully in the seat beside her.

Then they hit.

The OnStar service alerted first responders of the collision, and they arrived within ten minutes.

As she drifted in and out of consciousness, Maggie had only faint impressions of her rescue. The flashing colored lights. The paramedics. The incessant rain...

Then she was being pulled from her car and laid on a stretcher. Voices assured her she was going to be okay. She was staring up at the dark outlines of trees, her face pelted with rain, as they carried her to the ambulance and slid her in back.

Where was Katie?

"My daughter," she moaned in a strained voice barely above a whisper. She struggled to sit up but was gently pressed back down by a medic.

"They're taking care of her, ma'am," the medic sought to assure her. "Please, just lie back."

The medic knew this was a lie, but it was what she needed to hear. She was bleeding from multiple wounds, with possible spinal injuries, and her blood pressure was falling fast. There would be time for the truth later.

Someone had to survive this night.

The young girl, Katie Dunne, was already with God.

****

Cassie's heart stopped during the ambulance ride to the hospital. The medics frantically continued to administer CPR, while calling ahead with the Code Blue. The operating room was prepped and ready by the time they wheeled Cassie in.

They would need to revive her in minutes; or else, the night would claim another victim.

Surgeons and nurses sprang into action. They hooked Cassie up to a ventilator and administered epinephrine, while technicians wheeled over a crash cart. The heart monitor showed a steady flat line and filled the room with its sharp tone.

Seconds passed.

The paddles were quickly gelled, the defibrillator charged, and the paddles pressed on her chest.

Her body bucked with the shock. The heart monitor spiked momentarily, then returned to its flat line.

They were going again.

Again her body bucked... followed by the flat line and that terrible tone.

It was on the third attempt that Cassie's heart restarted. With a sharp gasp, her body bucked, then came to rest. But this time the monitor continued to rise and fall with a steady rhythm, and the clear ventilator mask fogged with her breath.

Cassie Stevens was back.

A wave of relief swept the room as they watched her heart continue to beat on its own. They had saved a life that night.

But in the excitement that followed her resuscitation, one thought never occurred to anyone —

Where had she been during those minutes of death?

CHAPTER EIGHT
Coming Home

Cassie spent the week in the hospital under observation. She was badly bruised, with broken ribs and cuts from the shattered glass, but she was alive. Somehow she had made it back from that night.

Alison had rushed to the hospital the moment she received the call about the accident. She had nervously paced the waiting room till Cassie came out of surgery, and agonized the entire time over the fight she had with Cassie earlier that night. Those couldn't be the last words they ever said to each other.

She prayed for the first time since Rick's death and promised to be a better mom if God just gave Cassie a second chance.

She collapsed into a chair with relief when a doctor told her that Cassie had been revived. Cassie had been moved to intensive care, but her prognosis looked good. The doctor suggested that Alison go home and get some rest. She looked like hell.

Alison returned home, but rest was impossible. She called work and arranged to take the next few days off. She was ready to quit if they refused.

Alison was back at the hospital the next day, and the day after that. Cassie's condition was upgraded to stable, and Alison was there when she opened her eyes for the first time since the crash.

Alison arrived early to pick Cassie up on the day of her discharge. There was so much they had to say to each other, and Cassie could finally express the remorse she had felt that night.

"I'm so sorry, Mom," Cassie said as they drove home. "All that stuff I said that night, and the way I've been acting... you didn't deserve any of that. And I'm not gonna be like that anymore."

It was the most heartfelt thing Cassie had ever said to her, and Alison felt a tear well up in her cheek. "I'm sorry too, Cass. I haven't been there. I guess I got so used to your dad taking care of you, I forgot how to be your mom. How about we both try to be better to each other."

Cassie smiled and gave her a nod. "Deal."

Cassie relaxed back in her seat and let her mind drift back to memories from that night; at least what remained of those memories, since most of them were clouded in a haze. There had been the rave, with its thumping techno music, dizzying lights, and sea of twirling glow sticks. The smell of alcohol and vomit. The drugs...

But what puzzled her was her detachment from those memories. Had they even been her memories, or had they been... the *Other's*? It almost felt like she was a spectator to them, rather than a participant.

It was like that for all her memories from the past few months. Ever since that thing had entered her, the line between its memories and hers was blurred. If there even was a line.

But it was no longer in her. At least she no longer felt it in her. Ever since the crash, her thoughts and mind and body belonged to her again. She felt free and liberated in a way she never could have imagined just a few months ago. And she was determined to keep it that way.

Alison turned onto the gravel drive leading to their house and parked out front. They headed inside, where Cassie was greeted by Rex. He was six now, and full grown, but still acted like a pup when he was excited. And he was excited at the moment. Cassie gave him a hug, being careful not to bump her ribs, then headed upstairs to her room.

Cassie was surprised to find her bedroom clean. All of the mess she had made that night was gone, and the clothes neatly folded and hung on hangers.

She walked over to her dresser and looked at the miniature juniper bonsai that sat on top. She'd named it Dodger, and it had sprouted new leaves while she was gone.

Her mom had done all of this while she was gone;

even after the way Cassie went berserk on her that night. Cassie felt those guilt pangs again over the way she'd been acting the past couple of months. And even before that. As she thought about it, she honestly couldn't remember the last time she felt like *Cassie*, but it was probably all the way back to the time *before*.

A knock on her door snapped her from her musings. "Yeah. Come in."

Her mom entered and walked over. "Hope you don't mind. I cleaned it while you were gone."

"No. That was really cool of you. Thanks. And thanks for watering Dodger."

"Couldn't let the little guy get thirsty while you were gone."

Cassie nodded. "I'm sorry again for the way I've been acting. And all that stuff I said."

Alison gave her a gentle squeeze. "Hey. It's all behind us. You and I are both moving onward. Cool?"

Cassie smiled. "Cool."

"So how would you like to take a drive with me?" Alison asked.

"Where are we going?"

"I thought it might be nice to go see your dad."

****

Cassie spotted the vase of fresh flowers next to her dad's gravestone as she and Alison walked up.

"You brought him fresh flowers," Cassie said.

Alison nodded. "I came here the day after the hospital told me our daughter was going to be okay. I figured your dad probably had something to do with it."

Cassie nodded. "I think so too."

"I saw the birthday card you left for him," Alison said. "I hope you don't mind that I brought it home. It was getting a little weathered."

"No. That's fine."

"That was really thoughtful of you to do that."

"I just wanted him to know I was thinking about him."

"I'm sure he does, honey," Alison said. She set her hand on Cassie's shoulder. "He was always your biggest fan, Cass. Along with me." She gave her shoulder a gentle squeeze.

"Thanks, Mom."

They stood in silence for a while as a pleasant breeze stirred through the grass. Then Cassie noticed a faint scent carried on the breeze.

It was the sweet, gentle fragrance of daisies, but Cassie couldn't think of any place around here where they grew. She turned her head to look around for the source, and saw another person in the cemetery.

She was a little girl, with soft blond hair, standing near a gravestone twenty yards away. She wore a pure white Communion dress, and in her hand she held a bundle of daisies.

She was watching Cassie.

"You ready to get going?" Alison asked.

"Huh?" Cassie snapped from her momentary daze and looked at her mom. "I'm sorry. What'd you ask?"

Alison looked at her curiously. "Are you okay?"

"Yeah, I just..." Cassie's eyes wandered past that other grave again, but the little girl was gone. "...thought I saw someone?"

"We should probably get going," Alison said, giving Cassie's shoulder a gentle squeeze. "I need to stop by the store so we have something to eat."

"Okay," Cassie said as she continued to stare at the other grave.

CHAPTER NINE
Father Sean

"To everything there is a season...
A time to be born, and a time to die...
A time to kill, and a time to heal..."

— *Ecclesiastes* 3:1

****

"Then shall come to pass the saying that is written..." The elderly priest stood at the foot of the small grave, reciting prayers from his missal for the Rite of Christian Burials. His name was Father Dennis Jenkins, and despite his advanced age, his eyes continued to reflect a sharp mind and sound clarity of thought. These were matched by his innate kindness.

"Death is swallowed up in victory," Jenkins continued, his eyes momentarily looking up from the missal to the several dozen mourners gathered around the grave.

They were at the Faulkner Cemetery, not far from the plot where Cassie's dad was buried. The mourners had been greeted that chill fall morning by a dreary sky and light drizzle that only felt appropriate for the burial of the seven-year-old girl. She was Katie Dunne.

"Oh, death, where is thy victory? Oh, death, where is thy sting?" Jenkins recited the prayers verbatim from the missal, yet couldn't resist a taunt in his voice as he pronounced this rebuke. Death could claim no victory over Katie. Jenkins was a simple, humble man, but of this much he was certain — Katie was with God and would spend her eternity in His bliss.

Jenkins had met Katie's mother, Maggie Dunne, shortly after Maggie moved to Capetown almost six years earlier. She had been a young widowed mother at the time, raising an infant daughter on her own. Jenkins appreciated the hardships she was facing in a new town and had reached out to his parishioners to find her a job.

Over the years, he had become like a grandfather to the child, offering assistance to Maggie whenever she needed it, and providing free tuition for Katie at the parish's elementary school. He had also presented Katie with her first Communion just six months earlier.

In all his years, he had never met a sweeter, kinder, more gracious soul than Katie, and he had been heartbroken to hear about her death.

"And with this promise of victory, we now commend the soul of Katie into the loving hands of our Lord." At this point he paused and turned his gaze toward the sky.

"Eternal rest grant unto her, oh Lord. And may perpetual light shine upon her. May she rest in peace." Then, bowing his head, he concluded with a final "Amen."

Jenkins' "Amen" was followed by a succession of "Amens" from the mourners.

Standing just outside the close circle of friends was another priest, considerably younger than Jenkins. The young priest was Father Sean McCready, but to everyone who knew him, he was simply Sean, or Father Sean, or, in the case of the teen girls in his religious education class, most of whom crushed on his tall athletic frame, thick hair, and firm jaw, he was Father-What-a-Waste.

Sean waited for the other mourners to depart before he approached Maggie. Condolences always felt so awkward and rehearsed, no matter how sincere they were, but he knew they were expected and even appreciated by the grieving party.

"I'm so sorry, Maggie," he offered, joining her beside the small grave. "If there's anything at all I can do..."

"There is, Father," she said, with her eyes never leaving the grave. "You can tell me why He did this. Why God let my daughter die."

It was harsh, and bitter, and brutally honest. And it was the way Sean had felt for the past several days since returning from that other funeral.

Abandoned. And empty.

He just shook his head. For a moment he considered giving her the usual canned responses — *she's in a better place*, or *God works in mysterious ways* — but all of those felt hopelessly inadequate in the face of this level of grief. Maggie deserved honesty; and at that moment, it wasn't something he could give anyone.

"I don't know, Maggie. I wish I did; but I just don't." It was the best he could offer her.

And himself.

****

No one was more surprised than Sean that his life's journey lead him to the priesthood. While he had grown up in an Irish Catholic family, where Sunday Mass was a part of the routine, he had never felt particularly religious. Like so many Irish families, Catholicism was just assumed; it was as much a part of their identity as sports and beer. Irish kids went to Irish schools, attended weekly Mass, and more often than not, were on a first-name basis with the parish priests. But the rest of the week, they were indistinguishable from the other kids on the block.

Sean was the youngest of three brothers — Brendan, the oldest, and Conor, who was two years older than Sean. They were all tight, but Sean was probably closest to Conor, since they were closer in age and shared the same penchant for mischief that usually got them grounded.

They grew up in the small town of Kenneth Point, thirty miles south of Boston, where their dad, Jack, was a cop and their mom, Cheryl, a homemaker. The boys were tough and athletic, like their dad, and learned to protect themselves at an early age. But they also learned compassion from their mom, and none of their classmates would ever describe them as bullies. Their mom wouldn't have put up with it.

Like his brothers, Sean excelled at sports and made the varsity teams his sophomore year for wrestling, baseball, and football. It was during summer football practice, where Sean played wide receiver, that he caught the eye of a cute young cheerleader named Amy Duval.

It happened on a warm afternoon, on the grass field that served as a football stadium for St. Augustine's High School. As practice ended and the team broke for the showers, Amy spotted Sean alone on the sidelines, loading his cleats into his duffel bag. Her friends on the cheer squad had watched her sneak glances at him all summer, and it was time she finally made her move.

"Would you just do it already," they pressed.

"Do what?"

Duh. "Talk to him."

"I don't know what to say."

"Just say hi," her friend Jenny said, and the other girls nodded in agreement.

"What if he doesn't say anything?"

"He will. Just do it."

A deep breath. "Okay."

Sean zipped up his duffel bag and rose from the

bench.

"Hi."

It was a girl's voice. He turned and saw one of the cheerleaders approaching. She was strawberry blond, with freckles, and lacked the deep tan of the other girls on the squad. But what she had was a cute charm that shined in her smile, and her awkward blush as she nervously approached.

"Hey," he smiled back. And she was instantly relieved. First part accomplished — he hadn't laughed at her.

"I'm Amy. And I just — well, you did really good out there. You know, catching the ball and stuff."

She bit down on her lip. Had she just said, *'catching the ball and stuff'?* Real smooth, Amy. She needed to extract herself ASAP, before she blurted out any more stupid lines.

"Anyway. Just wanted to say that." She turned to go...

"Amy."

She stopped. Looked back. He was smiling.

"Thanks."

She fidgeted. "Yeah. Sure. You're welcome."

Oh, geez. Could she suck any worse at this? She bit her lip again. But then she noticed — he was still smiling. He wasn't laughing at her or rolling his eyes at her lameness. He walked over and extended his hand.

"I'm Sean. You wanna grab something to eat?"

And just like that, he had put her at ease.

"Okay."

****

Amy was pretty sure she fell in love with Sean the moment he first smiled at her. It was the way he put her at ease over her clumsy approach and boosted her confidence. He made her feel good about being Amy.

Amy had no brothers, but she had an amazing dad, who was always doing kind things for her mom. She saw how it always made her mom smile, and she loved her dad all the more because of it. It was number one on her checklist of things she wanted in a boy — she had to find someone who would treat her the way her dad treated her mom.

Sean had that quality. And he was cute. But only the first part really mattered.

Love came slower for Sean. He had an adventurous spirit that made him — in his own words — commitment-ophobic. But Amy's quirkiness made her fun to hang around, and she soon became his partner in crime. They did most things together — studied, went to parties, watched movies, went sailing, took long hikes and bike rides, went on picnics (although he constantly had to remind the vegetarian Amy that guys like meat on their sandwiches). She also blushed easily, much to her embarrassment, so Sean's mischievous side had him always look for ways to make her blush. This usually got him a punch on the arm, which for Sean meant mission accomplished.

For their first Christmas together, Sean asked her what she wanted. That was simple — a bottle of her favorite perfume, Chanel No. 5. She made him repeat it till it stuck in his memory. There would be a quiz on it later, she assured him.

Amy's family was also Catholic, so it wasn't long before their families met for Mass on Sundays and would go out for brunch afterward. Amy's mom, Pamela, and Sean's mom also became quick friends and often met for coffee while their kids were at school.

Amy took her faith a lot more seriously than Sean and was trying her hardest to remain a virgin till her wedding night. It wasn't always easy, but she was relieved that Sean never pressured her to go all the way. It scored major points for him with her. So even if he was a jerk for making her blush, she could live with that. She really liked this boy she had fallen in love with.

Sean, of course, never told any of the guys about this virginity thing with Amy, or he never would have heard the end of it. But he knew it was important to Amy, so he just dealt with it. It also gave him a chance to get to know her as a friend, without the sex part overwhelming everything, so that was pretty cool.

Over the coming months and years, the two of them laughed, and teased, and played, and had fun. And Sean did eventually fall in love with Amy.

It continued that way till their senior year, and then something happened that would later haunt Sean in ways he never could have imagined at the time.

CHAPTER TEN

Innocence

The final score that Friday night was St. Augustine Knights 17, Wilshire Hawks 10. Seven of those points, and eighty-seven of the yards that got them to victory, were thanks to Sean. The team was headed to Troy the linebacker's home on the harbor to celebrate. Troy's parents were out of town, and his older brother had picked up some kegs, so it looked to be an epic party.

Sean and Amy arrived with the team and cheer squad and stuck around the party till late in the night.

Amy was small, weighing all of 105 pounds, so it didn't take much to get her drunk. Sometime around midnight, she stumbled off through the party to find Sean. She found him on the patio, playing beer pong with the guys. She strolled up and leaned into his ear: "Can we go for a walk?"

Sean and Amy strolled along the water's edge, far

away from the city noise and lights. Moonlight danced across the water, and waves lapped gently against the shore.

Amy stopped and looked up at him. Was he always this tall? Or was she just that drunk?

"I think I'm ready," she said.

"Ready for what?" He was pretty buzzed himself.

"You know. To..." She didn't want to say it; but from the puzzled look on his face, she was going to have to.

"Make love," she finished.

Oh.

She blushed at the sudden change of expression on his face. It was somewhere between dumbfounded and excited Neanderthal. He definitely had not seen that one coming.

"Are you sure? Or is that the beer talking?"

"A little of both," she admitted shyly.

"Maybe we should wait till it's just the one."

She saw the concern in his eyes; he didn't want to do anything unless she was absolutely certain. And it was that care that made her want him even more at that moment.

"I want this," she said, then broke into that blush that was so uniquely Amy. "But don't make fun of me if I do it wrong."

"Can I make fun of you just a little," he teased, and she smacked him on the chest. But it was all in fun. She wanted this.

At least she was pretty sure she did.

They sat down on the sand, with their backs against a bluff, and faced out over the ocean. She guessed it was around one in the morning, and there was no one around.

As they kissed, he noticed the scent of her perfume dabbed behind her ear. Chanel No. 5, he reminded himself. He made a mental note to buy her a bottle as a gift.

She leaned back and began unbuttoning her shirt. He watched as her fingers trembled. She was shaking.

"Amy..." He was worried again.

Shhh... she pressed a finger to his lips.

"Okay," he reluctantly nodded. But this was wrong. She wasn't ready. They shouldn't be doing this.

But they did it anyway.

And for Amy Duval, her first time was scary, and awkward, and wonderful, and oh so painful.

And devastating.

Amy leaned over in the sand and vomited. But not from the beer. It was a deep, gnawing guilt that clawed at her stomach.

Sean could only watch.

A desolate silence hung over them as they walked home afterward. Sean had no words. What could he even say? He wanted to kick himself for having agreed to it. If she had been sober, and knew what she was asking for, it would have been different. But she wasn't.

In the few words they exchanged during the walk home, they promised to never tell anyone. It would stay their secret. And as far as Sean knew, it had remained so.

What he didn't know at the time, but would later discover in the most horrifying way, is that nothing is ever truly secret.

They knew.

They were always watching.

****

Sean walked Amy to her door. There was a hug and quick kiss, but it felt staged, like she was simply going through the motions because it was expected.

Sean lay in bed all night staring into the darkness and replaying the night over and over again. He was an idiot.

He punched his pillow for the hundredth time that night. He didn't know how he was going to make things right with her, but he was going to do whatever it took. He was still awake when the sun came up, and he counted down the hours till the stores opened. By then, he had an idea.

Sean was waiting outside with his coffee when the department store opened at nine. He cut through the clothing departments and over to the cosmetics counter. He purchased a bottle of Chanel No. 5 and had it wrapped in a gift box.

Sean's next stop was a florist, where he bought a bouquet of roses. Now it was time to grovel.

Sean called Amy at eleven that morning, figuring it would give her time to sleep. It turned out she hadn't slept either. Their call was short. He asked if she wanted to grab lunch, but she said she wasn't feeling well. Besides, she had some studying she needed to do. She would just see him on Monday.

She was wounded. And Sean was crushed.

Monday couldn't come soon enough.

Amy arrived at school on Monday morning and found several of her girlfriends gathered around her locker. They were giggling and staring at a rose taped to the front of it. There was also a card inside a sealed envelope.

"Someone's got it bad," the girls teased. "Open the card."

Amy did. And despite the anxiety that gnawed at her stomach, she still managed to blush. Inside the card was a small hand-drawn map that went from her locker, down the hallway, through the doors at the end, and to a planter out front.

"What's it say?" the girls wanted to know.

Amy shook her head. "It's a map."

"To what?"

"I don't know."

"Awwww," the girls fawned. How cute. High school boys did things like that?

After the girls left, Amy followed the map to the planter. There was a row of bushes that ran along the front of the building. Amy looked behind the bushes and saw a small gift box that had been carefully wrapped with a ribbon and bow.

She opened it. Inside was a bottle of her perfume,

and a handwritten note:

To my best friend and partner in crime — please forgive me.

She smiled. And that knot in her stomach began to shrink.

"There's nothing to forgive, Sean," Amy said as they met for coffee at a small coffee shop down the block from school. "You didn't make me do anything."

He poked his finger in his coffee. "I could have said no."

"You did. A bunch of times."

"Obviously not enough."

He looked up and saw her watching him play with his coffee. He took his finger out and wiped it on his shorts.

She smiled. "I don't blame you, Sean. You've been wonderful to me about it. It's me I'm disappointed in."

"Buy why?"

"It was supposed to be my gift to my husband on my wedding night."

"It was still a gift."

She nodded. "I know. It just would have felt more magical on my wedding night."

"Instead of on the sand."

She couldn't help but smile. He was trying.

He reached for a napkin and wrote something on it, then slid it across the table to her. She read it:

To the girl I hope to share that wedding night with, thank you for the gift.

She reread it several times and felt that knot in her

stomach melt away. She flipped it over and wrote something on the back, then slid it over to him. He read it:

To the boy who always makes me smile. I love you.

CHAPTER ELEVEN
Drums of War

"Only the dead have seen the end of war."

— Plato

****

It was the fall of Sean's freshman year in college when the first in a tragic sequence of events would occur. He and Amy were at his parents' house for breakfast that morning when his brother Conor called to see if they were watching the news. The family turned on the TV and watched as thick plumes of smoke billowed from the sides of the Twin Towers. Two planes had crashed into them earlier that morning, and the FAA had already shut down airspace over the entire country.

There were no words.

Soon reports came in that a third plane had flown into the Pentagon, and it was clear now that these hadn't been mistakes, or tragic miscalculations; the country had been attacked.

It was shortly after the Pentagon strike that the unthinkable happened. There, on live TV, they watched the once-majestic towers crumble down in volcanic eruptions of ash and debris. And they, along with the rest of the country, could only stare in numbed silence.

America was at war, and she was a country wounded and grieving.

Sean met Conor for coffee on campus later that week. Conor was like a dog, pacing restlessly at a door for someone to let him out. He wanted in on whatever action was coming and had met with a Marine recruiter the day after the attacks.

He was enlisting, and he wanted his younger brother to join him. They could attend boot camp together on the "buddy program," and the recruiter told him there was a good chance they could be assigned to the same company, and possibly the same platoon.

Sean thought the idea sounded crazy. He had just started school. And what did they know about being soldiers? But Conor already had his answers planned. School could wait. There was still time to withdraw without failing his classes, and then he could attend later. And the Marines would pay for it. And as for the soldiering, that's what boot camp and infantry training school was for.

Conor was way too practiced at this. All their lives, Conor had always convinced Sean to join him on his misadventures — whether it was jumping off their roof with a bed-sheet parachute or egging the principal's house — the two brothers were inseparable.

And now they were talking about the Marines. Despite his initial misgivings, Sean soon found himself actually considering it.

The brothers rented a collection of war films, then binged them one afternoon in Conor's apartment over pizza and beer. It was John Wayne, and Rambo, and even an old Abbott and Costello Army comedy for the pure nostalgia of it.

Conor took Sean to meet with the recruiter the following Monday, and they spent several hours listening to war stories of his time in Operation Desert Storm. This guy reminded Sean a lot of his dad. Unflinching. Badass. A hero. That's what Marines were and why they were so feared and effective — they ran to the sound of gunfire.

Sean walked away from that meeting convinced. He knew it was the craziest thing he would ever do, but he was doing it with Conor. And that just made it feel right. Sean and Conor — that's how it always had been, and he always came out better because of it. Now he just had to tell Amy.

****

Amy couldn't believe her ears. The Marines? The idea had come so completely out of left field, she didn't even know how to react. But as soon as she heard Conor was the instigator, it all made sense. She knew the boys' bond and how they would walk through fire for each other. But she also knew the sway Conor had over Sean, and even if Sean had any misgivings, he still would have enlisted just to have his brother's back.

This really sucked.

But Sean's mind was apparently made up, and there was no way she would even think about getting between the brothers. No. That was a no-win battle, no matter how much Sean loved her. And although she was furious at Conor at the moment, she was also really fond of him. He had always been a big supporter of their relationship and a big fan of Amy in general. He had lent them his boat several times, had bought them Red Sox tickets, and he even lent Sean his car for a road trip she and Sean had taken up to Maine.

So no matter how much she wanted to hate Conor for dragging Sean into his craziness, she knew she couldn't. The brothers were simply doing what they had always done — they were being brothers.

This really, *really* sucked.

****

Amy was at Sean's graduation from boot camp, along with Sean's parents and brother Brendan. Brendan had a fun time giving his younger brothers shit about their latest rash decision, but it was all in fun. They were all proud of Sean and Conor, and that included Amy.

Sean had two weeks' leave before he had to report to the School of Infantry at Camp Geiger, so he and Amy were going to pack as much as they could into that time.

She noticed some definite changes in Sean that had taken place during his thirteen weeks of boot camp.

There were the obvious changes — gone was the thick hair, having been sheared off into a high and tight. He was also leaner, or, as Amy put it, ripped. She enjoyed that part. But there were subtle changes as well. He walked with a new confidence. Sean had never been shy or timid, but the way he carried himself now projected a real presence. He was also politer and more considerate, and she snickered when he addressed her mom as "ma'am."

"Stop that, Amy Joy," her mom scolded. "Sean's being a gentleman."

But the teasing resumed as soon as they were out of her mom's earshot.

The Marines also seemed to have tamed his more mischievous side, and she doubted he and Conor would be steeling any more golf carts to go joyriding across golf courses anytime soon.

That was probably a good thing.

But either way, he was still her Sean, and she had him for the next two weeks.

****

Following their leave, the brothers spent two intense months with the Infantry Training Battalion in North Carolina before being deployed to Afghanistan. There, they joined up with operating forces already on the ground and engaged with an enemy who lurked behind every crag.

It was the first of many successive deployments to that Godforsaken region. They were brutal and harsh, and when his enlistment was finally over, the Sean who returned home was not the Sean who had left all those years ago.

Conor had returned home two months earlier in a flag-draped coffin. They had been exactly sixty-three days and a wake-up from the end of their enlistments, and were already making plans with Brendan for a drunken trip to Europe, when a suicide vest worn by a young Afghan girl ended Conor's life.

CHAPTER TWELVE
A New Calling

Sean returned home broken and hollow. For weeks after his return, he numbed his thoughts with alcohol and long walks alone through the port area. His friends were calling, but he didn't want to see anyone. He wanted to turn everything off and withdraw to a place within himself where he didn't have to feel anything. And that included Amy.

He didn't want to feel.

"I don't know what to do," Amy told Sean's mom, Cheryl, as they sat down for coffee one day. "It's like he's completely closed himself off to me and everybody."

Amy had become like a daughter to Cheryl over the years, and it broke her heart to see Amy so hurt and helpless. "You do know this has nothing to do with you," Cheryl tried to assure her, but it wasn't sinking in. So Cheryl tried it again. "Amy, honey, listen to me. This isn't about you, or anyone else. Sean saw the devil over there, and it took a part of him that may not come back. You need to understand that." And this time it sank in.

"So what can we do?"

"We can pray," Cheryl said. "And we can be there for him when he needs us."

It had been two months since his return, and Sean found himself walking through a quiet neighborhood of Colonial houses and parks. It was there that he came across a small Catholic Church on the corner. It was built of red brick and white trim, set back from the sidewalk behind a neatly trimmed lawn. A sign out front said "Welcome to St. Francis."

Sean hadn't been inside a church since Conor's funeral, but something about this small church seemed to beckon him. Who knows, maybe God had some free time to chat.

Inside, the church was simple and basic, with two rows of wooden pews, stained-glass windows, and a small altar at the far end. But what it lacked in frills it made up for with intimacy and charm.

The church was empty at the moment, and Sean slid into a pew near the back, where a refreshing breeze from the door blew past. It felt pleasant and calming.

Sean sat there for almost an hour, just letting his thoughts drift and unload. There were thoughts of Conor, and Amy, and even just life. He had been drowned in a numbness he couldn't shake, and it was like the part of him that allowed himself to feel had shut itself off. But as he sat there in that small no-frills church, he felt that crippling weight lift from his shoulders. *Was this what peace felt like?* It had been so long, he could barely remember.

He was so wrapped in that warm feeling of calm that he barely noticed when someone entered from a side door near the altar. He was a small older man, maybe in his seventies, and wore the brown habit of a Franciscan priest. Despite his apparent age, there was a zest in his step as he went about the church placing missalettes in the pew pockets. He had been so focused on his task, whistling as he went, that he failed to notice Sean sitting in the back. He blushed with embarrassment when he finally did notice.

"Sorry about that," the priest said with a touch of Irish brogue. "Didn't realize I wasn't alone."

"No worries, Father," Sean said with a slight laugh. "I need to get going anyway."

"Not on account of me whistlin', I hope."

Sean shook his head. "No. Your whistling was fine. It's good to see someone happy."

"Well, let's hope a little of it follows yeh then."

Sean nodded his thanks and headed out the back. He stopped on the way out and picked up a bulletin to take with him. He planned to come back.

Sean was at St. Francis again the next day for the noon Mass. There were several dozen parishioners in attendance, and the same elderly priest was the celebrant. It was the abbreviated weekday Mass, without any singing (which Sean always hated) and with a brief homily that surprisingly held Sean's attention.

Sean stuck around after Mass to introduce himself. The priest was Father Ian O'Malley, an Irish immigrant who had come to America when he was just a little older than Sean. He had joined the Franciscan Order right out of high school and had been ordained a priest fifty-two years ago. And, as he put it in his Irish brogue, it'd been a helluva ride ever since.

Father Ian spotted Sean in the pews a few days later and recruited him to read the first reading at Mass. Sean agreed. And it would be the words from that reading that awoke something in him.

"Liked that one, did yeh?" Father Ian grinned knowingly as he and Sean spoke after Mass. "Always liked it meself." It was a particular passage from Song of Songs in the Old Testament, and it had left Sean deep in thought.

"Did it speak to yeh?" Ian asked.

"What do you mean?" Sean asked.

"Did yeh feel it in here?" Ian said, tapping his own chest above his heart.

Sean thought about it. "Yeah. I guess it did."

"That'd be the Spirit talkin' to yeh," Ian said and handed Sean a missalette. "Why don't you read it again out loud, the part that spoke to yeh, and tell me what it means to yeh."

Sean flipped through the missalette to the page for

the reading. He scanned through the reading till he found the particular part that had stirred him, and he read it aloud: *"Behold, my beloved speaketh to me: Arise, my love, my dove, my beautiful one, and come. For behold, the winter has past, the rain is over and gone. The flowers have appeared in our land, the time of pruning is come: the voice of the turtle is heard in our land: the fig tree hath put forth her green figs: the vines in flower yield their sweet smell. Arise, my love, my beautiful one, and come.'"*

Sean closed the missalette, and found Father Ian with a thoughtful faraway look in his eyes. "Yeh figure out what it means?"

"I'm not sure," Sean said. "It feels like it's there, but not quite."

"Don't think about it up here," the elderly priest said, tapping his head. "Let it speak to yeh in here." He again pointed to his chest, right above his heart.

When Sean arrived home later that evening, he dug out an old copy of the Bible his mom kept in the house. He read the passage again. And then reread it. Each time he felt the same lump in his throat, and it wasn't until late that night he finally understood why.

"It's about death, isn't it?" Sean said to Ian after Mass the next day.

Ian smiled and nodded. "It's about God callin' a soul home to Him after death, and showin' him all the wonders and beauty awaitin' him in Heaven." The old priest's eyes had become misty as he said this.

Sean let this sink in for a moment. It was powerful, and touching, and exactly what he needed to hear. "I lost my brother in the war in Afghanistan," he finally said, swallowing a lump in his throat. "I'd like to think that's how he was greeted when he died."

Ian laid a gentle hand on his shoulder. "Me boy. Yeh can count on it," Ian assured him, and there was no hesitation at all in his voice.

"You sound really sure."

"Course I am," Ian responded. "That voice yeh felt in yer heart when yeh read that, that'd be God sendin' yeh one of His love letters tellin' yeh yer brother's doin' jest great."

Sean stopped by Amy's on the way home from St. Francis that night, and the two of them went out for a late dinner down by the shore. Amy was shocked, but pleasantly so, to see him so alive. The gloom and despair were gone, and he was alive in a way she hadn't seen in years. At least not since going off to war.

Sean told her all about the small church he had been spending time at, and his talks with Father Ian.

"Let me ask you something," he posed to her. "Have you ever read the Bible and had a part of it jump out at you like it was written just for you?"

"Yeah," she answered with a big nod and smile. "Did it happen to you?"

He nodded. "Yeah. Just yesterday. And then again today. I talked to Father Ian about it, and he said it's God sending us a love letter."

Amy's smile broadened. It was such a beautiful way to describe it. "So when do I get to meet this priest? I want to thank him for helping bring my boyfriend home."

Amy joined Sean for Mass at St. Francis that Sunday, and they stuck around afterward so he could introduce her to Father Ian. Ian was of course pleased to meet her, and even more pleased to discover she was of Irish decent.

"An Irish lass, eh?" he told Sean. "You be sure to treat her like a queen."

Amy beamed and turned to Sean with a grin. "Make sure you take notes on this."

****

Over the coming weeks and months, Sean attended Mass at St. Francis almost daily, and he and Father Ian became fast friends. Ian had a great way of making God come to life, particularly with his examples and anecdotes. And Sean was also finding more of those passages that spoke to him on a personal level — God's love letters, as Ian had put it.

Things had rekindled with Amy as well, and Sean was reconnecting with old friends for weekends of football, baseball, and cookouts. He felt like the old Sean again, but with one glaring exception — and that came whenever the subject of future plans came up. He had none, and to be honest, nothing excited him the way discovering God did.

God had saved him from the pathetic slump he

had fallen into, and he felt an increasing need to share this.

"Have you thought about becoming a deacon?" Amy suggested over drinks one evening. "Or teaching religious ed?"

The truth was, he had thought of those options, but neither of them appealed to him. They felt like half steps toward something bigger and more meaningful.

But a bigger what?

Sean already suspected the answer but refused to admit it, because that answer terrified him.

This turmoil within him continued for a little over a month before Sean finally accepted that he needed to talk to someone.

"Question for you, Father," he asked Ian over beers after Mass one afternoon. "How did you know you were supposed to be a priest? And don't read anything into this. I'm just curious."

Ian chuckled. "Askin' the question for a friend, are yeh?"

Sean let out a chuckle himself. "Let's just say yes."

"Well, I'd tell that friend of yers it was when I found meself askin' that same question of a priest at me old parish back in Ireland. Fer a friend, of course."

Sean let out another chuckle. It was such a classic Ian response.

"Not the answer yeh was hoping for, was it?"

"Nope," Sean said with a shake of his head. "Definitely not. So, did it all feel like it just came out of left field for you?"

Ian nodded. "It usually does. Kinda hits yeh when yer busy makin' other plans. But yeh know how that sayin' goes. Yeh ever wanna make God laugh, just try tellin' Him yer plans."

There was something frustratingly truthful in that saying, and Sean saw the humor in it. But he wasn't amused. He could already see his life was on the verge of taking another huge turn.

Ian watched the frustration in Sean's face with empathy. He'd been there. "Tell yeh sumthin' else that priest told me back then," Ian picked up again. "And what he said was, 'A vocation isn't sumthin' you go chasing after; it's sumthin' that comes calling after you.'"

"What if you say no?"

"He leaves that up to you. But yeh gotta figure He had some reason He came callin' on yeh. Is that somethin' yeh wanna say no to?"

****

"I thought something like this might be happening," Amy said as she and Sean strolled along the shore. It was where they had spent so many days together growing up, and even planning their future together. And now it was a future that would never come to be.

Sean had fretted for weeks over telling Amy about what he increasingly felt was a calling to the priesthood. He had postponed it again and again, hoping that he would wake up one day and find it was all a fluke, that he had been let off the hook.

But that fire inside him had grown, and he could

actually picture himself now saying Mass and dispensing the Sacraments, and even telling a whole new generation of kids about these love letters God sends us. It could be wonderful for him, and amazing, and yet it meant closing a door he so desperately didn't want to close.

"How could you tell?" he asked.

"The way you light up every time you talk about God. Have you talked to anyone about this?"

"Just Father Ian."

"What did he say?"

"He said it ambushed him the same way. He said it's not something you chase after; it's something that calls you."

"Wow. So you're really thinking about this."

He nodded. "Yeah. I'm sorry."

"No." She stopped him, but there was no anger or bitterness in her voice. Only a touch of sadness. "You don't need to apologize, Sean. Not for saying yes to God."

"But I feel like I should. You didn't ask for any of this."

"You didn't either, Sean. But if God's calling you to be a priest, I think it's something you need to say yes to. We'll just call it another chapter in our hopelessly star-crossed relationship."

"I don't want it to be our last chapter."

They stopped walking. Amy turned to him and took his hands.

"It won't be. I will always love you, Sean. No

matter what. And I want you to know you have my full support on this."

****

Sean entered the seminary that fall, at the same time Amy began graduate school. They exchanged birthday and holiday cards over the years, but neither of them saw each other when they were in town. It was an unspoken understanding they seemed to have, that it would be too painful on both of them.

Their families, however, kept in close touch over the years, and kept each other updated on how their kids were doing. They each saw the other's kids as part of their own family, and there had never been any bitterness or resentment from Amy's parents that Sean had left Amy to become a priest. Amy wouldn't have tolerated it.

Sean handled his time in the seminary pretty well, especially for someone as phobic to commitments as he was. His biggest objection, however, was the heavy emphasis they placed on social justice issues, and the lack of focus on the "getting to know God" part that had attracted him in the first place. Why couldn't they emphasize both? After all, he had joined the priesthood, not the Peace Corps, and this aspect of his training annoyed him. He had written to Father Ian to voice his gripes about it several times and laughed at Ian's reply, in which Ian described much of modern theology as *"a whole lotta poppycock."*

Most detrimental, however, was the seminary's failure to teach the subject of demons, other than to dismiss them as literary license and metaphors. That left Sean wholly unprepared when he would encounter one several years later.

Sean was in his late twenties at the time of his ordination to the priesthood, and his first assignment was to the small parish of St. Matthew's in Capetown, Maine.

St. Matthew's church sat adjacent to its high school, and both were built of the same red brick architecture, with thick elm trees shading their grounds. And while it was considerably larger than Ian's tiny church back in Kenneth Point, Sean found it had the same welcoming intimacy.

The pastor was an elderly priest named Father Jenkins, who reminded Sean a lot of Father Ian (but absent the Irish brogue). They were both traditional in their faith, and had no qualms at discussing it over a pint of beer.

Sean was brought in to teach religious education at the parish's high school after the previous teacher, Mrs. Campos, had resigned suddenly. He never learned the full story behind her sudden departure, only that she felt there was something disturbingly wrong with one of the students — a girl named Cassie Stevens.

Cassie had once been a model student, described as a sweet, albeit shy, girl. All of that changed after her dad, who had taught physical education at the school, had died of a sudden heart attack.

Sean tried to talk to Mrs. Campos about her

concerns over Cassie, but Mrs. Campos had declined, stating only: "They'll know you're talking about them, Father. And that won't be good for you. Best to leave it be."

With that ominous warning in mind, Sean had no idea what to expect as he took on his role as teacher in the early months of Cassie's junior year. As he entered the classroom that first day, before having even looked at the seating chart, he knew which of the students was Cassie. She was a small girl sitting in back, slim and maybe five feet tall, with black dyed hair and thick eyeliner that clashed with her pale skin.

She watched him as he crossed the room, and there was something unsettling in her stare; he felt like she was sizing him up.

He stepped behind his desk and was unpacking his books when a voice spoke from the back of the room.

"Think you're ready for us, Father?"

Before even looking up from his books, he knew it was her. And when he finally did look up, he saw her staring at him with an unspoken challenge in her eyes. He also noticed, almost absently, that the other students were averting their eyes away from her.

"Guess we'll see, won't we?" Sean replied.

She merely grinned. "Guess we will."

At the time, he had assumed the "us" she referred to meant the other students. It would be much later that he realized she had meant *something* else.

****

Amy had attended graduate school in New York, where

she received her master's degree in English literature. She had been hired after graduation to teach creative writing at one of the State University campuses. It was only a four-hour drive to Kenneth Point, so she drove home often to see her family and friends.

Amy and Cheryl McCready had stayed close over the years, and they always arranged to meet for coffee when Amy was in town. Cheryl had been as heartbroken as Amy that she and Sean hadn't gotten married, but she still cherished Amy as a friend and happily updated Sean about her whenever he asked. Which was often. She knew the two of them still exchanged cards and gifts for each other's birthdays and holidays, and sent letters and emails back and forth.

Amy always went out of her way to find something sweet and meaningful to send Sean for his birthdays. This past year it had been a small gift box of dirt from home plate of the field where he had played baseball. Another year it had been a shell she had found while wandering the shore where he had told her about his vocation.

She knew he was an associate pastor at a small parish in Maine, where he was also teaching religious education and would be coaching the baseball team in the spring. They had exchanged teaching tips with each other, and his latest one made her laugh — *"Never let them see you sweat."*

She had just spent the weekend in Kenneth Point, and was back in New York teaching her creative writing class, when she collapsed at the front of the classroom.

CHAPTER THIRTEEN
Childhood's End

'For the moon never beams, without bringing me dreams
Of the beautiful Annabel Lee;
And the stars never rise, but I feel the bright eyes
Of the beautiful Annabel Lee;"

— *Annabel Lee* by Edgar Allan Poe

****

Sean was out jogging laps on the track that ran around the school's football field when the parish secretary came running out to find him.

"Your mom called, Sean," she said, huffing for breath. "She said it's important that you call her back right away."

Sean sprinted back to the rectory with the secretary and went upstairs to his room where he called his mom.

It was about Amy. She had suffered a ruptured aneurysm in her brain and was in critical condition. His mom was driving down to the New York hospital with Amy's family. She gave Sean the address of the hospital, and he booked a flight there as soon as he got off the phone.

Sean arrived at the hospital five hours later. His mom and Amy's parents were already there, and they exchanged warm but worried hugs. Amy had already been in surgery for six hours, and the staff had few updates at that point — only that there had been a massive amount of bleeding, and she had already suffered a second stroke.

Sean sank down in the waiting room chair. *This was real. This was really happening...* On the flight over, he had been sure he would arrive there and find her sitting up in bed and complaining about the hospital food and why everyone was making such a fuss.

But no — this was bad. This was bad on a scale like Conor. Sean just sat there with his mouth open and stared blankly at the wall across the room. There were no words. None. His mind was completely and terrifyingly numb.

It took an hour before Sean could even lead the others in prayer. They had gone into the chapel, but the words came heavy and forced.

A second stroke...

Sean felt no hope. There were none of God's *love letters* (hadn't Amy told him how beautiful that term sounded?) or sweet consolations that had carried him before.

God felt absent.

Amy was pronounced dead at 3:08 in the morning. Sean, his mom, and Amy's parents were still in the hospital chapel when the doctor delivered the news. It gripped Sean in another paralyzing numbness.

Amy was dead.

Those words. Had he really heard them? His mind was reeling.

The Amy of picnics and strolls on the sand, of long bike rides, tailgate parties, and road trips. The moist smell of her hair in the rain, and the sweet fragrance of her perfume.

Gone...

That day after practice, when she had first met him on the football field. How she had been so shy, and awkward, and endearing...

The way she blushed...

His best friend and partner in crime.

To the boy who always makes me smile, she had written to him on that napkin at the cafe. *I love you.*

"I love you too, Amy," he whispered to her memory through a grief too bitter for words.

Amy was dead.

And Sean's childhood died with her.

****

Amy's body was returned to Kenneth Point, where she would be laid to rest near the parks where she once played.

Her parents asked Sean if he would perform the Mass and burial, and he couldn't imagine a greater honor. He called Father Jenkins back at his parish in Maine and told him he would need several days off. His friend had passed away, and he needed to spend some time with her family, and his. Jenkins expressed his sincerest condolences and told Sean to take as much time as he needed. He also informed Sean that one of his students, Cassie Stevens, had been in a deadly automobile accident but was expected to recover.

Where was God in that? Sean thought to himself after their call. Amy died and Cassie lived. He had to agree with Mrs. Campos — there was something seriously disturbing about that girl. But he couldn't think about that now. He had his best friend's funeral to prepare for.

Sean spent an entire day writing and rewriting her eulogy. How do you sum up the importance of someone in mere words? Amy could have done it — she was great with words — but Sean was horrible at it. He finally decided to do it as a letter addressed to her.

"Dear Amy," he began his delivery the next day before the packed church. "My love, my dove, my beautiful one. You were a daughter, a teacher, and a friend to many. But to me you were my best friend, my love, my confidant, my companion, my partner. You were my light in the darkest times. You were quick to laugh, quick to forgive... quick to blush," he smiled at that one and was glad to see others in attendance also smile. Especially Amy's mom.

"You made life beautiful, and wonderful, and meaningful. You gave me the best years of my life, and I know that Heaven's a better place now because you're in it. So until we meet again, just know that I always have, and always will, love you. Sean."

And for the first time since he could remember, he wept.

Amy was laid to rest in the Whispering Pines Cemetery, not far from the shore where she and Sean had their first date, and it was consoling to see so many of their old high school friends in attendance.

Sean stuck around Capetown for another day after the funeral, just to spend some time with his family and Amy's. After that, it was back to Capetown and this life he had made for himself.

But something vital in him had died with Amy's passing. Something that gave life its zest and flavor. And by the time he had attended Katie Dunne's funeral three days later, God also felt gone.

CHAPTER FOURTEEN
A Warning

"Then the Devil approached Him and said, 'If you are the Son of God, command that these stones become bread...'"

It was Sean's first day back in the classroom after returning from Amy's funeral, and his students sensed a change in him. They had always related to him because he seemed like a big kid at heart. He wasn't uptight like that older priest, or any of the lay teachers. He joked around in class, answered questions they had about life as a teen, and even played sports with them. But the Sean who returned that day felt distant and somber.

There were rumors floating around that he had gone home to attend the funeral of an ex-girlfriend, and aside from the gossip that triggered, some part of him had been left behind; and it was the part that gave him life, and purpose, and made his lectures fun.

And Sean wouldn't have disagreed with this. He

knew he was just going through the motions that day. Ever since Amy's funeral, he'd been haunted by a torrent of what-ifs that called into question every major decision he had ever made.

What if he and Conor hadn't joined the Marines? Then his brother would still be alive.

What if he had gone to college, and played sports on his scholarship?

What if he hadn't become a priest?

And the biggest what-if of all — the one that curled his stomach into an agonized knot: *What if he'd married Amy?*

Would she still have died? Or could they have caught her aneurysm in time to treat it?

Could they have had their "happily ever after" together?

"Father?" One of the students spoke.

Sean snapped back, only then realizing he had chased those what-ifs down an endless rabbit hole. It was painful to return.

"Sorry," Sean said. "Where were we?"

"Jesus said in reply," answered a student.

Sean nodded. "Jesus said in reply, 'Man does not live on bread alone, but on every word that comes from the mouth of God.'" He set his Bible aside and looked up at the class. "Who wants to tell us what's going on here?"

Becca was a pretty teen who sat in the front row, and out of all of his students, she was usually the one most engaged in the class. She had just written some notes and quickly shot up her hand.

"Becca," he called to her.

"It shows that even Jesus was tempted by the Devil, but He was able to resist."

As he listened, something unsettling stirred within him. It was deep, and subtle, and something he couldn't recall feeling before.

It was a resistance.

He shook it off.

"I guess that's one way you could look at it," Sean said, "but if you take it so literally, you miss the bigger message the author was trying to convey."

Becca looked confused, and as Sean scanned the rest of the faces, most of them also looked confused.

"I should probably explain what I mean by 'bigger message,'" Sean said, and this was met by nods. "Okay, here's an example. In this passage, I think the lesson the author wants us to take away is self-restraint. Here we have Jesus, who's been fasting for forty days, so he has to be starved. And this guy offers him food, but Jesus resists. You see, that's a lesson all of us can apply in our daily lives."

A few students got it, but most of them still looked confused. Becca raised her hand again.

"Becca."

"But it uses the word 'Devil' to say who he was tempted by," she said.

Again that *resistance* stirred in Sean. Why was she so hung up on that word "Devil"?

"I don't think the author meant the literal 'Devil,'

Becca," Sean said. "I think it's just a figure of speech, or a metaphor for anything that tempts us."

It was also Cassie's first day at school since the accident, and she was at her desk in the back row against the window. She looked nothing like the girl her classmates had last seen. She'd washed the black dye from her hair, so it was back to its natural sandy brown color, and wore only a hint of makeup — far from the gaudy dark eyeliner she'd previously worn.

She'd been met by lots of stares as she walked the hallway that morning, and it felt weird. Although her memories from the time of the *Disturbances* were fuzzy, and the lines often blurred between what was real and what had been dreamed, she did recall that nobody stared at her; they were too scared to draw attention to themselves. But with that presence inside her gone now, the students felt free to stare and sneer and crack jokes about her and wonder why they had ever been afraid of this freak.

Not a single person said hi, or welcomed her back, or asked how she was feeling.

She was doing her best to pay attention and stay focused in class, but her mind kept wandering back to a poem she had begun in the library earlier that morning. It was about the loneliness she was feeling, and she was calling it "The Invisible Girl."

Father Sean had just called on the boy who sat next to her. She was pretty sure his name was Steve, but those memories of class introductions were still fuzzy.

"What about the other places in the Bible where it mentions the Devil?" Steve asked.

"Just mental illness, Steve," came Sean's response. "Back then, if you saw someone foaming at the mouth, your first thought was demonic possession. Thankfully, today we know it as epilepsy and treat it with medications instead of a witch doctor."

Most of the class laughed, and Cassie looked up from her poem to see Father Sean smiling at his own joke. It struck her as odd — *a priest who didn't believe in demons?* She almost raised her hand to say something but decided not to. She didn't want *Them* to know she was thinking about them. And they would know.

They were always watching.

It was then that she noticed a peculiar tingle in her mind, and a pressure beginning to build. It was blotting out sounds and filling her ears with a tinnitus-like ring.

As she looked around the classroom, she saw mouths moving and speaking words, but the actual sounds were distant and faded, like she was hearing them from across a great void.

Then a scent touched her nose — it was the soft fragrance of daisies she had smelled in the cemetery. She couldn't recall ever smelling it in here before, and a quick look around the classroom confirmed there were no daisies or any other flowers.

Someone was watching her.

This awareness came suddenly. It was from outside her window. She turned to look...

The window looked out on a grass courtyard with

a marble fountain in the middle and several oaks providing shade. It was surrounded on four sides by breezeways and classrooms built of red brick.

The *Little Girl* from the cemetery stood on the far side of the courtyard. She was in the same white Communion dress and holding a bundle of daisies.

She was staring right at Cassie.

Rather than feeling confusion or alarm, Cassie felt a gentle warmth wash over her. It was calming and relaxing, and dispelled much of the morose she had felt all morning.

"Cassie?"

From somewhere across that great void of silence came the sound of her name. But Cassie didn't want to let go of the peace she felt.

"Cassie?"

This time it came more forcefully, and sounds from the classroom came rushing back. She was met by a roomful of stares, including Father Sean, who had called her name.

"Yeah?" she said.

"Everything okay?" Sean asked.

Shit. He'd seen her staring out the window.

Before she could respond, a smartass named Daryl blurted out: "Uh. No."

The class erupted in laughter, and several kids seated around Daryl exchanged high-fives with him.

Cassie looked around at all the laughing faces and wished there was a way she could just disappear beneath her desk.

Sean blew into his fingers in a loud whistle to get everyone's attention. "How about we take it easy on Cassie. Okay?"

Most of the laughter died down at that point, but there were still a few giggles and snickers. Thankfully for Cassie, the bell rang, and everyone's focus turned to packing up their books.

Cassie took her time packing her books to give everyone else time to leave. As she did, she took one last look out the window. The *Little Girl* was gone. And the scent of daisies was also gone.

As soon as the last student left, Cassie grabbed her backpack and walked up to Sean.

"Hey," she said, stopping in front of his desk. "Sorry, I got kinda lost there for a bit."

"No worries," Sean said. "How are you feeling?"

She shrugged. "Not so great. But I'm alive. So I guess that counts."

He smiled and gave her a nod. He could already see a massive change in her since her accident. Her defiance and that odd quality about her were gone, but there was something else too; something he couldn't quite put his finger on.

"The new hair's a good look for you," he said.

"Oh. Thanks. Yeah, it's my natural color." She actually smiled, and Sean was pretty sure it was the first time he'd seen her smile. But then it faded, and she took a deep breath before continuing.

"I want to apologize for the way I've acted. There was something wrong with me, but I think I'm better now."

"Do you want to talk about it?"

She hesitated, then shook her head. "Maybe someday, when I get it all sorted out. But I just really want you to know I'm sorry about everything. I hope you won't hate me anymore."

With that, she turned and started for the door.

"Cassie," Sean called out to her. She stopped mid-step and turned. "I don't hate you. It's nice to meet this version of you. I hope she sticks around."

Cassie nodded. "Yeah. Me too."

****

See me.
Am I really that different?
I have cares.
I have dreams.
I hurt, and your smile could have cheered me.
I ache, and your nod could have healed me.
I mourn, and your words could have soothed me.
I died, and your touch could have saved me.
See me.

— "The Invisible Girl" by Cassie Stevens

****

Cassie maneuvered through the maze of students in the hallway, keeping her head low to avoid eye contact. After the ridicule she just took in class, she decided being ignored was easier than being seen. She noticed several conversations stop mid-sentence as she passed, but she still caught bits and pieces of them —

"What's she doing back?"

"Someone said she died."

"I heard someone was killed in the crash."

"Why isn't she in jail?"

"Why couldn't she have just stayed dead?"

She spotted an opening in the hallway crowd and squeezed through it to the bathroom.

She was relieved to find the bathroom empty. She walked over to the sink, splashed some water on her face, then looked in the mirror. Why did she even bother trying to look pretty that day? Nobody cared; they all hated her.

A few tears swelled beneath her cheeks, but she fought them back. They would only give everyone another reason to pick on her.

Voices were coming from outside the door. She quickly ducked into a stall and pulled the door shut. She stood on the toilet so her feet wouldn't show beneath the stall's door.

She heard the bathroom door open and two girls enter. She recognized their voices as Tina and Cindy from her religious ed class that had just ended. She'd known them both since fifth grade, and her dad had even coached Tina's brother on his Pee Wee league team. She and Cassie used to talk to each other in the bleachers while watching the games.

"I laughed so fucking hard when Daryl said that," Cassie heard Tina say to Cindy, and then she mimicked Daryl's voice: "Uh. No."

Cindy exploded in laughter. "I know, right? Oh, and the way Cassie just sat there with her mouth open."

"Duh!" Came Tina's voice again. "Loser. You couldn't even die right."

Both girls burst out in laughter.

"I mean, seriously," Cindy jumped back in. "How hard is it? You're halfway there already."

"Just don't start breathing," came Tina's voice again. "Boom! Done!"

They were laughing again. Cassie heard the faucets turn on briefly then the air dryers.

"Maybe we'll get lucky and she'll forget to wake up tomorrow," said Cindy, and they laughed as they walked to the door and headed out.

"Fingers crossed on that one," came Tina's voice, then the door clicked shut.

Cassie waited inside the stall for the bell to ring. When it finished ringing, she grabbed her backpack and hurried from the bathroom. The hallway was empty as she raced down it and out the double doors at the end.

****

The cafes and shops along the town's Main Street were closing down for the night. Many already had their "Closed" signs in the windows as Cassie strolled past.

Main Street passed for downtown in Capetown. It had its rows of elms like the rest of the town, and its sidewalks were lined with gas lamps. Cassie hated that it closed so early, because it's where most of the cool shops were at.

She stopped outside the pet shop, which had

already closed for the night, and looked in the long window that lined its front. The lights were already off inside, but there was enough light from the gas lamps to see in.

A cage of young puppies sat near the window, and they watched excitedly at the stranger staring in at them. It reminded her of when they picked up Rex as a pup, and she wanted to adopt them all.

Something stood behind her in the reflection. It was tall and dark, like the silhouette of a man.

She startled and spun around... but no one was there. She looked both ways down the block, but there were only a handful of pedestrians at the far end. She turned back to the window, but there was nothing in the reflection this time.

The hairs on her arms prickled. She hurried off down the block to the wharf district, where its cafes and taverns stayed open late. She bought a soda, then took it with her down to the pier.

She strolled out onto the town's wooden pier, passing boats that rocked gently in the tide. She sat down at the end and let her feet dangle over the side. A crescent moon hung in the sky, and its light rippled across the black waters of the sound.

Just a hallucination, she told herself. Nothing had been behind her in the reflection. It had been the gas lamps playing tricks on her eyes.

A chill breeze had picked up while she sat there, and it whistled through the masts of the nearby boats. Something in its sound caught her attention. It was subtle, and there wasn't any particular quality in it she could pick out; it just felt *off*. She looked back at the masts as they swayed gently, and flags flapped in the breeze. It was gone now, whatever that odd feeling was.

It would be much later, as she looked back on that night, that she realized the breeze had borne a warning.

He was coming.

CHAPTER FIFTEEN
The Lighthouse

It was her second day of school, and Cassie woke up already dreading it. Alison had breakfast cooking by the time she stumbled downstairs and plopped down at the table.

Alison looked over from the stove and gave her a smile. "There's coffee made, if you want some."

She did. "Thanks," Cassie mumbled as she shuffled over, poured herself a cup, and took it back to the table.

She'd barely slept at all that night after returning from the pier. That reflection, or hallucination, or whatever it was she'd seen in the window, had her worried.

"Eggs?" Alison asked.

"Okay."

Alison scooped some eggs on a plate and set it on the table in front of Cassie. "You ready for your second day of school?"

Cassie shook her head. "Nope."

"How was your first day?"

Cassie poked at her eggs. "Sucked."

"Oh, honey. I'm sorry. Do you want to talk about it?"

"Not really."

"Were the kids being mean?"

"Can we not talk about it."

"Okay," Alison said and walked back over to the stove. There was a photo on the counter next to the stove that she picked up. "I found this photo in an old scrapbook last night and thought you might like it."

She took it over to the table and set it in front of Cassie. It showed two eight-year-old kids in their Halloween costumes — they were Cassie and Justin, dressed as a princess and a cowboy.

Alison couldn't resist a chuckle. "You two were so cute. Have you talked to Justin lately?"

Cassie shook her head, continuing to stare at the photo. It was yet another reminder of the happy days of the *before*. "No. Not in a while," she said.

"That's too bad. You two always seemed so happy together."

Cassie nodded. They had been. And she missed it. She set the photo down and poked at her eggs again.

Alison watched this. She had hoped the photo would make Cassie happy, but it obviously hadn't. She wrapped her arms around her from behind and gave her a kiss on top of her head. "I love you, Cass. Things are gonna get better. I promise."

"I hope so."

****

It was a lot more of the same for Cassie as she walked through the school hallway that day. There were the blatant stares and abrupt stops to conversations, but there seemed to be less snickering. Hopefully that meant the novelty was wearing off.

She spotted Justin down the hallway as he tugged his backpack from his locker. He and the other jocks were in their football jerseys for game day, and the cheer squad was running around in their cheerleader skirts. It was all part of the school spirit camaraderie Cassie had once felt a part of, back in the *before*. And along with goofy Halloween costumes, and dollar nights at the Mayflower, it was something she missed.

"Hey," she said as she strolled up to Justin. "Remember me?" She had decided to wear a smile to see how it felt, but right now it was feeling really forced and fake. Hopefully he wouldn't notice.

"Hey," he said back as he slammed his locker shut, then noticed her hair. "You got your old hair back."

She had forgotten about the hair. She drew several strands in front of her face to give herself something to fidget with.

"Yeah. Black wasn't really doing it for me."

"Brown looks better."

"Thanks," she said, and this time her smile was real.

Cassie was lucky that Justin had never encountered her up close during the months of the *Disturbances*, so what he knew of them came only second hand. They mostly sounded to him like BS, or people exaggerating. He'd seen her with the black hair and goth clothes from a distance but didn't see how that made her dangerous or scary.

But still, a lot of people did fear her, or at least used to, and even more disliked her, as was becoming apparent from the stares they were receiving as people walked past.

Cassie seemed oblivious to the stares; she wasn't, but over the years she'd gotten used to them.

"So. Game tonight?" she said, nodding to his jersey.

"Yeah. We play Oakwood."

"Oh. Cool. Good luck."

"Thanks." He noticed even more stares now and felt like he had broken some rule. Cassie also noticed, and now she noticed Justin noticing.

"I should get to class," he said. He didn't want to hurt her feelings, but he felt like he was under a microscope from all those stares.

"My mom found this in a scrapbook," she quickly cut in before he could escape. She dug through her backpack and handed him the photo of them.

He cringed and let out a chuckle as he looked at the eight-year-old him. "My cowboy phase."

"And my princess phase," she said with a cringe herself.

"How old were we back then?" he asked.

"Eight. And I'm using temporary insanity as my

excuse."

"I'll use that one too."

He handed it back to her, and finally let his eyes meet hers. They were that light shade of blue he remembered, almost like the sky, and for a brief moment he forgot about all those stares.

"You doing okay, Cass? I heard about the accident."

She thought about it and nodded. "I think so. Except these stupid broken ribs. They make it suck trying to sleep."

He cringed and nodded. "Been there. It does suck."

"Hey, Mahoney, you pussy," came a boy's voice from the adjoining hallway behind him. "Drop and give me twenty."

Justin looked back and saw his buddies Daryl and Tim watching him. They were also in jerseys.

Cassie knew Daryl — he was the asshole who had ripped on her in class the day before. Tim, she didn't know, but she knew who he was.

Justin turned back to Cassie and this time had difficulty meeting her eyes. The weight of peer pressure was back on.

"I should get going," he said.

"Yeah. Me too. I'll let you know if my mom finds any more blackmail photos."

He smiled at this, then headed over to the boys.

Daryl shook his head with dismay. "The fuck were you doing with that weird chick?"

Cassie had only taken a few steps down the hallway when she overheard this. She stepped into the doorway of an empty classroom and stood there to listen.

"Talking," replied Justin, sounding defensive. "What'd it look like?"

"Looked like you two was being all friendly."

"Do you know her?" Tim asked.

"Sort of. Her dad used to coach my baseball team."

"Well, she ain't her dad," Daryl said. "That chick is seriously messed up."

"What was the picture she showed you?" Tim asked.

"Just some picture." This was feeling like an interrogation now.

"Of what?"

"None of your fucking business. Okay?"

"So there is something between you guys," Daryl said with a smug smile.

"No. I told you. I knew her dad."

"Then why are you getting all defensive about it?"

"I'm not. Why are you guys up my ass about it?"

"Just looking out for you, man," said Tim. "That is one fucked-up chick."

"Fine. Whatever. It's not like I'm friends with her."

"Hope not," said Daryl with a smirk.

"Fuck off," said Justin. "Let's get to class."

Cassie missed the rest of their conversation as the boys disappeared down the adjoining hallway. But she had heard enough. She slipped from the classroom doorway and hurried off down the hallway.

Once outside the building, she raced across the parking lot to the bus stop on the far side. She was cutting her last two classes and getting out of there before she did something stupid. Like cry.

She boarded the bus and headed down the aisle to the backseat. She slid across it to the window, then put in her earbuds and pulled up a playlist on her phone. She turned up the music loud enough to drown out her thoughts.

Normally the ride across town took about fifteen minutes, but traffic that day was at a slow crawl. Cassie removed her earbuds and looked out the window on her right to see what was causing the delay.

They were nearing an intersection, and she saw that traffic had backed up behind a crash. She could only see one of the cars — it was flipped on its side in the middle of the intersection, with its front end completely crushed. There was glass and metal parts everywhere; enough to let her know that someone had probably died.

On the sidewalk was the usual crowd of spectators that gathered like vultures at wrecks.

Cassie glanced up the aisle to the large front windshield and saw police directing traffic around the wreckage.

With a lurch, the bus groaned forward and steered into the left turn lane. Cassie sat back and was inserting her earbuds back into her ears when she felt that sudden tingle again of being watched. She looked around at the other passengers, but their focus was on the wreck. Even passengers on the left side of the aisle were craning for a peek out the right-side window.

Was it outside?

Before she could look, the *Stench* hit.

It was the fetid odor of rot and decay, of maggot-infested meat left in the sun; or a bloated corpse whose organs had liquefied. Her stomach heaved, and bile filled her mouth. It burned as she tried to choke it back down...

Something was outside her window.

A ghoulish *Face* was there, staring at her from its hollow eyes. She only caught a quick glimpse before it vanished, and she noticed the *Stench* fade off with it. But she was sure something had been there, and a deep crushing fear gripped her as she continued to stare at the empty window.

It was back.

****

Father Jenkins' study was on the second floor of the parish rectory. It was decorated like a small shrine, with dark paneled walls, paintings of Christ and the saints, a small angel statue on his desk, and rows of bookcases. His desk was near the back wall, and behind it was a window that overlooked the school's courtyard.

Jenkins was at his desk reading, when a knock came at the door on the far side of the room. He set the book aside and looked over.

"Yes?"

The door opened, and Sean poked his head in. "You wanted to see me, Father?"

"Yes. Yes, Sean. Please, come in."

Sean closed the door behind him and walked over. "Is something wrong?"

"That's what I'd like to find out," Jenkins said. "I had several parents call and tell me you were teaching their kids that demons don't exist. Is that so?"

"What I told them was that the Bible uses them as metaphors. Not literal demons."

Jenkins looked aghast. "And wherever did you get such an idea?"

"It's what they taught us in the seminary."

"Oh, good Lord," Jenkins muttered and ran a hand through his thinning gray hair. "I'm going to need you to forget everything they taught you about demons, Sean, because they're wrong. And dangerously so."

"So, you believe demons are literally real?"

"Oh, yes, Sean," Jenkins said with a big nod. "In fact, I'm quite certain of it. And not only are they real, their actions can have dire consequences for us."

Sean couldn't get over how much Jenkins reminded him of Ian at that moment. "What kind of consequences?"

"Well, it varies considerably, depending on the individual. In lesser instances, you might find inexplicable mood swings, or sudden thoughts that feel alien to you. But as it progresses, you might find yourself compelled to behaviors, or presented with thoughts you feel are abhorrent, and yet an inexplicable attraction draws you to them. The common factor in all these stages is that these outside thoughts are presented to you as your own. It's the way in which the demon disguises itself. You see, by presenting these thoughts to you as your own, it's much more likely you'll consent to them and act on them. And eventually, if you continue to allow your consent, it can reach a stage known as possession. This is where the demon now inhabits its victim and exerts direct dominion and control over them.

As Sean listened, that odd feeling of *resistance* stirred again. It was more than a simple disagreement with Jenkins over his superstitious beliefs; he felt resentment toward the old man for believing that way.

"You believe that actually happens?" Sean asked, and it held a note of condescension that surprised Sean. But Jenkins didn't seem to notice.

"Oh, yes, Sean," replied Jenkins, "I have no doubt whatsoever. You see, I've had the unfortunate experience to have encountered such an individual, and to have felt the threat presented by the demon that inhabited her."

****

The bus groaned to a stop at the turnoff to the lighthouse. Cassie climbed out and headed down the wooded path that lead past the lighthouse and over to a grassy the bluff at the end. From there, it plunged steeply to the rocky shore below.

This was where she had always come for inspiration for her poems. On a clear day, she could sit and watch the ocean roll out over the horizon. But this day wasn't clear — it was gray and murky, which matched her spirits.

She sat down and unpacked her journal from her backpack, then spent several minutes staring out over the haze. She had spent the rest of the bus ride convincing herself that the *Face* she saw in the bus window was only her own reflection. And that thing she had seen reflected in the pet store window? It had been the gas lamps creating an illusion.

It couldn't be back. She almost didn't survive it the first time.

What she couldn't deny so easily was Justin's rejection. *He was ashamed of me.* Her heart ached in a way it hadn't in a long time — maybe even since her dad died.

She needed to escape her thoughts and hoped immersing herself in poetry would work like it had in the past. She picked up her journal and browsed through her old poems. The earlier ones she recalled vividly — she had written them during the happy days of the *before.* Her dad was alive to her again in those memories, and life was filled with simple wonderments and innocence.

A pronounced shift in tone came with the loss of her dad, and the advent of the *after.* They became bleak, and dark, and filled with ruminations on death and all things of darkness and night. Particularly disturbing was one she had titled "A Requiem in Black." It had been an ode to *Death.*

Cassie shivered as she read the dark words on those pages. She and her friends had been idiots to think they could seduce something as cold, powerful, and uncaring as *Death*. And now that she had seen its face, and the eternity of horror it held for her, she wanted nothing to do with it. It would come someday, as it did for everyone, but until then it was to be resisted.

She looked back at the ocean and sky and took a moment to shake off those disturbing thoughts. She needed to put herself back into the mind of that happy hopeful girl from the *before* — a girl she hoped still lived inside her somewhere.

With a deep breath, she flipped to a blank page and began writing. Her initial inspirations were of the colorful autumn days of her youth when the world had seemed magical. It had been filled with the innocent delights of spending afternoons at the park while her dad coached; of raking leaves with Justin, and jumping into them; of long strolls through the forest, enjoying the sights and smells; of playing with Rex; of the fresh smell that followed a New England rain shower; and of the rainbows that had colored her childhood skies.

She continued on, but as she wrote, she felt those memories drifting further and further away till they were mere specks in the distance; and something ominous was taking their place. She began to feel a peculiar pressure in her head, as if something was seeking entry into her thoughts and mind. Somewhere, just beyond the reach of her awareness, thoughts were forming and being pressed on her. And while it was her mind that was being forced into consent, those thoughts hadn't come from her.

She panicked — *something was forcing its way into her mind*, and it was doing so with brutal determination. She struggled to resist, but it proved relentless, as it probed for openings into her thoughts and imagination.

She needed to shut off her imagination and thoughts. Even the thought of thoughts needed to stop, as she no longer trusted her mind to discern which were hers and which came from outside.

She closed her eyes and focused on one singular mantra — *don't think*.

Despite her efforts, pieces of that outside filth oozed in, flooding her imagination with grotesqueness and horror. A crushing despair seized her. She would see her dad one moment, happily coaching baseball on those summer afternoons... then watch as maggots burrowed from his bloated corpse...

Daisies...

The smell came suddenly, and as it did, those alien thoughts retreated from her mind.

She opened her eyes and exhaled sharply. Without even looking, Cassie knew *She* was there.

The *Little Girl* stood near the lighthouse less than fifty yards away. She appeared as she had the previous two times, and as before, a gentle warmth washed over Cassie.

Cassie sat like this for several minutes, with neither of them saying a word, and then the girl slipped away around the lighthouse corner.

Cassie looked up at the slowly darkening sky, and it was only then she realized it was getting late. She had no idea how long she had been there, but it must have been a lot longer than she thought. It felt odd that she couldn't remember most of that time.

She went to close her notebook when her eyes fell on the page she had been writing on. And she froze. She had been writing the entire time, without having been aware of it, and there were several pages filled with one word repeated over and over.

It said, *"Dead."*

****

"Into that maw of darkness I stare;
aeon's ode to eternal despair;
then whispered it taunts from chasms deep —
'Fear the night, child; for I walk while you sleep.'"

— "Requiem in Black" by Cassie Stevens
****

Cassie's nerves were still on edge as she returned home from the lighthouse. The house was dark as she entered, and flipping on the lights, she found a note from her mom taped to the fridge, along with a ten-dollar bill — *"They need me to work late tonight to make up for the week I took off. Use the money to buy dinner. Love, Mom."*

Great. She was alone in this big house. It wasn't like she could fault her mom — she had taken the week off to be with Cassie at the hospital — but the thought of being alone still left her feeling uneasy.

She thought about crashing out on the couch in front of the TV till her mom got home, but who knew when that would be. Plus, she would have to explain why, and she wasn't sure if she even knew the answer to that.

"Rex," she called out, looking around for her dog. He could be her bodyguard and chase away all the bad things that came in.

"Rex," she called out again, but apparently he was outside. She could always go get him, but he was probably covered in mud from the sprinkler. Anything wet and muddy was like catnip to him. She finally decided to just suck it up and headed upstairs alone to her room.

As she entered, she noticed it felt cooler than the hallway. She looked across the room to the window, but it was shut, and there weren't any other openings for a draft to come in.

She took a step back into the hallway, then stepped again into her room. It was definitely colder in here. She didn't really give it any more thought at the time, other than thinking it was odd. It would only be much later that she would understand the significance of this and the ominous forewarning it portended.

She tossed her backpack on the floor, slid out of her school skirt, and pulled on a T-shirt. She climbed into bed and pulled the blanket over her.

She lay there for a moment, giving her mind time to settle. Maybe all of this could be explained — the

Face, the writing, the *Stench*... Maybe all she needed was a good night's sleep, and everything would be okay in the morning.

Maybe...

But it wouldn't.

And that night, the *dreams* began.

CHAPTER SIXTEEN
Dreams

*"Is all that we see or seem,
but a dream within a dream?"*

— *A Dream Within a Dream* by Edgar Allan Poe

****

Cassie wandered down the dark forest path. Through a thick canopy of leaves overhead, thin slivers of moonlight filtered down to light her path in its ghostly pall.

All around her was darkness and mist. Within the darkness, unseen eyes watched, and hungry things prowled. Baleful spirits wailed their hideous cries as they drifted through trees, and Cassie's skin crawled with supernatural dread.

It was a forest of the dead, and yet it lived with unnatural life. Its air whispered a haunting chorus that circled and teased —

Caaasssiiiieee it beckoned in whispered taunts.

Come to us, Caaassssiiiee...

Play with us...

Casssiiiiieeee...

Stay...

Be with us Cassiiiiieee...

Come...

Fear gripped her and she hurried on, desperate to escape this haunted forest where dead things hunted and prowled.

She finally emerged into a desolate clearing where nothing grew. All plant life ceased at the forest's edge, and as she looked out across that broad windswept plain, she saw the reason.

In its center, some distance from the boundary of the forest, rose the grim specter of a massive foreboding manor.

It loomed mightily in the night, with the moon to its back, revealing only the dark dimensions of its immense breadth. And from inside its unhallowed walls, echoed screams of infinite torment carried across the plain.

As much as she feared the forest from which she had just come, she dreaded that manor even more. Its essence was of such unbounded evil that it held the night in terror.

It was what the night feared.

Cassie felt the icy fingers of a paralyzing terror grip her soul.

She knew this place.

And it wanted her back.

Cassie startled awake. She was drenched in a cold sweat, and her pulse pounded in her ears. The nightmare had felt so real and vivid that its dark aura breathed into her mind for several more minutes.

It was the sting of the cold room on her bare legs that finally drew her attention away from the nightmare. Her blanket was gone. As her eyes adjusted to the dim moonlight that sifted through her curtains, she spotted it on the floor across the room. She started to rise to get it, then suddenly froze.

Something was in the room.

It wasn't that she'd seen or heard anything. It was an awareness that came as an instinct; a prickling of hairs on her arms.

She gripped her sheet and tried to pull it over her, but it was matted up beneath her. She turned back to the room and slowly swept her eyes across it. There was just enough light for her to see the dark forms of her furniture. There was her dresser, with the mirror above it, her desk, a chair...

It was in the corner.

From the corner of her eye, she had caught a subtle movement in the shadows near her closet; but when she turned her head in that direction, nothing was there.

A loud bark came from outside and nearly startled her from her skin. She clenched her teeth for a moment to settle her nerves.

It was of course Rex, and this gave her a sense of relief. At least he was also awake.

Then came another bark, and then another, and that relief she had felt was gone. Something was outside.

She hopped from bed and sprang across the room to the light switch and flipped it on. Nothing was in her room.

She pulled on some jeans and went over to the window. She drew the curtains aside and looked down at the grass clearing behind her house. The moon was just a sliver in the sky, but in its cold light she saw Rex in the middle of the yard, tugging at his leash.

And barking at the dark woods that bordered her yard.

Cassie climbed down the wooden steps from her back porch and crossed the damp yard to Rex. He was tense like she had never seen him and focused completely on those dark woods. He startled as she reached down to pet him, then returned his attention to the woods.

Something was out there, and Cassie was beginning to feel it herself. And whatever it was, it was able to scare a large German Shepard.

"Hey, buddy," she said, stroking his back. "You see something?" She followed his gaze to the woods where she could see the dark outline of the trees along its border, but the moonlight failed to penetrate beyond that.

Rex took a tense step back, and all at once, the night grew still. There were no more sounds of insects, or animals, or even the breeze. The night was holding its breath, as something ominous moved through it.

The fur on Rex's back bristled, and a low growl rumbled in his throat. He sensed the change too. But then his growl faded, and a terrified whimper escaped him. He took several steps back. Whatever was out there, it had met his challenge, and this was Rex's whimpering retreat in the presence of a dominant predator.

Cassie watched his reaction. "Come on, buddy. Let's get inside." She reached for his collar...

Rex suddenly jerked away and bounded off across the yard to the house where he hid beneath the porch.

And now Cassie was all alone; just her, and whatever was in those woods. She slowly turned back to them and tried to see into the darkness beyond its border. Something was there. She sensed it now even more than before. And it was watching her.

"What are you looking at?" came Seth's voice, and Cassie nearly screamed. She saw that he was standing beside her, and next to him were Silvia and Trish. She had been so focused on Rex and the woods that she hadn't even heard them approach.

"Shit!" Cassie swore when she regained her breath. "Don't do that."

"Don't do what?" he said, feigning innocence.

"Don't sneak up on me like that. It's not cool."

"But it's funny as hell."

"So is me macing you."

"What were you looking at, Cass?" Silvia asked.

Cassie nodded to the woods. "There's something out there."

"What is it?" Trish asked.

"I don't know. But I think Rex saw something."

"Is that why he ran away?" Silvia asked.

"Yeah."

The others turned to stare at the woods.

"Maybe it was like a rabbit or something," Silvia offered. "Or a fox."

Seth snorted. "You think a rabbit scared the shit out of Cassie's dog."

"Then you then tell me what it was," Silvia shot back.

"Something a lot scarier than a rabbit. You know animals can see shit that we can't."

"Like what?" Cassie asked.

"Ask your dog the next time you see him growling into an empty room."

Trish nodded in agreement. "They say animals have a sort of sixth sense."

"Which means what exactly?" Cassie asked.

"It means you've got a ghost in your backyard, Cass," Seth said.

Trish and Silvia nodded in agreement. Cassie looked back at the woods for a moment, then again at her friends.

"So, what are you guys doing here?" Cassie asked.

"Was that you saying how good it is to see us?"

said Trish.

"Sorry. It's good to see you guys. And what are you doing here?"

"We came to see you, bae," Silvia said. "We missed you."

"Hug it out, bitch," Trish said and grabbed Cassie and Silvia in a group hug.

"We tried to see you at the hospital," Silvia said when they finally broke off the hug, "but we couldn't get in."

"They said it was family only," Trish added. "No scary goth kids."

"So, how've you been?" Silvia asked.

Cassie shrugged. "Surviving? They said I was dead."

"That's what we heard," Trish said. "So, what was it like?"

Cassie thought about it a moment and shook her head. "I don't know. I don't really remember any of it."

"No bright light or anything?" Silvia asked.

Cassie shook her head. "Nope."

"Oh, fuck that," said Seth. "How could you not remember?"

"'Cause I don't."

"You got to actually see the other side, and you don't remember."

"Nope."

"Well, that sucks. Next time you die, be sure to take better notes."

"I'll keep that in mind."

Seth smirked. "Now, if everyone could please gather around..." He held up his fist in a tribute. "I'd like to offer tribute to our friend, Cassie Stevens, who got to taste death, and then cheat it. And even if she can't remember any of it, which is totally lame..." He shot Cassie a wink to let her know he was just messing with her. "It's still good to have you back, Stevens."

****

While Cassie dreamed of the dark Manor in the clearing, across town Father Sean was deep within his own dream...

A gray sky clung over a dozen mourners gathered around a grave. Father Ian read from his missal, while the mourners listened and wept.

Sean observed this from beneath the shade of a tree some distance away and only caught pieces of Ian's sermon.

"I am the resurrection and the life..." he heard Ian saying...

A peculiar feeling struck Sean as he watched. It felt oddly familiar, like he had been here before and knew who these people were and who the funeral was for. The answers seemed to be on the tip of his tongue, yet remained frustratingly elusive. All he knew for certain was that he was observing a funeral, and it was being presided over by a priest he also felt he should know.

"Whoever believes in me shall not die, but shall have eternal life..."

Several mourners stepped aside, and behind them Sean saw Amy's parents. Now he understood why it felt so familiar — he was at Amy's funeral.

At this point, Sean became strangely cognizant that he was in a dream. It was the recurrence of a dream he previously had of Amy's death and funeral, only in that dream Sean had presided over her funeral.

Of course Amy wasn't dead in real life, and Sean's dreaming self knew this; it was only in this dream and the previous one that she was dead. But it worried him that his dreams kept returning to this theme.

"And I will raise him on the last day..."

He also observed that he was a priest again in this dream and the recurrence of this theme also troubled him. Of course he wasn't a priest in real life, and his dreaming self knew this. He was a college student, attending Boston College on a baseball scholarship with Amy. They had plans to marry. And he obviously had no intention of telling her about these dreams, as they would only worry her.

He turned his attention back to the funeral and found that it was over and everyone was gone.

Father Ian. That was the priest's name. But how did he know this?

An unease came over Sean. There were large gaps in his memory, and so many pieces of this puzzle were missing; pieces he knew were significant.

How did he know that priest? He was certain they had met somewhere, but he had no idea how or where.

He began to suspect that these memories of his sleeping self might not be the memories of his waking self. But where had they come from? And what would he awake to find?

At that moment, the answer came to him, and it was like a door to his waking memories had suddenly opened. He was, in fact, a priest... and Amy was, in fact, dead.

A sudden grief hit his stomach the way it had at Amy's real death. He stared numbly at her casket — at where his hope for happiness lay dead...

Then he felt its approach.

It came in the bitter wind now blowing through the trees and in the dark storm clouds forming overhead. Something monstrous and obscene was coming, an affront to all that was pure and good...

Amy was coming... but it wasn't his Amy.

Sean struggled to back away but was now caught in the full force of the dream and the ominous game master that controlled it. Whatever had placed him here, it wouldn't allow him to leave until he saw *what she had become.* It needed to dash against jagged rocks of despair every last ounce of hope and faith he had clung to.

She was closer now...

As the wind moaned its ghostly hymn through the trees, Sean struggled not to listen, because he knew if he listened, he would hear her voice. And yet the more he struggled to block out sounds, the louder they came.

And closer...

Sean knew he would soon hear it... and within seconds he did.

"Sean..."

It was the sound he had feared. It was her voice, carried on the wind, in the hollow echo of an empty tomb.

Then he saw her — *Amy's ghostly figure*. She stood twenty yards away, covered in her death shawl and looking pale and emotionless.

"I'm so cold, Sean..."

He closed his eyes to shut it out. That thing wasn't Amy. It was a blasphemy. Don't look at it. Don't listen to it...

"You left me, Sean... You left me alone..."

With his eyes still closed, he now felt it next to him — the presence of something cold and unloving. He made the mistake of opening his eyes.

She stood in front of him, with black soulless eyes that bored into his.

"Come inside me, Sean... like we did on the beach..."

"You're not Amy..." he muttered.

"No one will know..."

"You're not Amy!" This time he shouted.

Her skin began to darken and crinkle. Dark splotches spread across her face, and clumps of hair fell from her scalp. The skin of her face shriveled and tore like thin sheets of paper, and her lips peeled back from her teeth in a grim death's face.

She raised a skeletal hand and reached for his face...

And he felt it touch him.

Sean shot awake in his bed at the rectory. His pulse

pounded in his ears, and his shirt was drenched with sweat. He breathed heavily, clenching his fists and forcing his mind away from memories of that dream. They had disturbed him on so many levels — not just in their degradation of Amy, but in the despair and confusion they had sought to instill in him. And to some extent, they had succeeded.

As he lay back on his pillow, he couldn't shake the truth of one thing that counterfeit Amy had said.

"You left me, Sean... You left me alone..."

CHAPTER SEVENTEEN
It Came Back

The large bus rumbled down the street on its morning commute. Cassie sat in the back again and watched the town awaken through the window. Shopkeepers flipped the "Open" signs in their windows, and vendors wheeled their pastry carts onto sidewalks. There was the usual morning crowd of early risers, relaxing over coffees at outdoor cafes and reading the morning paper. A few joggers ran past.

The bus turned onto a new street, and they were soon passing more colorful wooden shops and pedestrians.

Two men were walking their dogs in opposite directions as the bus groaned to a stop at a streetlight. The man coming from her left had a dark lab, while the man coming from her right had a pit bull. The men exchanged greetings and continued on. They had walked a little ways farther when their dogs stopped and turned to stare at the window Cassie was watching from. The dogs appeared confused at first, cocking their heads to the side, then suddenly burst into barks.

They lunged forward, yanking the leashes from their startled owners' grips, and leaped at Cassie's window.

The pit bull's head crashed into it like a mallet, shattering it into jagged shards. Cassie dove from her seat and across the aisle, and passengers screamed. The dogs leaped again, and their paws caught the bottom edge of the broken window. They barked furiously as they scrambled to climb in.

"Go!" a frightened passenger shouted to the driver, who had been watching all of this through his side mirror. He laid on his horn to alert traffic then pressed down on the gas. Cross-traffic skidded to a stop as the bus lurched forward through the intersection.

The dogs lost their grips on the window and fell to the street but were quickly back up and chasing the bus.

Cassie raced back to her window and looked out at the chaos behind them. Cars had piled up in the intersection and the dogs bounded through them after the bus.

The bus sped down the block and quickly spun the corner onto a new block. Cassie watched the dogs fall farther and farther behind till they finally gave up the chase.

The dogs had accomplished what they wanted — they had chased away that ghoulish *Face* they had seen watching them from the window.

****

"You left me, Sean... You left me alone..."

Sean sat in the front pew of the empty church, alone with his haunting memories of the dream.

In front of him was the tabernacle, where they stored the consecrated Communion Hosts, and to the right of that was the altar, where a large crucifix hung from the ceiling above it. But Sean barely noticed any of this; his thoughts were on the dream. And try as hard as he could, he couldn't shake off those words from the dream —

"You left me, Sean... You left me alone..."

It was like a stone had lodged in his shoe, and his foot rubbed over it till blisters formed and bled.

He tried praying, but it came forced and dry... and he felt nobody was listening on the other end.

What kind of priest couldn't even pray?

A bad one, an inner voice whispered to him. *A fraud.*

It troubled him that he didn't disagree with this.

Maggie Dunne entered at the rear of the church. She looked around the empty sanctuary and spotted Sean at the far end. She headed down the aisle toward him, paying little attention to the religious trappings around her. Those stained-glass windows depicting gospel themes, and statues of saints, meant nothing to this widowed mother of a dead child.

"Hey, Father," she said, sliding into the pew beside Sean. "The office said I could find you here. Can we talk?"

Sean glanced at her and tried not to let his annoyance at her intrusion show. "Sure, Maggie," he offered reluctantly. "How are you?"

She let out a breath. "Honestly, it's been hard." And it was clear from the worn look on her face that it had been. Sean felt his initial resentment subside. She was grieving and lost, and it was something he could relate to.

"I'm sorry, Maggie. I know how painful it is."

She nodded in acknowledgment. She knew he had lost his brother in the war, but she wasn't aware he had also lost a close friend in Amy. She stared down at her hands, which she had begun to wring into knots, and took a deep breath.

"So I guess you heard they're not going to be filing any charges in the crash."

"No. I hadn't heard."

"Well, they're not. So that means my daughter's dead, and nobody's being punished for it."

Her hands continued to twist into knots as the rage boiled inside her. Sean wasn't sure how to respond.

"That's gotta be hard," he finally offered. "Is that what you wanted to talk about?"

She cleared her throat. "I understand Cassie Stevens is a student at this school. Can you help me find her?"

This caught Sean off guard. He sympathized with Maggie and her frustration, but turning over a student to what would be an obvious chastisement wasn't something he could do. Especially not one as troubled as Cassie seemed to be.

"I don't see how that's going to help anything, Maggie."

"Well, it will," she shot back sharply. "That girl needs to know the hell she's put me through. Katie was all that I had, and that girl took her from me." Maggie's hands were now squeezed into fists, and her nails dug into the flesh of her palms.

"I want her to know that I wish she died instead."

****

Coach Bobbie blew her whistle, and the girls' PE class hustled out onto the field. One girl kicked a soccer ball with her as she ran.

Cassie was suited up in her gym shorts and ready to play, but Coach had sidelined her because of her ribs. This was the last thing Cassie wanted or needed. She knew everyone already thought she was a freak, and would have preferred having the rest of her ribs broken than giving the girls another reason to hate her. And she could tell from their angry stares that was already happening.

She let out a sigh and walked over to the coach.

"Look. I know I'm not supposed to play, but what if I was really careful? Do you think maybe you could let me?"

The coach shook her head. "Sorry, Stevens, but Principal Hall would have my ass if I let you play. Excuse the French."

"So I'm supposed to just stand here and have everyone stare at me?"

Coach looked out onto the field and saw the angry glares Cassie was getting from the girls. Cassie had a point.

"Okay. Go ahead and change back into your school uniform. But I want you in the library studying. Do we have a deal?"

"Yeah," Cassie nodded. "Thanks."

****

Cassie pulled her uniform from her gym locker and pushed it closed. She quickly slid out of her gym shorts and into her school skirt. There was still enough time to make it to the library and maybe get some reading done before her next class.

She started to leave when Coach Bobbie's voice called to her from the far end of the locker room. "Cassie, can you come here a second."

That was weird. Cassie hadn't heard anyone else come in.

"Yeah," Cassie called back. She grabbed her backpack and headed down the rows of lockers to the back of the room.

When she reached it, nobody was there. And she hadn't seen anyone down any of the rows.

"Coach?"

A shower came on in the adjoining shower room. Seconds later another shower came on, then another, and then another...

Did the class return without her hearing them?

"Coach?"

There were no other sounds except the showers.

She walked back in that direction and looked through the opening into the shower room. It was filled with thick clouds of steam, and even from across the room, she could feel the water was scalding hot.

Yet there were people in there.

She could only see their blurred outlines through the steam, but there appeared to be at least six of them.

"You wanted to see me, coach?"

There was no answer.

The steam slowly billowed through the opening, and Cassie felt its damp warmth surround her. She took a step back into the locker room, and noticed those dark shapes approaching her in the steam.

She took another nervous step back. Then another...

A hand touched her back.

It felt cold and clammy. She spun around but saw only the empty locker room, with steam now drifting into it. She turned back to the shower, and those shapes were almost on her.

Cassie quickly staggered back and tripped on a bench. She fell to the floor and landed hard on her ribs.

"Ow!" she cringed. But as she looked up, the steam billowed in around her like a dense fog. Tentacles of steam traced across the ceiling, and with loud pops, the lights went out and left the room in complete darkness.

Cassie felt the steam's damp warmth surrounding her now — and things moving within that steam. She scrambled as quickly as she could across the floor in the direction she hoped the door was.

Casssiiiieeee... a hissed voice came inches from her ear.

Come, Casssiiiieeee...

Cassie screamed! Then the school bell rang in the hallway outside. The door was in that direction. She sprang to her feet and ran in that direction till her hands hit the wall.

Caaassssssiiiieeee... a voice hissed beside her.

Cassie patted her hands along the wall till she found the door. She grabbed the handle, but it wouldn't budge.

Things were moving in the darkness around her.

Caaassiiiieeee... A foul breath brushed her ear.

Staaaayyyy Caaasssiiieee... hissed a voice in her other ear.

"Hey! Hey! Help!" she screamed, pounding on the door.

Staaaaayyy... A breath brushed against her neck.

"Hey! Help! It's locked!"

The door swung open, and Coach Bobbie and the girls stood outside it.

"What the hell, Stevens?" Coach Bobbie said, then saw past Cassie into the dark locker room. Before Coach could say another word, Cassie squeezed past her and the girls and raced off down the hallway and out the doors at the far end.

****

Cassie was still a terrified mess by the time she arrived home from school. *It was back.* Everything added up —

the *Face* in the bus window; whatever Rex had seen in the forest that night; whatever had happened to her at the lighthouse; and now the locker room... all of it couldn't be her imagination, or hallucinations, or whatever her doctors at the hospital had warned her she might experience. There were just too many of these things happening to her, and they were happening more frequently now.

It was back.

As she looked around the empty house, she decided there was no way she was going to stay home alone inside till her mom got home. And who knew when that would even be.

"Hey, Rex, wanna go for a walk?" she called out, and seconds later he came bounding in. She snatched his leash from the broom closet and patted his side as she attached it to his collar.

"Hey, buddy. I need you to protect me, okay."

Neither of them could know it would be their last walk together.

CHAPTER EIGHTEEN
The Grave

Pioneer Road was the narrow stretch of cracked asphalt and dry leaves that ran from the town's northern border through grazing fields and forests, and finally up Pioneer Hill. There, it veered a sharp left and ran parallel to the town.

On its southern side, the road looked out across the town, with its canopy of elms and wood-sided houses and shops. And beyond that lay the tip of the peninsula, where its lighthouse stood against a boundless span of blue.

On its northern side was the Faulkner Cemetery, which was divided into two sections. The eastern half was the historic portion of the cemetery, with graves dating back to the town's founding centuries earlier. Its terrain was rugged and steep, and monuments and graves had shifted over the years as the ground beneath them eroded. It was surrounded by a fence of wrought iron bars, barricading it from the road. This section was known simply as the old cemetery.

On its western border was the portion known as the new cemetery. Its terrain had been graded into the hill and was well kept with trimmed lawns and gravestones. It was the portion where her dad and Katie Dunne had been buried.

Cassie and Rex had just reached the top of the hill, where the road curved left to run parallel to the town. She stopped a moment to rest and take in the view of the distant town. It was early evening, so people were just getting off work, and the town's streets were already lined with cars. In the distance, dark storm clouds were gathering over the ocean, so she and Rex would need to head home soon to beat the rain.

She turned to look at the old cemetery behind them and found that even in the dwindling daylight, its aura was foreboding. With the sun low on the horizon beyond the hill, a grim pall was cast over its monuments and aged gravestones, and long shadows crept toward her like skeletal hands. A few leaves tossed about in the growing breeze.

It felt like the approach of *Death*, and she shuddered at memories of the fascination it once held.

She patted Rex on his side. "Come on, buddy. Let's get going." She had spooked herself enough for one day.

As they turned to head back down the hill, she suddenly froze.

Something was moving in the cemetery.

In the growing dusk, something barely perceptible had hovered in the far corner of her peripheral vision like a shadow. Only it wasn't a shadow, and she knew this. It moved upright, apart from any objects a shadow could have been cast on; and as had happened with that *Face* in the bus window, it was gone when she turned in its direction.

It was something she would come to refer to as the *Shadow*.

A low growl rumbled from Rex. She looked down at him and found his eyes fixed on a spot in the cemetery near a large granite vault. Every muscle in his large body was tensed, like he had been in the clearing behind her house that night. He was watching something out there among the graves, and his canine instincts had already determined it was a threat.

You know, animals can see shit that we can't, Seth's words flashed in her memory.

Ask your dog, next time you see him growling into an empty room.

"Rex. Come on. Let's go." She patted his side again, and this time she found him trembling. He seemed completely oblivious of her or anything else — every nerve and muscle in his body was focused on the unseen threat that watched them from the graves.

Without warning, he suddenly lunged forward and yanked the leash from her grip. He bounded across the road to the fence and quickly squeezed between the bars.

"Rex, stop!" she shouted, racing over to the fence,

but Rex was already bounding up the hill on the far side.

Cassie ran along the fence till she found an opening where two bars had rusted away. She squeezed through, then hurried up the hill as fast as she could.

"Rex!" she hollered again as the barking grew farther away. The grass came up to her knees in parts and concealed holes where the ground had eroded away. She stumbled through several of them and nicked her ankle on several gravestones that were hidden by the grass.

"Rex! Dammit, Rex, just stop!" She paused a second to catch her breath.

Then the barking stopped.

****

The sun had set, and a brisk wind from the approaching storm swept through the grass and fallen leaves of the old cemetery.

"Rex!" Cassie panted as she trudged up the hill. It had been over twenty minutes since she'd heard his last bark, and the first drops of rain had begun to fall. The ground would soon be slick with mud, so she hurried as fast as she could.

She reached the northern boundary of the cemetery at the top of the hill and turned to look back down the rugged slope. There was nothing moving below.

"Rex!"

She leaned back against the fence and thought about it for a moment. She looked over to her right, where the old cemetery stretched till it reached its western border with the new cemetery. Maybe that's where he went.

The rain hit harder now, and the ground was slick with mud. She sloshed through it till she finally reached the fence along the western border. On the far side of it, the ground sloped sharply downward till it reached the fresh-cut grass of the new cemetery. There, the earth had been graded level into the hill.

She searched along the fence till she found an opening in the bars. She was squeezing through when a sound from the old cemetery caught her attention. She turned to look back at it. Trees and statues and gravestones appeared now as dark silhouettes against a stormy sky. She cupped her hands over her eyes to shield them from the rain but couldn't see anything out there. At least nothing dog-shaped.

A sudden crash of lightning lit the cemetery.

Something was coming toward her.

In the brief flash, she had seen the *Shadow* floating toward her across the rugged ground.

Cassie's heart jumped. She spun back to the fence and quickly squeezed through the opening in the bars. In two steps she was on the steep slope, sliding down it on her bottom to the new cemetery below.

She reached the bottom and sprang to her feet. She spotted the dark outline of a crypt not far away and raced across the lawn to it. She ducked around its corner, keeping her body close to the wall to avoid being seen. A narrow eave high above deflected most of the rain.

She waited a moment to catch her breath, then eased over to the corner and peeked around it. It was dark, and the rain made it difficult to see, but it didn't look like anything was moving.

Then, over the harsh patter of rain and the rumble of thunder, came a distant howl. It was faint, but Cassie would have known it anywhere. It was the howl she used to tease Rex into making. She leaned back around the corner and listened to see if it came again.

It did, from the direction of another crypt maybe fifty yards away.

The rain beat down harder now as she dashed across the slick grass toward that other crypt. She slipped halfway across the lawn, and fell in the mud covering a fresh grave. She hopped to her feet and backed away, brushing the mud from her jeans.

Then she caught the name on the gravestone, and a lump filled her throat.

KATHERINE "KATIE" DUNNE. SLEEP WITH THE ANGELS, BABY GIRL

Cassie stood there panting, unable to take her eyes off that grave. A drenched bouquet of flowers lay at its base, but it was the name that held her focus.

"Why this one, Cass?" came Silvia's voice. She stood beside Cassie on her right, and Seth and Trish were on her left. Cassie hadn't heard them approach.

"'Cause she's the girl we killed," said Seth, stepping over to the gravestone. He looked down at the small grave and gave the gravestone a mocking pat. "Ain't that right, Katie?"

"It was an accident," Cassie muttered.

"You trying to convince us of that, or yourself," said Seth. "Cause I'm not buying that you believe it."

"You were the one driving," Cassie shot back.

"I didn't hear any complaints."

"We didn't tell you to let go of the wheel like an asshole."

"Trish wouldn't beer me."

"Fuck you."

"Look, guys, everyone just chill," Silvia cut in. "There's nothing we can do about it now, so just drop it."

"Fine. Dropped," said Seth. "You cool with that, Cass? No more playing blame game?"

Cassie shook her head. "Whatever. So, what are you guys doing here?"

Trish shrugged. "Hanging with the dead. What else?"

"In the rain?"

"It's when they're the most restless."

"What are you doing here, Cass?" asked Silvia.

"Trying to find Rex. He ran off earlier."

"Geez," said Seth, shaking his head. "Get a hamster or a mouse already. Something you can keep in a cage."

"I don't want a hamster. I want my dog."

A faint howl arose over the storm. It sounded closer.

"I think your dog just said he wants a new owner,"

cracked Seth.

Cassie ignored him. "Did you guys hear where it came from?"

"I think it was over by that crypt," Silvia said, nodding to the crypt Cassie had been running toward when she slipped.

"Come on, you guys, help me get him," Cassie hollered back as she raced off toward the crypt.

She reached it and found its heavy iron door ajar. The gap was just wide enough for Rex to squeeze through.

"Rex," Cassie called in through the gap, "you in there, buddy?" She listened and a faint whine seemed to come from inside.

"Rex?"

She eased the door open a bit farther, and its rusted hinges groaned with a heavy creak. Her friends caught up.

"Wait," said Silvia. "You're going in there?"

"Yeah. I think I heard Rex inside."

"That's a bad idea, Cass," said Trish. "You don't want to enter a crypt during a storm."

"Why not?"

"Remember what I said about the dead being restless."

Cassie stopped. She looked at the girls then back at the gap. She tried calling him again, but this time a lot quieter.

"Rex?"

And again came that faint whine from inside.

Cassie turned to her friends.

"Shit. I think I hear him. Will you guys watch the door if I go in there really quick to check?"

"Yeah," nodded Trish. "But I'm telling you, it's a bad idea."

"I'll be quick."

Cassie squeezed through the opening and found the inside much larger than she would have thought. Its outer walls were built of stone, about twelve feet in height from the crypt's floor, with stained-glass windows along their top halves. To her left was an inner wall with marble plaques over the vaults where the bodies were interred.

Cassie descended the five stone steps down to the crypt's floor. There was little light in there from the stained-glass windows, so she flipped on the flashlight on her cell phone and shined it around. The narrow beam cut through the gloom to the far wall, and she could see it was empty.

"Cass, it's closing!" Silvia called down, and Cassie heard the heavy door groan on its hinges. She bolted back up the steps and reached the top just as it clanged shut. She threw her weight against it and pounded.

"You guys, this isn't funny!" she hollered through the door.

"We didn't do it, Cass," came Silvia's muffled voice from the far side. "It closed on its own."

"Shit!" Cassie swore and pressed against it again. "It won't open. Can you guys all try tugging on it."

She waited for a response... but none came.

"Silvia. Can you guys try tugging on it, while I push?"

Again, no response came.

"Silvia? Seth? Are you guys out there?"

She pressed her ear against the door and listened, but all she heard was the storm.

She looked at her cell phone, and there were no bars. *Shit. She was so screwed.* She looked up at the stained-glass windows, and they seemed to be the only way out. She could see they were set back in the wall about six inches, so there was just enough ledge for her to grab onto.

The window was about a foot beyond her reach, so she leaped up and her fingers caught on the ledge. She chinned herself up, and was placing her forearm on the ledge, when she slipped and fell.

Shit. She leaped up and tried again... and again she slipped off.

A third try ended the same way. As she was preparing for a fourth try...

A sound came from behind her.

It was something clinking against marble. But the only marble in the crypt was the plaques covering the vaults.

Cassie turned to face the wall of vaults and shined her cell phone's flashlight along their marble plaques. As the light reached the end, a knock came from behind a plaque.

A rush of panic gripped her. She turned back to the windows and leaped up, this time clinging to the ledge with every ounce of muscle she had.

Another knock...

She braced her left forearm on the ledge to hold herself in place, then swung her cell phone against the window.

The force knocked her grip lose, and she fell back to the floor.

Another knock came from the plaque at the end of the hallway.

She leaped up again and braced her arm on the ledge. It was probably killing her ribs, but she was oblivious to everything except getting out of there.

Knock... then a clink...

It was the sound of a marble plaque hitting the floor.

One of the vaults was unsealed.

Cassie hit her phone against the window with all her strength. Then she hit it again and again. It finally cracked.

Something was moving behind her...

Cassie pressed her palm against the cracked glass, and a large shard peeled lose. She shoved it out, then grabbed the glass next to where it had been and broke it off.

A soft thud hit the floor at the end of the hallway...

Cassie didn't dare look behind her. She frantically peeled away those broken shards and tossed them onto the lawn till she had made an opening wide enough to squeeze through.

Bracing herself on her elbows, she pulled her body

up the wall then eased her torso through the window...

Something grabbed her foot.

Cassie screamed! She squirmed and kicked with her free foot and felt it connect with something. The grip on her foot released. She grabbed the outer rim of the window and pulled herself through.

She fell to the grass below and the air knocked from her lungs. For seconds she could only lie there helpless.

Something was coming toward her across the lawn.

She caught it from the corner of her eye. She spun her head to look in its direction, but it was gone.

It had been the *Shadow*. The one she had seen in the car the night she died; and then earlier in the cemetery that night. Each time she saw it was from the corner of her eye. This reminded her of an old saying she heard as a child — *"Evil hides in the periphery."*

Her breath was back now, and she struggled to her feet. She cupped her eyes and looked around the cemetery, but as far as she could see, she was all alone.

She raced off across the cemetery toward the road. From all around her came new sounds, mixed with the wind and fury of the storm. These were sounds of ghostly wailing, and moans, and terrified screams.

As she finally reached the road, and raced off down it toward the town, one final disturbing sound carried over the storm...

It was a low moanful howl.

CHAPTER NINETEEN
Voices

It was the morning after Rex had run off. The storm had passed, but a dreary gray sky clung over the town. Cassie rose from bed with an aching groan. She was crisscrossed with bruises and cuts, and her ribs hurt like hell, but none of that mattered as she raced downstairs to see if Rex had come home during the night.

He hadn't.

Her mom was still asleep when Cassie trudged back to the cemetery. The grass was damp, and the frosty morning air drilled into her sore joints, but she still combed every inch of the new cemetery.

While it wasn't as scary in the daylight, it still retained a disquieting air, especially in the eerie silence that seemed to hang over it. There were no calls of birds, or insects, or even the wind — nothing that gave a place life.

It felt dead.

She stopped at the crypt she had fled from the night before and saw the glass shards spread across the lawn. There was also the indent where she had landed.

It hadn't been a dream.

She spent one more hour retracing the grounds, but without any luck. She returned to the road and took it over to the old cemetery. She stood outside its wrought iron fence and peered through the bars. The eroded turf would be like quicksand from the rain, so it was too dangerous to go inside.

As she swept her eyes across those crumbling monuments and gravestones, she felt a forlorn emptiness hanging over the ancient grounds. It was the quiet stillness of names and families long forgotten.

"Rex?"

She waited... but there was nothing. Nothing moved on those desolate grounds.

She returned home shortly after her mom left for work. She pulled up some old photos of Rex from her cell phone's camera and pasted them onto "missing" fliers she designed on her laptop. She offered a twenty-five-dollar reward. She knew it was measly, but it was all she had.

She caught the bus down to the print shop and had a stack of fliers printed. She then spent the afternoon stapling them to telephone poles around town.

She returned to school the next day and taped a dozen fliers around campus. They listed her cell number to contact her.

Less than an hour later, the texts started coming in.

The texts that flooded her cell came from anonymous numbers, and many of them had grotesque photos of dead dogs and animals attached. The messages were equally cruel, and one in particular hit her like a punch in the gut: "First you killed a child, now you killed your dog. Would you just die already."

****

Cassie's last class was English literature, and by that time she'd been beat to hell by all the texts. Not a single one had expressed sympathy or offered to help; they just vented their hatred toward her.

Hate them back.

It was a small voice in her head that came from out of nowhere, but it clicked — if they hated her, it gave her license to hate them back.

Hurt them.

It was another thought that came from out of nowhere, but it gave her an odd pleasure. She looked across the room at Becky Styles, who Cassie was pretty sure had sent that last text about her dying. Becky had always been a bitch to her, even before the *Disturbances*, and Cassie imagined her slipping in the shower and bashing her brains out on the tile floor. Or Justin's buddy Daryl, the asshole who'd always made her life hell, she could see him being crushed by a car.

And Molly Daniels. English lit was Cassie's only class with Molly, who sat with the popular girls across the room. Cassie was pretty sure Molly hadn't sent any of the texts, but she still hated her because Justin liked her. Would Molly still be queen bee if those tanned legs and flawless face were covered in deep scars?

Why am I thinking this?

Cassie froze at the sudden realization that these weren't her thoughts. They came from outside of her. Something wanted her to hate, and it worried her that she had indulged in it so willingly. She tried to shift her focus away from them and onto happy thoughts — memories of hanging out with her dad, and playing with Rex...

Rex is dead.

No! He isn't! Cassie shook her head.

Then why didn't he come when you called?

It was like the lighthouse all over again — no matter how hard she tried to shut out those outside thoughts, they kept forcing their way back in...

A scream from across the classroom snapped Cassie from this turmoil. She looked over and saw that everyone had scooted their desks away from Becky Styles. Cassie leaned forward to see what happened, and she almost puked. Becky's head lay on her desk in a pool of blood, with a ballpoint pen stuck in her eye.

****

Paramedics loaded Becky Styles into the back of an ambulance while Cassie and dozens of students watched from the parking lot. It didn't escape Cassie that this had happened to Becky just moments after her revenge fantasy.

Nobody had seen Becky do it, so speculation ran wild. And Becky hadn't made a sound either — she'd jabbed a pen in her own eye, and didn't make a sound.

It had been Jenny Scanlon's scream that everyone heard.

A new concern troubled Cassie as she looked around at all the grieving students — she felt no pity for Becky. Becky got what she had coming.

Karma's a bitch, Becky.

She saw students crying in the parking lot...

Becky didn't give a shit about you.

Others hugged each other. She even saw the old priest consoling some students by their cars.

Did Becky even know your names?

She looked back at the school and saw several girls on the steps outside the entrance crying into each other's shoulders. But all Cassie felt was satisfaction at their grief.

And it terrified her.

Across the parking lot, Molly held Justin's hand while she explained what happened. Nobody had any idea why Becky did it. She never seemed depressed or anything and had been laughing with Josh Taylor just a few minutes earlier.

A few people tried to explain it away as an accident, but seriously? Someone accidentally had a pen aimed at their eye, then accidentally jabbed it in without making a sound? Molly didn't buy it.

As Molly's eyes skimmed the parking lot, she spotted Cassie standing on the far side near the school's main building. She was alone, and it looked like she was watching several girls on the steps outside the building.

Molly had never really talked to Cassie beyond an occasional "hi" as they passed in the hallway. She knew Cassie's dad had coached PE at one time, and Cassie had seemed normal enough back then. But after that she had gotten weird, and then outright creepy earlier this year. Molly had never experienced the *Disturbances* firsthand, but several of her friends said they had, and that was enough to make Molly avoid Cassie whenever possible. She had no idea if Cassie was still that way, but as she watched her watching the girls on the steps, she felt something was off.

"How well do you know Cassie Stevens?" Molly asked Justin.

"Pretty well, I guess." He shrugged. "Why?"

"Just be careful. There's something really wrong with her."

****

Like most Catholic churches, St. Matthew's held confessions inside a small room that sat off to the side of the main church sanctuary. The confessional had two doors that led inside it, one being for the priests to enter by and the other for the penitents, to allow them anonymity.

Inside, it was a little larger than a closet and divided into two halves by a wall. There was a mesh window in the wall that let the penitents speak to the priests while maintaining their privacy.

Father Jenkins and Father Sean rotated days on which they heard evening confessions, and that day had fallen on Sean's rotation.

They had opened the confessional early that day on account of Becky Styles' "accident," and several students had already come in to discuss their distress over it. Sean did what he could to counsel them.

It was toward the end of the afternoon that Sean heard a girl enter on the other side of the mesh screen. She began with the usual opening...

"Bless me Father, for I have sinned..."

Most of the penitents that day had been students, and he had recognized several of their voices, but this girl's voice was one he didn't recognize.

"How long since your last confession?" he asked routinely.

"It's been a while, Father. I'm not really sure how long."

"Not a problem. What did you want to confess?"

"Well...," she began, "there's this boy at school I like, and I finally got up the nerve to meet him after he finished football practice one day... and he was so sweet and took me out to eat and everything..."

Here she paused, and Sean wasn't sure if she expected him to say something. "It sounds nice," he offered.

"It really is... or at least it was..."

"What happened?"

Sean heard her take a deep breath before continuing. "Well... you see, I was saving myself for marriage... and... well, we were at this party one night after a game, and I got really drunk, and we went for a walk on the beach, and then... we... you know... had sex..."

Sex was probably the most common thing he heard confessed by the students, so that came as no shock. And he certainly was in no position to judge anyone, nor did he have any desire to. But what struck him was the similarity this girl's story had to his and Amy's night on the beach. They were identical.

"Are you sorry about this?" he asked the girl. It was obviously why she was there.

There was a pause before she answered; and when she did, there was a subtle shift in her voice.

"Were you sorry?" she said.

An icy chill ran up his spine — not just at her question, and the way it was presented, but in the familiarity of the voice.

"Excuse me?" he asked.

"Were you sorry you fucked me, Sean?"

It was Amy's voice.

Sean hopped from his seat and went around to the penitent's side of the confessional. He flung the door open... and there was no one inside.

He stepped back and ran his eyes across the entire sanctuary.

It was empty.

****

It was dark by the time Cassie arrived home, and she was an emotional wreck. The voices were gone by then and it sickened her at how willingly she had indulged them.

School was let out early after Becky's incident, so

Cassie had spent the rest of the day on the pier, just staring out over the water.

Her mom's car was gone, and the lights were off in the house when she entered. There was no Rex to greet her this time with his antics. What greeted her was an eerie stillness and the cold November moonlight that sifted in through the living room curtains.

She flipped on the lights and breathed relief that nothing was hiding in the corners. She slung her backpack over her shoulder and headed upstairs.

At their top, the stairs opened into a long hallway with Cassie's bedroom at one end and her mom's bedroom at the far end. Her mom's door was closed, like she always kept it during the day.

Cassie headed into her bedroom. She tossed her backpack on the floor and flipped on the lights. Nothing was hiding in there either.

She kicked off her shoes and lay back on her bed. She really needed Rex at that moment. Ninety pounds of Rex therapy could always snap her from even the darkest morose...

A door creaked.

Cassie stiffened. It came from down the hallway. She held her breath a moment and listened into the silence...

It creaked again.

Cassie sat up. "Mom?"

Suddenly the lights went out and plunged her room into dim moonlight.

Cassie sat there frozen for a moment, staring into

that darkness for any signs of movement.

Another creak...

"Mom..." Her voice shook this time. She reached into her backpack and pulled out her cell phone. She flipped on its light and shined it toward her doorway. Thankfully, nothing crouched there.

She slowly rose from bed and walked to her doorway. She shined the flashlight down the hallway, and its faint narrow beam showed her mom's door cracked open.

Her skin crawled like ants as she stared at that door, expecting something to step through it at any moment.

"Mom?" she called out meekly. But there was only silence.

She stepped through her doorway into the hallway and saw there were no lights coming up the stairs from the living room. That meant it was a circuit breaker, which was easy enough to fix. She just needed to get to the breaker box in her kitchen.

She used her flashlight as a guide as she walked down the hallway to the stairs. She shined her light down them and didn't see anything moving. She took a step down...

Her mom's door creaked.

Cassie swept the flashlight back to her mom's room — *the door was wide open.*

Cassie took a breath. She had to get out of the house. And fast. She started back down the stairs...

"Cassie..."

It was her mom's voice whispered softly, and had come from her bedroom. Cassie stepped back into the hallway and shined her light toward her mom's bedroom...

Was it a trick of her eyes, or did something just move inside her room?

"Mom? Are you okay?"

She began easing down the hallway toward her room, keeping her flashlight aimed on that open door. There was no more movement, and Cassie was certain now it had been a trick of her eyes.

She should leave.

Cassie slowly backed toward the stairs, keeping her flashlight trained on that door...

"Cassie..."

It was her mom's whispered voice again, and Cassie was certain it had come from her mom's bedroom.

Why wasn't she coming out?

"Mom?"

She took a slow step toward her room... and another... and then another... till she stood just outside the doorway. She shined her light in. It was the master bedroom, with a large queen-sized bed in the middle, dressers, and a nightstand in the far corner.

No one was in there. The bed was untouched, and the curtains were closed.

She was alone in the house.

"Come in..." an eerie voice whispered from the dark. And it was no longer her mom's voice. It was no longer

a human voice.

Cassie backed down the hallway to the stairs, never taking her eyes off her mom's doorway. She turned and shined her light down the stairs...

Something stood at the base of the stairs.

It vanished in the light, but it had been tall, like a man, yet made only of shadow and darkness. And while she could no longer see it, she still felt its presence watching her.

It was coming up the stairs.

Cassie dashed down the hallway into her bedroom. She locked her door then hurried behind her bed. She crouched down and waited... and watched... and listened...

Her room suddenly exploded into chaos — objects rattled and quaked. Pictures shook from their hooks and fell to the floor; a glass on her dresser shattered like it had been squeezed in powerful hands; her closet door whipped open, and clothes flew from hangars across the room; books flew from her desk and crashed into walls.

Then a scratching sound arose from the wall behind her and circled the room. It was like deep nails being torn through wood. The ceiling fan swayed, and its lights flickered on momentarily, then exploded in bright bursts.

Cassie lunged over to the window behind her and tugged it open. She climbed through it onto the roof and scooted across it to the trellis. She scrambled down the trellis to the backyard then backed away till she stood in the middle of the yard. She was far enough away that she could flee if anything came out.

She stood there for several minutes watching the house, then finally sat down in the grass. And waited...

She was still there when Alison came home from work three hours later. Never taking her eyes off the house.

CHAPTER TWENTY
The Periphery

It was a gray overcast morning, and Cassie felt like death. She hadn't slept at all that night. Alison had come home to find her shivering in their backyard, but when Alison asked her about it, Cassie told her she thought she had seen Rex. It was easier than telling her she saw a ghost.

Cassie went to school early that morning, and sat at the marble fountain in the courtyard typing search terms into her laptop.

The first search term she tried was "ghost shadow," and millions of results came back. That was pretty much useless. So next she tried "ghost near-death experience," since everything seemed to have started after her revival from the crash.

Fewer results came back this time, and as she scanned through them, some of them seemed relevant. One result was about a rock band member who had died of a heroin overdose. She clicked that link and quickly skimmed through the article. Like Cassie, this guy had died, and after being resuscitated, claimed to see a ghostlike figure from his peripheral vision.

This gave Cassie an idea. She typed in "ghost peripheral vision," and this combination came back with even better results. She scrolled down the results page and found an obituary for a teen who had killed himself after being haunted for several months by a specter he claimed to see from the corner of his eye.

Below that one was another obituary, and she clicked that link. It was a young prostitute who had died from a knife wound inflicted by her pimp. She had also been resuscitated and later claimed to see spirits from her peripheral vision. She had been sent to the county mental health hospital, where she was later found hanging from a shower head. Foul play wasn't suspected.

It was a link on the second page of search results that proved to be the most relevant. The link was to a blog titled "Evil Hides in the Periphery." She clicked the link, and as the home page loaded in her browser, Cassie gasped...

There on the home page was a charcoal drawing of the *Shadow* she had been seeing. And which the website's owner was also seeing.

The owner's name was Kyle Martin, and his photo was posted on the right margin of the home page. She clicked his photo, and it expanded into its own window. *Holy shit*, she thought, this guy looked scary as hell. He appeared to be in his late twenties, or early thirties, with long unkempt black hair that ran past his shoulders and dark circles around his eyes that told of long sleepless nights. There was also something tattooed on his forehead. She zoomed in on the photo and saw the tattoo was of an upside-down five-pointed star within a circle — a *pentagram* — an occult symbol Cassie had become all too familiar with during her time with the goths.

Beneath the photo were links to his blog entries. Cassie clicked the link for the most recent entry that was dated two days ago. It read: "It came again last night. I know what it is now, and why it's after me. Kyle."

That was it? She returned to the home page, where she was again greeted by that charcoal drawing of the *Shadow*. She scrolled down the list of blog entries, and found one from two weeks ago captioned "Deceased." She clicked on this link, and it pulled up a list of links to obituaries. Several of them Cassie recognized from her search, but Kyle had listed more. Lots more. As she scrolled down the list, she found that Kyle had added his own comments alongside the links. Things like "rest in peace brother," or "vaya con dios." Kyle knew these people. They had all shared this same experience of being haunted by this thing they saw in their peripheral vision.

And now they were all dead.

She returned to the home page and bookmarked it. She needed to contact this guy, no matter how strung out and sketchy he looked.

"Whatcha doin', Cass?" It was Silvia, who stood beside her. Cassie hadn't noticed her before.

"Just searching for stuff."

"You're searching for scary ghost drawings?" Seth stood on her other side, staring at the drawing on her laptop screen.

"It was on this guy's home page."

"Evil hides in the periphery?" Trish's voice came from behind her. She was reading the laptop screen over Cassie's shoulder. "What's that about?"

"It's nothing. Just some stuff I was looking up."

"Which brings us to the question — why?" said Seth.

"'Cause I wanted to."

"Bullshit. What aren't you telling us, Stevens?"

Cassie took a deep breath. "I've been seeing something."

"Is it that thing in the drawing?" asked Trish.

"Yeah."

"How long have you been seeing it?" asked Silvia.

"Since the accident."

"So, what is it? A ghost?"

"I don't know. But I think so."

"Do you know what it wants?" asked Trish.

"No. That's what I'm trying to find out."

"Why don't we do a séance, and see if we can contact it?"

"No way," Cassie shook her head. "I'm not doing that stuff anymore."

"Why not?"

"'Cause that's how all this stuff started."

"But you want it to go away, right?" said Trish.

"Yeah. But I also don't want anything worse to happen."

"It won't. All we're doing is finding out what it wants."

"And what happens if things go bad?"

"Then we just stop it and close the channel."

Cassie hesitated. "I don't know…"

"I promise nothing bad's gonna happen. We'll be extra careful."

"Where would we do it?"

"It would need to be your house."

"Why my house?"

"Because that's the place you have the strongest connection to."

"Shit. My mom would freak if she found out."

"What time does she get home?" asked Silvia.

Cassie shrugged. "I dunno. Late."

"Like, nine late? Or ten late?"

"Ten-ish."

Silvia turned to Trish. "Does that give us enough time?"

"It should," said Trish. "We could start at maybe eight. Does that work for you, Cass?"

Cassie thought about it and finally nodded. "I guess. But we stop if anything goes bad."

"I Promise," Trish said.

****

Sean stood behind the altar with his head bowed over the small Communion wafer that lay on the tray. "... Then Jesus broke the bread and gave it to His disciples saying, 'Take this, all of you, and eat of it, for this is my Body, which will be given up for you.'" He then raised the consecrated Host for the several dozen parishioners to see.

It was a weekday noon Mass, so attendance was small, and it was usually the same faces day after day. It tended to be an older crowd, and it was rare to see someone younger than thirty and much rarer to see someone in their teens.

Amy had been an exception to that. She had attended weekday Masses even when she wasn't forced to go by the nuns that taught their school.

You left me, Sean... You left me alone...

Sean clenched his teeth as those haunting memories from the dream continued their taunts. He replaced the Host on a silver platter and picked up the chalice that sat beside it. He bowed his head over it and resumed the words of consecration.

"When supper was ended, He took the cup, and again He gave you thanks. He gave the cup to His disciples saying, 'Take this, all of you, and drink from it, for this is the chalice of my Blood. The Blood of the new and eternal covenant, which will be poured out for you and for many for the forgiveness of sins. Do this in memory of me.'" He then raised the chalice of Christ's consecrated Blood in benediction for the parishioners to see...

Were you sorry you fucked me, Sean?

It wasn't Amy, he mentally repeated to himself, that voice I heard in the confessional wasn't Amy. It was only his imagination, dredging up horrors of subconscious guilt he had buried long ago.

Then who was in the confessional with him?

This question he didn't have an easy answer for and could only assume there had been nobody there. All of it, even before hearing Amy's voice, had been in his imagination.

Then what does that make you? Crazy?

He finally had to close his eyes to keep his thoughts from spiraling down that bottomless rabbit hole of questions he didn't have answers for.

He had no idea how long he had held the chalice raised, but when he opened his eyes, he saw the parishioners watching him with awed looks. Maybe they thought he had experienced a moment of rapture or devotion. But it was anything but that.

As he lowered the chalice, an unease stirred within him. It was the *resistance* he had felt in the classroom, and then again in Jenkins' office.

He stood there for a moment, staring down at the consecrated Host and chalice, but he no longer saw them through the eyes of faith as the Body and Blood of Christ as he once had. He saw only bread and wine in their physical appearance.

Behold your god, an eerie voice whispered in his thoughts.

He looked up from the altar to the parishioners,

who had bowed their heads again in silent reverence. They believed. For them, these elements were now sacred.

All sheep, that voice whispered again.

Baaaa baaaa baaaa.

****

A foul wind howled through the night. Trees swayed in the woods surrounding Cassie's house, and things that normally crept from their dens at night stayed hidden. The night was preparing for the arrival of the dark essence Cassie and her friends sought to conjure.

Despite the noise outside, an eerie calm lay over Cassie's bedroom. She lit a candle and placed it on her dresser. Six other candles already flickered around the room.

Seth, Trish, and Silvia sat around a Ouija board spread out on the floor. Trish sat at the head of the board and would act as the medium. She looked over at Cassie. "We're ready, Cass."

Cassie joined them around the board, taking her seat between Silvia and Trish on the side facing the window.

Silvia gave her hand a squeeze. "You nervous?"

Cassie nodded. "Kinda."

"We don't have to do this. It's your call."

Cassie shook her head. "No. It's fine."

Seth frowned. "None of us is gonna be doing this if we don't hurry up before Cass's mom gets home."

Trish nodded and turned to the others. "Everyone, put the fingers on your left hand on the planchette."

She waited until they all did. "Now, whatever happens, make sure you don't break the circle until we move the planchette to the word 'goodbye.'"

"Why? What happens if we do?" asked Cassie.

"You leave the channel open. Then anything can come through."

Seth sneered. "I thought the whole reason we're doing this is 'cause Cassie already let something through."

"Do you want to let more through?"

"Not really."

"Then shut up, and just do it." Trish looked at them all. "Do any of you guys have any questions before we start?"

Seth did. "Yeah. How come we're having to help Cass clean up her mess?"

The girls rolled their eyes. Trish turned to Silvia and Cassie. "Do any normal people have any normal questions?" They shook their heads. "Then let's get started. Everyone take a deep breath... hold it... now let it out slowly..."

Trish waited as they did. She took a deep breath herself, and closed her eyes. "We're gathered here tonight to speak to the entity that's revealed itself to Cassie. If you're here, spirit, speak to us..."

"Yeah. Speak, dammit." Seth said, never passing up a chance to be a dick. Trish shot him a frown, as did the others. "It's not gonna work, unless we're all serious. You think you can manage that?"

"No problem. Here's me being serious." He put on

a look that was supposed to be serious, but it looked more constipated than anything. Trish shook her head.

"Just don't say anything. Okay?"

He mimed pulling a zipper across his mouth.

"Good. Now stay that way." Trish closed her eyes again and took another deep breath to center herself. "If you're here, spirit, speak to us. Tell us what you want." She hesitated a moment, then added: "We command it."

Outside, the wind howled, and nocturnal creatures watched from their dens. But nothing had arrived yet.

Cassie and her friends had been at it for a while now. They still sat with their eyes closed and fingers on the planchette, but nothing had happened.

"I don't think it's working," Silvia finally said.

Trish shook her head in frustration. "If there is a spirit that's reached out to Cassie, speak to us now. She needs to know what you want. This we command."

This time she said it forcefully.

And this time something heard.

A violent crash on the window shattered the calm. They all jumped.

"What the fuck?" Seth was on his feet, hurrying over to the window. Deep cracks edged through it where something had hit it.

"What was it?" Silvia asked.

"I don't know," he said, straining to see the grass below. "I don't see anything." He returned to the others, but a new atmosphere had settled on the room. It was something dynamic and energized, and something they all felt.

"I think we've made contact. Everyone put your fingers back on the planchette," Trish instructed, and they did. She closed her eyes again. "We know you're here, spirit. Speak to us. Tell us what you want with Cassie."

Within the room, the air was calm, yet the candle flames waved... then snuffed out.

Trish was the first to sense it — something subtle stirred in the air. She turned to her friends, and there was apprehension in her eyes. "He's here."

And now the others felt it. Something was there with them. It seemed to be all around them, and each felt an inaudible hiss in their mind's ear.

The planchette slid.

Everyone froze. "What the fuck?" Seth muttered.

"Make sure you keep your fingers on the planchette," Trish cautioned. "He wants to communicate." She looked down at the letter framed in the small window on the planchette. It was on "D."

"D," Trish said. "The first letter is D."

It began sliding again and stopped on the letter "E."

"E," Trish noted. "D - E."

It slid again and stopped on the letter "A".

"A. D - E - A."

A scratching sound came from the wall behind Cassie. It was like claws dragged through wood. They all heard it, and followed it with their eyes as it circled the room.

Then it was gone.

"You guys, look." Trish nodded to the board. The planchette's window was centered on the letter "D." It had moved on its own while they were focused on the scratching.

"D," Trish muttered. It took a second, and then she realized. "Dead. It wants you dead."

Cassie stared in horror. "You guys, that's not funny. Did one of you do that?"

They all shook their heads, and it was obvious from their scared looks that they hadn't. As she searched their faces, her eyes drifted past the window...

The *Face* was there. It was the same ghoulish one she had seen in the bus window.

Cassie only caught it briefly before it was gone. She screamed and fell backward from the board.

"Cass?" said Trish. "Are you okay?"

Cassie shook her head. "There was something in the window watching us."

They all turned to the window, but it was now empty.

"I don't see anything," said Silvia.

"No. It disappears when you look at it directly."

"What's it look like?" asked Silvia.

"Evil," said Cassie.

"You wanna vague that up a little more?" said Seth.

"That's what it looks like," said Cassie, still freaked

out of her mind. "Think about the scariest things you could ever see, and put that in a face, and then times it by a million."

Everyone scooted back from the window. "And you saw it outside?" asked Silvia.

Cassie nodded.

Seth climbed to his feet. "Well, Cass, it's been real, but I'm outta here." He hurried out the door.

"I'm sorry, Cass," said Silvia, "but I gotta go too." She hurried out the door after Seth.

Cassie turned to Trish, who was packing up the board. "What do we do?"

Trish shook her head. "Nothing. There's nothing we can do."

"Wait," said Cassie as she followed Trish down the stairs and across the living room to the front door. Seth and Silvia were already gone. "Don't we need to close the channel?"

Trish stopped at the door and shook her head. "We didn't open the channel. It was already open before we started."

"How could it be open?"

"Because it's you, Cass. You're the channel. It came in through you."

"How?"

"It followed you back from death."

Cassie's knees felt like Jell-O.

"There's gotta be a way to stop it."

Trish shook her head. "There isn't, Cass. I wish I

could help, but I can't. I've never even heard of anything like this happening before." She looked around nervously, then grabbed Cassie in a quick hug.

"I gotta go, Cass. I'm sorry." She raced off.

Cassie slammed the door shut and turned back to the dark, empty house. After everything upstairs, it now felt... still...

It felt too still...

All at once it unleashed. Furniture shook and toppled over. Paintings fell from walls. Books flew from the bookcase shelves...

Then the scratching sound came from the wall behind her and traveled through the walls and ceiling.

Cassie backed toward the door. She reached behind her and grabbed the doorknob.

Everything stopped, and the house was again plunged into silence. But it was a wreck.

Cassie flung the door open and raced out onto the gravel drive. Her mom's headlights were pulling up. Cassie raced over to her car screaming and crying hysterically.

And she couldn't stop screaming.

CHAPTER TWENTY-ONE
Dr. Switzer

"I already told you guys," Cassie groaned in frustration, "it wasn't me that did it. It was that thing." She sat on the couch in the office of Dr. Benjamin Switzer, MD, who sat across the small office behind his studious desk. She felt like she'd been there for hours rehashing the same story while this guy observed her like some lab rat but never listened. She'd already answered his questions about the night of the séance a million times, yet he kept asking the same questions over and over.

She'd made the mistake of telling her mom the truth about what happened that night — about it being a spirit that had torn through their living room — and it had landed an appointment with this shrink.

So much for the truth. She should have just said it was burglars or a drug gang.

Switzer's office was at the Hillview Mental Hospital, the oldest freestanding mental health institution in the state. Built in the early half of the twentieth century, it stood isolated in the wooded foothills at the end of a long winding drive. Its walls were built of red brick and towered three stories in height. Barred windows looked down on a broad lawn, surrounded by a perimeter wall. Clusters of old oak trees were spread across the lawn and partially concealed the building's facade from the drive.

In Cassie's words, the place looked haunted.

The doctor was Alison's idea, and she had insisted on Cassie meeting with him after she had returned from work to find their home in shambles and Cassie blaming it on a ghost.

Switzer was in his late sixties and had developed a considerable renown for working with disturbed and troubled youth. That description fit Cassie to a T.

"Why don't you tell me what you think this spirit wants, Cassie," Switzer proposed. He had a gentle, if not slightly arrogant manner, but Cassie was tiring quickly of neither him nor her mom believing her; even if her story was admittedly difficult to believe.

"That's easy," she said, continuing to fidget with her backpack. "It wants me to kill myself."

Instantly, alarm bells went off in Switzer's head. Whatever lackadaisical air he had before was gone, and he scooted up in his chair. His poker face was also gone.

Cassie watched all of this with a bit of amusement. "That got your attention."

"Yes. Very much so," Switzer admitted with a nod.

"But you still think I'm full of shit about the whole ghost thing. You're just worried that crazy Cassie's gonna go off herself, and then you're kinda screwed 'cause you were treating me."

He was speechless for a moment. He sat back in his chair and adjusted his glasses.

"Is that really how you think I feel about you, Cassie?" He sounded wounded. "Or any of my patients? That I'm only concerned about protecting my reputation?"

"Are you?" she asked.

"No. In fact, it's quite the contrary. Most of my peers retired long ago, but I've continued to practice for the simple reason that my greatest reward in life comes from seeing my patients recover from their difficulties."

Cassie watched him as he said this, and for the first time in the session, she saw what she felt was honesty. She decided to soften. Maybe this guy really did mean well.

"I'm sorry," she said. "That was uncool. I should probably warn you that I can be a bit of a bitch at times. I'm trying not to be, but it still comes out."

He smiled and nodded his acceptance. "Understood. And I offer my own apology if I appeared inattentive."

"Apology accepted. So. Question for you. Do you have many patients seeing ghosts?"

He nodded. "I have, over the years. Quite a few."

"Were you able to help them?"

"I believe so. Yes."

"Do you believe in ghosts?"

He hesitated, probably a little too long, before finally shaking his head. "Honestly, Cassie, I don't know. I've heard compelling arguments for both sides."

"What if I told you there's other people seeing this thing? Would that be compelling?" She dug through her backpack and pulled out a sheet of paper. She walked over to his desk and set it in front of him. "I got this off the Internet." The paper was a printout of the drawing of the *Shadow* from Kyle Martin's website.

She sat down in a chair opposite him and watched his expression as he studied the drawing. She was surprised to see him actually take an interest. He stirred a bit and even took a second look at it before setting it down. Something about it had clearly unsettled him.

"This is what you've been seeing?" he finally asked, looking up from the image.

Cassie nodded. "And what other people have been seeing." She made sure to emphasize this point.

Switzer took one more glance at the image, then slid the paper aside. "Cassie, I'm certain that these visions are quite terrifying, but my immediate concern is the effect they're having on you. Why you think this spirit wants you to kill yourself."

Cassie shook her head. Had this guy even been listening? She leaned forward and fixed her eyes on his so there could be no misunderstanding what she was about to say. "Because that's what it does. The website where I found that picture, that guy has a list of people from all over who've seen this thing. And they're all dead."

****

Alison anxiously paced the lobby at the Hillview Hospital. She was regretting the fight she had with Cassie that morning, but her daughter clearly needed help. And this crazy story about a ghost trashing their house...

But this is what moms are supposed to do, right? They're supposed to make the hard decisions, even if they aren't popular with their children. Cassie had to understand she was only trying to help her. Right?

She checked her watch for the tenth time and was frustrated to see it was only twelve minutes since the last time she'd checked. They'd been here two hours now. What was going on in there?

Shit. Okay, deep breath, Alison.

It was a short while later that Switzer strolled in from the long hallway that ran behind the check-in window. Alison hurried over to meet him.

"So, how is she? Did you find out what's wrong with her?" Her mind was going at a million miles per second.

"Why don't we take a seat over there," Switzer calmly pointed to the chairs across the lobby. Alison followed him over, and they sat down. She took a deep breath.

"First of all," Switzer began, "I'm reasonably certain that Cassie is not lying when she says a ghost was responsible for the damage to your house."

Alison did a double-take. "Wait. You're not saying

there really is a ghost, are you?"

Switzer shook his head. "No. What I am saying is that Cassie believes there is a ghost, and it's causing her considerable frustration that everyone dismisses her as a liar."

"Okay... so what am I supposed to say?"

"Simply hear her out. It's important to remember that this ghost is very real to Cassie, and you need to be open to hearing what she has to say."

Alison thought about this and nodded. "Okay. Yeah. I can do that."

"Good. Because it's critical that Cassie has someone she can talk to. And I'll address that point in a moment."

"So, what is it? Is she hallucinating?"

"Perhaps. I've reviewed her records from Saint John's Hospital, and they do indicate that she sustained some mild trauma to her brain from her accident. It's possible that something like that could trigger psychotic breaks like we seem to be seeing."

"Psychotic?"

"These hallucinations."

"Oh," Alison nodded, clearly relieved her daughter wasn't an actual psycho. "So, is this something that can be treated?"

"There may not be a need to physically intervene. If it's simply a swelling of the brain, as her physician at the hospital seemed to think, then these hallucinations will go away with time as the swelling subsides."

This again came as a relief to Alison. But then

Switzer's appearance took on a more dire tone.

"Now, while these hallucinations are certainly of concern, my more immediate concern is Cassie's belief that this ghost wants her to kill herself."

"Wait. What?" Alison's eyes were instantly wide with shock.

"I take it you weren't aware of this."

"No." Alison shook her head. "Is that what she told you?"

He nodded. "I'm sure you can appreciate that this is considerably more urgent."

"Yeah," Alison nodded. "Wow. I had no idea."

"No. No, I was quite alarmed when she said it."

He took a moment to adjust his glasses. "My hunch, were I to take a guess after only having had our first session, is that Cassie is suffering from a rather extreme form of survivor's guilt and that it's triggering these suicidal idealizations. And it's quite possible, it may also be contributing to these hallucinations."

"But why would Cassie have survivor's guilt?"

"It could be any number of reasons. Foremost would be the death of the young child in the other car."

"But Cassie wasn't driving."

"Clearly Cassie doesn't draw the same distinction as you do. In her mind, she was an active participant in the child's death, and perhaps she sees this ghost as some form of retribution for her actions."

"Is there anything I can do?"

"Yes. You can be there for her, in a very non-judgmental way. She's feeling very alone and isolated right now, so it's important that she has you she can openly confide in, without fear of ridicule or reprisal."

Alison's head sank. She could almost hit herself for the way she'd acted the past few days after Cassie mentioned the ghost.

"So, I need to be the exact opposite of the way I've been acting."

Switzer gave her a sympathetic nod. "I don't expect it to always be easy. But it's important that you try. And that Cassie sees you making the effort. I believe that will go a long way toward rebuilding her trust."

****

"He seems nice," Alison commented as they drove home from Hillview.

Cassie shrugged. "He's okay."

"What'd you guys talk about?"

Again, the shrug. "Just stuff."

"Was he helpful?"

"He's trying to be. But I don't think he can help me."

"Why's that?"

"Because he doesn't think it's real. He thinks I'm imagining it. And fixing my brain isn't going to make that thing go away."

Cassie watched as her mom took a deep breath, then relaxed.

"Look, I get it, Mom. I know it sounds crazy, and I don't know if I would believe it if someone was telling me all this, but it's real. And I really need you to believe me."

Alison glanced over at Cassie and could see the desperation and sincerity in her eyes. Switzer was right that Cassie really did believe this. "I'm trying, Cass. And for the record, I don't think you're making this up."

"But you don't believe there's a ghost."

Alison thought about it for a moment. "I'm going to be honest with you, Cass. It's still too new to me."

"Will you at least try?"

Alison nodded. "I will. And will you work with the doctor?"

"Okay."

Alison gave her a smile. This was going well. But there was something still pressing on her. "I need to ask you something, Cass. And please don't get upset."

"What?" She could already feel herself tensing.

"Have you been thinking about killing yourself?"

Cassie just stared at her. Unbelievable. So that's why she was being so nice. "Is that what Switzer told you?"

"Don't be upset. I'm just asking."

"Would it matter if I said I was? You guys don't believe me anyway, so why would you believe that?"

"Can you cut me some slack here, Cass. I'm trying."

Cassie looked at her again and could see the pain in her eyes. This really was tearing her up inside, and she did seem to be trying.

"The answer's no, Mom. I don't want to kill myself. What's waiting for me after death is way scarier than life."

It was dark by the time they arrived home. The remainder of the drive had been quiet. Cassie regretted the tone she had taken with her mom. It was obvious Switzer had told her something when they spoke after her session, and whatever it was, at least her mom wasn't yelling like she had earlier. Points for Switzer.

As soon as she got inside, she headed upstairs to her room and booted up her laptop. She pulled up Kyle Martin's website blog, "Evil hides in the Periphery," and there was his drawing of the *Shadow* to greet her.

She looked again at Kyle's photo, and he honestly creeped the hell out of her. Like Charles Mason creepy. And that's exactly why she needed to talk to him — because if anyone had answers about that thing, it was him.

She hesitated a moment, then scrolled down to the "Contact" button at the bottom. She was only going to ask him about that thing, and that was it. No harm in doing that, right?

She clicked the "Contact" button, and a messenger window popped open. She typed in the message: "Kyle? Are you online?" and clicked "Send."

She waited several minutes for a reply, and when none came, she headed to her bathroom to get ready for bed.

She returned several minutes later, brushing her teeth, and found he had replied: "Yes."

She sat down with a mouth full of toothpaste and

quickly typed a new message: "I see it too. What is it?" Again she clicked "Send."

This time his response came within seconds. It consisted of only two words, but those words froze the blood in Cassie's veins.

"A demon."

Cassie stared at those words for almost a minute before sending a new message: "How do you know?"

Again, his response came within a few seconds, and she felt another chill: "The same way you know."

She thought about his message for a moment, and he was right. She did know. She had known since the night of the Black Mass, and maybe even before then.

Her hands shook as she typed back a message: "Can we meet?" As scary and odd as this guy seemed, there was something much scarier after her. And she needed to talk to someone who understood.

Seconds later his response popped up, and Cassie wasn't sure whether to feel relieved or frightened.

"Sure. Just say where."

CHAPTER TWENTY-TWO
Kyle

Justin was at his locker, talking to his buddies Daryl and Tim. They'd been at it for a while now, and Cassie knew this because she'd been watching them from behind her locker door down the hallway. She needed to talk to Justin, but there was no way she was doing it in front of his asshole friends.

She was supposed to meet Kyle that afternoon, and in case he turned out to be as scary as his photo looked, she wanted someone there with her. And that someone was Justin. She knew the old Justin would come in a second — he'd always had her back. But that was in the pre-Molly days, and this new Justin was uncharted territory. And asking him in front of the assholes almost guaranteed a "no."

So she had waited and waited for the assholes to leave. But now it was almost class time, and there was still no sign of the assholes leaving. She was going to have to do this in front of them. And this really sucked.

She strolled over while they were in the middle of laughing at some joke Tim had cracked. Instantly the laughter stopped, and the boys all turned to stare at her.

This definitely sucked.

"Hey," she said to Justin, ignoring the stares from the assholes. "Can I talk to you for a second?"

"Well, check this out," Daryl jumped in. "Thought you said she wasn't your girlfriend, J."

"She's not." Justin frowned at Daryl before turning back to Cassie. "What is it?"

"Can we do it in private?" She was noticing the assholes' stares now.

"Ooh, private," Daryl jumped back in. "You know what that means, don't ya? Means the little pee stick came up positive."

Justin spun around. "What?"

"Means you're gonna be a daddy, J." Daryl and Tim cracked up.

"Would you just fuck off," Justin said, then turned back to Cassie. "I really need to get to class."

Cassie took a deep breath. Here it goes. "Okay. I'm supposed to meet someone after school today, and I was hoping you would come with."

"Why do you need me to come?" he asked.

"In case something goes bad."

"Oh, so you want Justin to be your bodyguard?" Tim clarified.

Cassie looked at him and nodded. "Kinda. Yeah."

"Well, ain't that sweet," Daryl jumped back in.

"Justin, the bodyguard."

"Will you carry my books for me, Justin?" Tim cut in.

Daryl cracked up. "Will you wipe my ass for me, Justin?"

Justin shook his head in annoyance. "Will you kiss my ass for me, Daryl?"

"Only if you wipe it," Daryl laughed back.

Cassie watched this back-and-forth exchange and finally turned back to Justin. "Please. It's really important."

"Ya hear that, J?" Daryl hopped back in. "Your girlfriend here says it's important."

That was it. She'd taken this asshole's shit for too long. She turned to him. "Why do you always have to be a dick to me? I never did anything to you."

It caught Daryl momentarily off guard, but he quickly recovered. "Uh, maybe it's 'cause you're freaky as all fuck."

"But I'm not like that anymore," Cassie protested. "Can you just cut me a break? Please."

"Guess we'll see, won't we?" he said smugly.

She knew her plea with him had gone nowhere. Way too much damage had been done during the *Disturbances*. She couldn't recall if she had encountered Daryl during that period, but she had encountered people he knew, and those people had talked. And they had been scared shitless.

Cassie turned back to Justin to make a final plea. "Will you help me?"

Daryl looked at her, then turned to Justin. "Maybe you oughta cut your girlfriend some slack there, J. The chick needs your help."

"Would you just shut the hell up?" Justin was growing impatient. "She's not my girlfriend." Then, turning to Cassie, "You said it was this afternoon?"

She nodded. "Yeah. We're supposed to meet at three."

Justin's face looked visibly relieved. He turned to the assholes. "Didn't coach want us to meet him after school?"

"When did that ever stop you," Tim looked at him with a smirk.

"Yeah. We'll just tell coach you're busy being a bodyguard for your baby mama." Daryl cracked up at his own joke, and Tim joined in. Justin wasn't amused.

And neither was Cassie. She took a final look at Justin, and just shook her head in disappointment. "Forget it."

She turned and hurried off down the hallway. She had to get as far away from those assholes as she could. And that now included Justin.

****

It was early afternoon when Sean spotted Father Jenkins locking the back door of the church. He walked over and joined the elder priest.

"I need to talk to you about something, Father. You have a couple minutes?"

"Of course," Jenkins replied, sliding the keys into his pocket. "Shall we do it on our way to the rectory."

"That's fine," Sean said, and they began walking. This would be a conversation Sean had rehearsed most of the afternoon, but finding a place to start was proving more difficult than he had expected.

"I don't think I'm over Amy's death," Sean finally admitted, "and it's affecting me in more ways than I would have thought."

"How so?"

"I think I first noticed it during that class lecture where the topic of demons came up. It was subtle, but it was something I don't recall feeling before."

"And what might that have been?"

Sean shrugged. "Hostility, maybe? Like I said, it was subtle."

"Might it perhaps have been a resistance?"

Sean thought about it and nodded. "Yeah. I guess you could describe it that way."

Jenkins seemed to nod knowingly. "And did you feel this when you and I spoke about demons?"

Sean nodded. "Yeah. I felt it then too."

"And how does this relate to Amy's death?"

"I never felt it before then. I'll be honest with you, Father, I came back from her funeral with a lot of nagging doubts, and they've only grown worse."

Again, Jenkins nodded. "The age-old paradox — how can a loving God allow bad things to happen to good people?"

"I'm one of those people who's asking that question now."

"And what is it you tell yourself for the answer?"

Sean shrugged. "That's the problem. I don't have an answer. At least not one that's adequate."

"Then tell me what answer it is that comes to you."

"I don't get what you mean."

"When that voice inside whispers to you, what does it say?"

"You mean the first thing that comes to mind?"

Jenkins nodded. "Most often that's the case. Yes."

"That the whole thing's a fraud. That if there is a God, then he's indifferent to us."

Jenkins seemed to anticipate this answer. "When these doubts come, do you find yourself engaging with them?"

"What do you mean?"

"Suppose I were to say something that you knew was untrue, would you attempt to correct me?"

"It depends on what it was. But probably."

"And you would be right to do so. Now let me ask, when those doubts come, do you attempt to correct them?"

Sean thought about it. "I think maybe I did at first."

"And you encountered that resistance when you did?"

"Yeah. It was persistent."

Again, Jenkins nodded knowingly. "I suppose those doubts have a thing or two to say about the Eucharist."

Sean stopped walking just outside the rectory door, and Jenkins stopped along with him. Sean looked at him as his memory flashed to the Mass he had said earlier that week.

Jenkins seemed to read the answer in Sean's expression. "I'm going to assume it was rather derisive."

Sean thought about it another moment then nodded. "It was."

"Did those doubts have anything to say about those in attendance at the Mass?"

Again, Sean's memory flashed to the moment he had concluded the Consecration, and his derisive thoughts of those parishioners who watched in awe and reverence. "It wasn't kind."

"And is that how you feel?"

Sean shook his head. "No. Not at all."

"I see," Jenkins nodded.

"There's something else, Father. The other day when I was hearing confessions, I heard Amy's voice come from the other side of the screen. There was no one in there."

Jenkins raised his eyebrows at this. "And what did this voice say?"

Sean hesitated a moment. "It's pretty vulgar."

Jenkins smiled. "I'm quite sure I've heard it before."

"It said, 'Are you sorry you fucked me, Sean?' Amy and I had had... an encounter once. No one knew about it."

Sean watched as Jenkins again nodded knowingly. It was as if a final missing piece of the puzzle had fallen into place for Jenkins. "You know something about this," Sean observed.

Jenkins nodded. "I know that those thoughts, and that resistance you felt, none of them were prompted by yourself."

"Then where did they come from?"

"Come inside with me for a moment," Jenkins said, opening the door to the rectory. "I have something that may provide you with some clarity on this."

Sean followed Jenkins upstairs to his study, where Jenkins removed a book from his bookcase and handed it to Sean. Sean flipped it over and read the title — *A Case for Demonic Possession.*

"The danger with demons, Sean, is that to disbelieve in their existence is to be disarmed against them. It's why a demon will strive to sow seeds of doubt to undermine one's faith. And you, my friend, are in the process of being disarmed."

****

The autumn sky had grown dreary and overcast, and a light rain peppered down on Cassie as she shuffled down the lonely neighborhood block.

The street was lined on either side by wood-paneled houses, set back from the road behind grass yards spotted with leaves. Tall elms arched their branches over the road in a canopy of shade.

With the exception of the soft rain, as it pattered down on the leaves and sidewalk, the neighborhood was quiet. There were no sounds of traffic or animals or anything to disrupt Cassie's memories of the bruising she had just taken from Justin and the assholes. She felt completely alone.

She was so lost in this morose that she failed to notice the man walking his small dog, who had just rounded the corner onto the street. The man paid no attention to Cassie, but his dog seemed curious about her. It was in the way animals detect subtleties beyond humans' five senses.

And it sensed something was wrong.

Suddenly the dog barked and startled Cassie from her thoughts. She looked across the street and saw it tug furiously at its leash to get loose and come at her.

Cassie was annoyed, like everyone gets when stupid yapper dogs won't stop barking. But something vicious spoke in her mind's ear — something subliminal, vague, and ferocious.

I could crush you.

It was the influx of hate she had felt forced on her in class the day Becky Styles jabbed the pen in her eye. The barking stopped abruptly as the dog sensed something no human eye could detect. It continued to stare at her a moment, with the knowing look in its eyes that it had challenged something it shouldn't have.

Within a span of seconds, the dog's look went from confusion, to wounded, to scared. With a terrified whimper, it retreated behind its owner's leg and began trembling.

I could crush him too, and you both die.

The dog urinated on itself. Its startled owner

looked down at it, then over at Cassie. But all he saw was a young teen girl standing there. Or was there something more?

With a worried look, he scooped up his trembling dog, then hurried off down the street.

As they disappeared around the corner, Cassie snapped from the momentary daze that had gripped her. She had heard those thoughts as they pressed on her mind, and in her annoyance at that stupid barking dog, she'd allowed herself to indulge in them. And that willingness to let them in scared the hell out of her. She had to get to Kyle and find out what to do.

She had just started down the block again when she became aware of a sudden stillness — all around her, the sounds had faded. Even the patter of rain was gone. It was the eerie stillness she had felt outside her house the night she saw Rex staring into the forest.

Something was coming.

She first sensed its approach in a light breeze that stirred through the trees. On that breeze came a faint echo of *whispers*. It was a cacophony of them, each overlapping the other, like multiple recordings played in reverse. There was no language, or pattern, or even actual words — only a single message, conveyed in her thoughts.

Die!

A car horn and screech of skidding tires brought her around. She had wandered into the street while entranced by those sounds and now stood within a foot of the front end of a car. The driver's door opened, and a boy stepped out that she recognized from the photo on the website.

"Hey. Your name Cassie?" he asked.

"Yeah."

"I'm Kyle Martin. You were hearing them just now, weren't you?"

How did he know?

She nodded. "I think so."

He nodded knowingly. "You better get in."

He was every bit as scary and sketchy as he appeared in his photo, with his long black hair, dark circles surrounding his eyes, and that pentagram tattooed into his forehead. She also noticed a twitch as he spoke, like someone maxed out on their nicotine dosage. Yet no matter how alarming or unsettling he might appear, he represented her best hope. So she got in.

****

Kyle ground out his cigarette in the ashtray and quickly lit another. While she hadn't actually kept count, Cassie guessed this was his third cigarette since she'd gotten in the car several blocks back. They had stuck mainly to side streets, so he could talk without the distraction of dealing with traffic. That suited Cassie just fine, as he seemed distracted enough just talking. Plus, if he tried anything, they were going slow enough she could jump from the car and make a run for it. She doubted he would, but you never know.

Kyle Martin gave new meaning to the term "basket case." He had all the signs of someone on the verge of a nervous breakdown — the jitters, the shaky hands, the glazed-over eyes, the hundred-mile stare, the million-words-per-minute speaking — it was all there. And yet he was convinced that he was holding himself together.

There was one thing that kept Cassie in that old run-down car with him — Kyle Martin was haunted, and by the same tormentor as she was. And so far he had survived (if that's what you wanted to call his existence).

Kyle had grown up within the rock and roll culture and had been one of the founding members of a death metal band called Black Plague. They played fast, and hard, and loud, and the band's name was an indication of the dark themes their music contained.

While the band never became a success financially, it managed to pay the bills and kept Kyle and his bandmates in a lifestyle of drugs, sex, and rock and roll. And all in excess, with dealers on speed dial and a harem of groupies always ready for a backstage quickie.

Kyle's wild days and nights of excess came to an abrupt end when he overdosed on heroin during a hotel room binge. Had the groupie he was with not awakened in time, Kyle's story would have ended there. But fortune was with Kyle, and the young groupie had the sense to dial 9-1-1. Kyle was rushed to the emergency room, where he was successfully resuscitated.

With a new lease on life, Kyle gave up his former life of vice, although he retained chain smoking as his fix. He moved back home with his deeply religious mom, who assisted him with his detox. Sex obviously had to go as well, as she refused to allow any of that under her roof.

It was shortly after he'd moved home that his mom began to suspect something was deeply wrong with her son; something beyond the delirium tremens and violent outbursts that accompany a heroin detox. Something evil had attached itself to her son. She had reached out to the local minister and asked him to meet with her son. He had agreed, but before the meeting could take place, Kyle's mom was killed when the brakes and steering on her car simultaneously failed and caused her car to slam head on into a large semi-truck.

There had been nothing wrong with her car before that night.

The meeting with the minister never took place.

From their onset, Kyle's hauntings closely paralleled Cassie's, as he began catching glimpses of the *Shadow* lurking just outside his peripheral vision, and experiencing the unnerving sense of the *Presence* that accompanied it. This had been going on for several months longer than Cassie's, and rather than abetting, these attacks had intensified. Kyle was no longer sleeping, and he experienced waking visions of grotesque images. He was also plagued with audio torments, which, as he attempted to describe them, were on the verge of shattering his sanity.

He began reaching out to others on the Internet who were suffering similar experiences and had started his blog in an effort to build an online community of survivors. He hoped there would be strength in numbers, or perhaps someone out there held the key to beating this thing. But over the months, the other survivors had died, with the vast majority being from suicide.

"How come you think it's a demon?" Cassie asked from the passenger seat. She watched Kyle's hands shake with the rush of nicotine. Or was it just nerves?

He shot her an incredulous look. "Really? You really just asked that?" He shook his head. "You and me, we're being honest here. And your soul knows exactly what that thing is. 'Cause there's nothing else in existence that's evil in the way this thing is. It's not just something that does evil things; the evil is its essence. It's what it is." He looked over to make sure she understood. "You can't play around with this thing, Cassie, and pretend it's not what you already know it is. Do you understand?"

She nodded.

"Good. So, is it showing you things yet?"

"Like what?"

"Like really fucked-up stuff. You know, madness... death... mutilation... the worst shit you could ever imagine."

She shook her head. "No. Not like that. But I'm having nightmares."

He nodded. "That's how it starts. It's digging its roots into you." Then he turned to her and for the first time seemed to actually be looking at her; not from behind some veil. "But it won't stay in your dreams."

She shivered, and not just from what he said, but from how he said it. This guy was haunted by what he saw. And she had to wonder if that's why he was hiding behind those veils.

Just as she thought this, that veil clouded back over his eyes, and he was again hiding. "What about people you know getting killed? Any of that happen yet?"

She shook her head. "No."

"Good. But it can happen. Happened to my mom."

"Can it kill us too?"

He snapped the fingers on his free hand. "Like that, if it wanted to. But it doesn't. It needs you to choose death and kill yourself."

"Why?"

"'Cause then it has your soul."

An icy chill ran down Cassie's spine.

"How close is it when you see it?" Kyle continued.

"It's usually like across the room."

He nodded. "Good. That means you've still got some time. It's when it gets close that you need to worry."

"Why?"

"'Cause that's when the shrill happens."

"What's the shrill?"

His jitters were back as he flicked his ash out the window. "It's this crazy, intense sound in your head that blasts the fuck out of your mind. And I mean this — there is nothing you can imagine that will prepare you for it. And when it hits, you need to do something quick to get your mind to focus on something else."

He placed his cigarette in the ashtray, then rolled up his sleeve. "Here's something I tried." He showed her the deep cigarette burns that traced across his forearm like craters. "Hurts like fuck, but still nothing compared to the shrill."

"This sometimes works too." He unbuttoned his shirt and pulled it aside to reveal a safety pin shoved through his chest muscle. "You twist it around, and it gives your brain a new pain to focus on."

Cassie could only watch in horror. She hoped that most of this insanity was unique to Kyle, but she suspected it wasn't. "Did those other people do that too?"

He nodded and fished the cigarette from his ashtray. "The ones who survived longest did. Knew one guy who pounded a nail through his hand. This other girl used a razor to slice her tongue open." He glanced at her and saw the scared look on her face. "You're getting freaked out by all of this, aren't you?"

She nodded. "Yeah. Pretty much."

"Good. 'Cause you need to be. This thing that's after us is no joke. It hates us. And it's going to torture the fuck out of you to make you chose death. And once you feel that shrill hit, you need to do everything it takes to get your mind off it. 'Cause the people who couldn't, they're the ones that chose death. And now they're His."

****

By the time they finished their talk, Cassie and Kyle had spent almost three hours together. They had driven laps through the same neighborhood streets over and over, with the rain pattering the windshield and the cigarette smoke clogging her sinuses. When she finally stepped from the car, her legs almost buckled, and she realized she had been tensed the entire ride.

As much as she wanted to disbelieve Kyle — particularly with regards to this thing he kept calling the *Shrill*, she knew she couldn't. He had known most, if not all, of the people in those obituaries she had read, and they all had those two things in common — they had suffered near-death experiences, and they were tormented by this *Thing*. Although Kyle had never participated in a Black Mass, he knew several of them had, and he admitted he would have been open to it back in his death metal band days.

The sun had already set by the time she returned home, and her mom would still be at work for several more hours. She thought about crashing on the sofa till her mom got home — she was still spooked by the idea of being alone in the house — but she decided to just crash in her room.

As she entered her room, she noticed a sharp temperature drop. It was much colder now than it had been even earlier that week. And even then it had felt cold. She went over to the window and made sure it was closed and locked. It was.

Then she noticed her small bonsai plant, Dodger, and her heart sank. It was dead and had already wilted.

She hurried over to the plant and ran her fingers along its tiny trunk. It was dry and lifeless, like something that had been seared by the sun for weeks without water. *But it had been fine just that morning, when she had watered it before school.*

She sank down on her bed and lay back. She closed her eyes, and sleep eventually came upon her. But the night would soon bring the most terrifying and traumatic encounter she had experienced up to that point.

CHAPTER TWENTY-THREE
What the Moonlight Brings

In the progression of possession, the possessing spirit seeks to both isolate its target, and instill feelings of despair and hopelessness.

No better vehicle serves to accomplish both tasks than a beloved pet. The sense of betrayal at seeing a once-loyal companion converted to the enemy is catastrophic.

> — From "Into the Periphery" by Rev. Sean McCready. Reprinted with permission.

****

It was on a cold autumn night that Cassie would again see Rex. A full moon hung in the sky and cast its ghostly pall over the quiet town that slept beneath it. It hung as a beacon and a caution that dared the unwise to explore down lonely forest paths in its light.

It was a *witches' moon*, as it was once called by the

early settlers to the area, and considered a harbinger of doom. But on this cold November eve, it came as a harbinger of something sinister and uncanny.

Cassie stirred from a restless sleep to the moanful sound of a distant howl. Her eyes snapped open, filled with the startled alertness of someone shaken from their sleep.

Something was in her room.

As her eyes adjusted to the glow from the moonlight that sifted through her filmy curtains, she sensed the presence of something hiding in the shadows.

She pulled the covers to her neck and let her eyes slowly scan the room. There were so many places for something to hide — behind the dresser or desk, inside the closet or adjoining bathroom...

Beneath her bed.

"Mom?" she squeaked in a voice barely above a whisper. But there was no response, which confirmed what she already knew — that Presence she felt wasn't a person.

As would always happen when she awakened at night, her imagination populated the dark corners with those things of nightmare that stalk us while we sleep. Always there, waiting for us to close our eyes.

We're never really alone.

Then it came again — that moanful howl, and it was no longer distant. It could be as close as the tree line beyond their yard. She turned to the window, where the curtains billowed softly in the night breeze.

She had closed and locked the window.

Icy fingers ran up her spine. The full moon was framed perfectly within the window's corners like a giant eye. It was watching her.

It had something to show her.

There was something out there beyond the window. Something in the dead of night it wanted her to see. And like a ghoulish siren, it beckoned her to come.

That low deep howl came again.

It was right outside her window.

Was it Rex?

She sat up in bed. It hadn't sounded like his howl, not even those she had heard in the cemetery, but that had been over a week ago. She pushed aside her night terrors and hurried over to the window. She pulled aside the curtains and looked down at the yard.

In the moonlight stood the dark silhouette of a large dog, watching her from eyes that reflected back the moonlight.

It was Rex.

Cassie could barely contain her excitement as she raced from her room. She bounded down the stairs to the first-floor hallway, and raced down it past the kitchen and dining room doors to the laundry room at the end. On the far side was the door to the back porch.

The porch door was open.

Muddy paw prints tracked across the floor and out the laundry room door. The tracks were fresh and wet from the damp ground out back. Rex had come inside and she'd missed him.

As she stared at those tracks, the hairs on her arms prickled. Didn't he hear her racing through the house to let him in?

Her instincts screamed at her to get out of there. Something had come in through that door that she was never meant to see.

But it was only Rex, she tried to assure herself.

"Rex," she said in a hushed voice ignoring that warning. She looked back out the laundry room door to where the tracks took a right turn into the kitchen.

Maybe he was just hungry...

"Rex? Are you okay, buddy?" She used the same hushed voice as she began slowly following those tracks.

She reached the opening to the kitchen and peeked around the corner inside it. The full moon hung like a ghastly eye in the window above the sink and gave just enough light to see by. She inched inside...

Something crashed to the floor.

Cassie jumped. It had come from the adjoining dining room.

"Rex?"

She crept across the kitchen to the opening to the dining room. In its center was a long table with three chairs around it and cabinets along the walls. She started to turn on the lights, then stopped. It might startle him. And there was still enough moonlight from the kitchen to see by.

"Rex," she said quietly as she stepped inside. "It's me, buddy." There were fragments of a glass bowl on the floor. She stepped around these as she eased over to the table and crouched down to look beneath it...

The dog watched her from the dark opening to the hallway. Warm saliva oozed from its jaws as it contemplated the soft flesh of the girl's throat. He could lunge and tear it open within seconds, and her screams would drown in a gurgle of blood.

But tonight wasn't the time. It could come later.

With a final glare, the dog turned and stalked off on silent paws. Seconds later, a bucket hit the floor in the laundry room.

Cassie spun around. "Rex?"

She raced back through the kitchen and into the laundry room. A bucket lay on the floor next to the washer, and now there were paw prints leading out the door.

Cassie stepped out onto the back porch, and her blood froze.

The dog stood there in the moonlight. It was halfway across the yard, but she could see its eyes reflecting back the moonlight like glowing orbs. In those eyes she saw neither kindness nor friendship. There was only a cold malevolence. It was the predator, basking in the fright of its prey.

Cassie knew she needed to retreat into the house, but a strange thrall held her fixed. And when it finally released her, a parting message was conveyed in her mind — it would be back, at a time and place of its choosing, and there was nothing she could do to stop it.

The dog that had once been her best friend then stalked off into the night and Cassie was again able to move. She backed into the laundry room and closed the door, sliding home the deadbolt. She sank to the floor trembling and pulled her knees to her chest. She was too terrified to mourn over the loss of her friend. That would come later.

Rex belonged to Him.

CHAPTER TWENTY-FOUR
The Breaking Point

The definitive investigation into the matters regarding Cassie Stevens was known as The Dawkins Report, named after its lead investigator, Dr. Jerome Dawkins, PhD, chair of the Department of Parapsychology and Paranormal Sciences at the Simpson Institute.

The investigative team was tasked with examining certain forensic evidence and conducting extensive eyewitness interviews over the course of two years.

Upon its completion, the committee concluded that there was "sufficient and credible evidence to support a finding of persistent and sustained occurrences of paranormal phenomena directly attributed to Cassie Stevens."

What was noteworthy is that while the report drew no conclusions as to the diabolical origins of the phenomena associated with Cassie, owing primarily to the lack of forensic evidence and a heavy reliance on subjective opinions and observations, the report refused to rule it out. In preparing the report, Dr. Dawkins noted that, "If one were to accept the existence of these supernatural beings, commonly known as demons, one would find no more compelling a case than that involving Cassie Stevens."

Indeed, the findings of diabolical influence in the matter were so compelling that at least two members of the investigative committee — men with no history of religious bias — reached out to priests and ministers following the investigation to express their fears and distress over their findings.

— Excerpts from "The Dawkins Report" published by the Simpson Institute. Reprinted with permission.

****

Flames roared through the interior of the decrepit garment mill and set the building aglow in their fierce light. They raced along walls and across the floor and ceiling. Massive lights that hung from the rafters exploded and showered sparks down on the crowd of partiers below.

The crowd screamed and scrambled for exits as flames quickly blocked their paths. Thick flaming chunks of roof and rafters crashed down on them and sent burning timbers through the air.

Those partiers who reached the exits found them closed and unable to be forced open.

Something held them shut.

And their dying screams echoed into the night.

****

November 21

Cassie awoke on the forest floor to the feel of wet pellets peppering her face. She opened her eyes and found herself staring up at the outline of trees against the dark nighttime sky. It was so startling and confusing, it took her a moment to realize she wasn't dreaming.

Where am I?

She slowly sat up and brushed the water from her face. She was cold, and wet, and caked in mud and twigs. And she had no idea how she got there.

She searched her memory for clues, but it came up blank. The last thing she remembered clearly was going to school that morning. *If it had even been that morning.*

She climbed to her feet and swayed dizzily as the blood rushed from her head. She gave it a second to pass, then took a look at herself. She was in a black dress that clung to her like a wet washcloth from the rain. It was something she had worn to raves back before — *before she died.*

She had thrown this out along with the rest of her "rave" clothes.

She remembered doing it. She had even thought about burning them, but in the end she had packed them in garbage bags and hauled them to the trash. It had been part of her cleansing.

She looked around through the forest and spotted a road through the trees. She trudged off through the mud toward it, and as she reached it, a sense of déjà vu struck her. She knew this road. *It was where she died.*

Why couldn't she remember anything? As her thoughts swam in a murk of confusion, she heard distant sirens quickly approaching. Colored lights soon rounded a bend as three fire engines sped toward her. She stepped aside onto the muddy shoulder as they roared past. They were headed toward the old garment mill where they had attended raves.

A fire. There had been a fire. She didn't know how she knew this, but it was there in her memory. Images flashed of flames sweeping across the floor, and walls, and ceiling; kids stampeding for exits; kids burning alive; the roof crashing down and crushing people beneath it... She felt their desperation as they pounded on doors; but they couldn't get out.

He wouldn't let them.

A numbness gripped her. So many of them had died. But how did she know this? Had she been there? She had the memories of seeing it, but those memories didn't feel like hers — it felt like watching someone else's memories on a movie screen.

And if she had been there, how was it that she woke up in the forest?

She knew that was where the fire engines were heading, and she also knew they were too late. She started to head in that direction, but then stopped. She couldn't go there; she couldn't see it; because seeing it would make it real.

She turned and trudged off toward town.

****

It was hours later that Cassie finally shuffled into town. By then, her mind was a numb haze from the rain, and the cold, and the fatigue... and the images of the fire that continued to assault her. It was there on the outskirts of town that she finally collapsed.

She lay there in the street next to the curb and stared numbly at the dark sky overhead. Maybe if she just lay there long enough, she could sink into the street and dissolve into oblivion. *To just be gone.*

She had just closed her eyes when she felt the first whisper in her mind's ear. Something was there with her. She opened her eyes, but there was nothing for her to see — only to feel and sense. And dread.

A pressure began building in her mind, and she felt its foul rot seek to invade her. It fingered and probed at her will, seeking vulnerabilities in the meager resistance her fatigued mind could muster. It wanted inside her and would persist as long as it took to force her into submission.

"No," was all she could mutter in her pathetic groans. But she was locked in a battle of wills with a being that refused to accept "no." And it pressed harder. And harder...

And then the *Shrill* hit.

The warnings Kyle had given her about the *Shill* did nothing to prepare her for the excruciating reality. Cassie convulsed in sheer agony as dark talons tore through her mind in searing pain. It lasted only a moment but had felt like an eternity. It shattered through her resistance like wet paper and left her broken and beaten... and without any will left to resist.

And the demon entered her.

When Cassie rose from the pavement, she was no longer guiding herself. *It* was in her, and *It* directed her movements. And each time she fought to resist, a searing pain shot through her mind.

Dark toxins of hatred and filth spilled through her as the demon seized an ever-increasing control over her. It led her down the street, past quiet houses where families slept.

Fear the night, for I walk while you sleep.

As she passed one such house, a large dog rushed at her, barking. She turned her gaze on it and watched as it shrank back in terrified whimpers. A terrible fear showed in its eyes — something a mouse might have when cornered by a cat, with no hope of escape or mercy as it faced imminent doom.

This thing inside her took pleasure at the dog's terror, but the Cassie who lay buried deep within the rot of her own mind felt sickened. And powerless.

****

The demon led her several blocks down, where she came across a party. It was still going strong at the late hour, and she watched as kids from her school hauled a fresh keg from the back of a truck and into the house.

Cassie stalked in the door like a predator, her hair and clothing drenched from the rain. There were kids in the living room where she stood, and they all stepped back to give her a wide birth. Those who hadn't experienced the *Disturbances* before, were sensing it now, and no one dared to question her presence at the party.

Cassie crossed the living room and over to an opening to the kitchen. Several jocks were in there, lowering the fresh keg into a tall bucket of ice. She watched quietly from the opening as they tapped the keg and began filling cups with beer.

Then she moved from opening, and every eye in the kitchen turned toward her. They all stopped what they were doing, and a hush fell over the room. What they saw was a small slim girl most of them recognized from school, whose black dress clung tightly to what was obviously her naked body beneath it; and yet it was like a lion had just stepped among them.

Nobody dared to speak as she took a cup from the counter and filled it with beer. Behind her, a few more students had crowded the opening to watch what was happening.

When her cup was filled, she turned to see all those faces watching her, and a sinister smile spread on her lips. Their eyes all showed the same cowered terror she had seen in the dog.

"Wendy," she began, fixing her cold gaze on a pretty blonde who stood beside her basketball-player boyfriend. "How's the baby doing, Wendy?"

Wendy staggered back, her eyes suddenly wide with terror.

"Oh, that's right. You killed her, didn't you? Never even gave her a chance to be born." Cassie's grin spread as her voice took on the eerie sound of a little girl.

"Why did you kill me, Mommy?"

This voice sounded nothing like Cassie; it was like another person's voice had spoken through her. Wendy spun around and raced from the room. Cassie then turned her gaze to one of the jocks. "Peter," she said mockingly with a shake of her head. "Peter the eater. Peter who likes to suck cocks and take them in his ass." Her grin widened as she watched the boy's face fill with horror.

Then she turned to another one of the jocks and locked eyes with his. "And Jeff. Does Stacy know you've been staring at my tits since I came in?" Then her look turned seductive, but with an alarming air of menace — she would fuck your brains out, then rip out your eyes. "Would you like to see them, Jeff?" she said, as she undid the zipper on her dress and allowed it to slide from her naked body onto the floor.

"Cassie?" came a boy's voice from the other room, and something inside her shifted. She felt a dark veil lifting from her eyes and the presence inside her slipping...

"Let me through," she heard the voice say, and it was a voice she recognized and one she thought she knew. If only she could clear her mind...

"Cassie?" The voice was closer now, and she saw the crowd part as someone squeezed through...

It was Justin.

Cassie blinked, and the presence was gone from inside her. Her lucidity was back. Instantly the dynamic in the room shifted, and the kids snapped from the terror that had held them in its strange thrall. Cassie dropped to the floor and grabbed her dress in complete humiliation and scorn. She struggled to pull it on as Justin rushed over.

"Cassie," he said, helping her slide the dress on. "What are you doing? Are you okay?"

She broke into deep choking sobs and shook her head. "I don't know what's wrong with me."

"Come on. Let's get you out of here." He took her hand and helped her to her feet.

Molly raced in and saw Justin helping Cassie steady herself. "What's going on?"

"Give me a hand," he said to her. "We need to get her home."

"Can't she just walk?"

Cassie looked over and saw the disgusted look on Molly's face. "I gotta go," Cassie said to Justin, then bolted off through the crowd.

Justin started after her, but Molly grabbed his arm. "What are you doing? Let her go."

He hesitated a moment, then shook his head. "I can't. There's something wrong."

"I know. She's crazy."

"It's more than that. Just wait here."

He shook his arm lose, then squeezed off through the crowd.

By the time he got outside, Cassie was gone. He looked helplessly up and down the street.

"Cassie!" he hollered, but all he heard back was the

storm and the music from inside the house.

He thought for a moment about driving to her house across town, but he'd had way too many beers.

"Justin." Molly raced outside to join him. "What was all that about?"

"I don't know," he said, shaking his head. "I saw something in her eyes. She was terrified."

"She was drunk and took off her clothes. And said some really weird stuff. Everyone's talking about it in there."

"She wasn't drunk," he said, shaking his head. "It was something else."

"Look. Whatever it is, you'll see her on Monday. Just talk to her then."

"What if Monday's too late?"

"It won't be. Just trust me. There's nothing you can do for her tonight."

Justin let out an exasperated sigh. He hesitated a moment, then finally nodded. Molly was right. He would see her on Monday. Everything would work out.

He hoped.

****

Cassie was destroyed by the time she shuffled into her bedroom. The demon had led her into a public humiliation and scorn, and she knew she could never see any of those people again. She had never known it was possible to feel so broken, and beaten, and alone. And defeated.

She slipped out of her dress and into a T-shirt, then slid into bed. Maybe sleep would clear her mind, if that was even possible.

As she lay there, she became acutely aware of the silence that surrounded her. It was the type of silence that tempts the ears to probe into its depths for any sound at all. The sound of a faucet drip, or footstep, or...

Her door creaked open...

Cassie tensed. She looked over at the door and it was now cracked open.

"Hello?" she said in a hushed voice. She waited... but there was no response.

She rose from bed and went over to the door. She looked out it into the dark hallway, but nobody was there. Only darkness.

She closed the door and this time made sure the latch clicked shut.

She climbed back into bed and pulled the covers up to her head.

She lay like this for some time, just staring at the ceiling and listening to the silence. She finally rolled onto her side and closed her eyes. But even with the darkness beneath her eyelids, her ears still probed into the silence.

She didn't want to hear anything. Especially not her door creaking again.

She tugged her covers around her like a cocoon, as if that would keep the bad things away.

And she was certain there were bad things. They were just waiting.

She opened her eyes, just long enough to give the

room one final sweep to make sure nothing was coming at her from the dark corners. Nothing was.

She closed her eyes again and practiced breathing to relax. It took some time, but a while later she was finally on the cusp of sleep. Her mind had entered that twilight area between sleep and consciousness, where imagination blurs between dreams and reality. She watched in her mind's eye as dark ghostly forms emerged from shadows and hovered through the air around her bed...

Something lay in bed beside her.

A foul breath had touched her neck from behind. She froze. Too terrified to move, or breathe...

A hand reached across her...

Cassie sprang from bed and bounded across the room. She braced herself against the wall and scanned the room...

No one was there.

Then what touched me?

The *Shrill* suddenly hit her again, and millions of hot daggers tore into her mind. The pain was beyond comprehension. It blasted every fiber of sanity, and she screamed and convulsed in grotesque agony. She dropped to the floor, gripping her head, and slammed it over and over again into the wall. She needed out of it, to be out of her head. Her vision darkened, and her senses failed; her whole existence was swallowed in unbearable pain.

She had no idea how long it lasted, only that at some point it began to fade, and she began to feel an awareness of her senses. Her vision was returning, along with touch, and smell, and sounds. She felt the warm puddle of vomit she lay in and the thick mucus strands that hung from her nose. Her breathing was harsh and came in gasps.

She slowly sat up and staggered to her feet. She shuffled over to the bathroom and stumbled in the door. She caught herself on the counter and propped herself up. Still gasping for breath, she looked up in the mirror...

The *Face* stared back at her.

"Get out!" she screamed. She spun around, but only the empty doorway stood there. She turned back to the sink, and broke into deep bitter sobs.

The *Shrill* hit again and screeched into her mind with excruciating fury. She vomited over the sink, then fell to the floor. She squirmed across it, gripping her head and screaming till her throat bled.

It lasted only seconds, but it could have been forever. Cassie staggered to her feet, still reeling in pain. She clenched her teeth, then smashed her fist into the mirror, shattering it into jagged shards.

Her knuckles were torn and bloodied. She gripped the counter to steady herself, then glanced down at those angry shards that mocked her from the counter.

Just one quick slice across a vein, and it would all be over.

No! She shook her head to fight that temptation. Death wouldn't be an escape; it would be the beginning of an eternity of torment. She had to fight it, and as she looked back at those shards, she realized that maybe she could use them for another purpose.

She picked one up and twisted it around in her fingers. She touched her finger to the sharp point and recalled the urgency of Kyle's warning — *"Once you feel that Shrill hit, you need to do everything it takes to get your mind off it."*

Everything it takes... She clenched her teeth and prepared for this. She could do this. She had to do this. She had to shut it off if it came again, or she would lose her mind.

She glanced over at the shower, where the frosted glass door was open. That's where she could do it.

She took the shard and stumbled over to the shower. She climbed inside and sat down on the edge. She touched the shard's sharp point to the back of her hand. Does she do it there? Or maybe her arm...

Yeah. It would need to be her arm.

The *Shrill* hit again. She tumbled down into the tub, dropping the glass shard as she fell. She threw her hands to her ears, but the *Shrill* wasn't coming in through her ears; it was in her mind. She blindly fumbled with her hand for the shard and finally found it. Gripping it tightly, she pressed it down on the back of her arm till the point broke the skin.

It wasn't working. Her mind refused to turn from the excruciating pain that blotted out everything.

Slice the vein, the voice in her head told her. *It'll all be over.*

"No!" she screamed. She dug the shard's point deep into the back of her forearm and dragged it down.

She screamed in pain, but it had worked. The *Shrill* began fading to a dull background drone. She pressed her hand to the deep cut to stem the flow of blood, but she had dug too deep. She tried to rise, but faintness was overcoming her, and she teetered on the edge of blacking out.

She fell back into the tub and felt the warm flow of blood trail down her arm. There was so much of it, and she was growing so cold. And sleepy...

"Help," she pleaded pathetically, but her voice came out as barely a whisper. She no longer had the strength to cry out.

She was dying...

From somewhere in the distant blackness, a voice called her name. Then there were footsteps outside the door, racing across her room.

The last thing she saw before drifting into unconsciousness was her mom racing in through the bathroom door. Alison was screaming, and so scared.

Help me, Mom...

Then everything went black.

CHAPTER TWENTY-FIVE
Old Friends

Cassie was again in that moonlit clearing, where faceless eyes watched from the haunted forest beyond its border. She stood in the shadow of that foreboding manor, whose massive bulk loomed darkly against a full moon. She was close enough now to feel its dark aura, and its reek of rot and despair fouled her soul.

The building was evil made manifest. Every stone and block in its immense build was born of evil, and it would exist through all eternity in that state.

A deep gong rang from its great bell, and the dead summoned forth from the surrounding forest. They came bloodied, and burnt, with torn shreds of flesh hanging from skeletal bodies.

These were the *damned* — those miserable souls doomed to an eternity of torment and despair. They shambled forth across that vast plain, with ghostly moans and wails that stirred the night.

As Cassie watched them pass, flashes of déjà vu flinched her memories. Despite the burns and rot, there was something familiar in their faces. She felt like she had seen them before but couldn't quite place it.

"You see their faces, Cass?" said Seth, who now stood on her right. "It's your fault they're here."

The manor's heavy iron door groaned open, and screams of unimaginable terror and pain echoed from deep within its haunted bowels.

"How's it my fault?" said Cassie, still unsettled at the familiarity in those faces.

The procession flowed past Cassie and through that door to their fate. Theirs would be an eternity of horrific suffering, unmitigated by any hope of escape or repose.

"You brought *Him* to the rave with you," said Trish, who now stood on her left.

Cassie shook her head. "I haven't been there since the night we crashed."

"You were there the night of the fire," said Silvia, who now stood beside Trish. "That's the night these people died."

Cassie again shook her head. "It wasn't me. I wasn't there."

Cassie felt a strong traction grip her, and she stumbled several steps toward that door.

"You were there, Cass," said Trish. "And you brought *Him* there."

"And they died because of you," said Silvia.

A powerful force now held Cassie in its grip and

was pulling her along with the procession. "You guys, help me," she pleaded. "It's pulling me inside."

"We can't help you, Cass," said Seth. "This is your fate."

"You chose this, Cass," said Trish.

"It's your destiny," said Silvia.

Cassie struggled to break free but the force was too strong. She was inching ever closer to that door.

"Just accept it, Cass," said Seth. "Stop fighting it."

Those faces of the damned turned to Cassie, and recognition flickered in their dead eyes. They reached out with skeletal hands and tore the flesh from her arms.

Cassie screamed!

"This is where you belong," said Silvia.

Cassie was now within feet of the door, and its sickening aura filled her senses with bile.

"Time to abandon hope, Cass," Seth's voice called out above the screams and shrieks from inside. "Welcome to your eternity."

Cassie let out a horrific scream as the shadow of the doorway fell over her. She screamed! And screamed! And from somewhere in the night, a distant voice called —

"Cassie! Cassie!"

"Now!"

****

Cassie awoke from the hypnotic trance on Dr. Switzer's couch. He hovered over her while she panted for breath, and laid a reassuring hand on her shoulder.

"That's it, Cassie. That's it. You're okay now. You're in my office."

Cassie's forearm was bandaged to protect the wound that had been stitched together. Her screams that night had awakened her mom, who had raced into Cassie's bathroom just as Cassie fainted from blood loss and fatigue. She rushed her to the hospital, where Cassie had spent the rest of the night hooked to IVs.

Switzer was the first call Alison made the next day. He scheduled an emergency appointment and arranged for Cassie to stay at Hillview where he could closely monitor her.

When Switzer saw that Cassie had calmed down after awaking from the trance, he sat back down in his chair next to the couch.

"What just happened, Cassie?" he asked. "You were screaming with considerable alarm."

"It was that place. The one I keep dreaming about. I was outside it again, and it was trying to pull me inside it. And there were all these dead people going inside it too. They were all burnt and rotted."

She shivered at the vividness the memory still held.

"Go on," Switzer said calmly. "You were saying they were burnt."

"They were. And Seth, Trish, and Silvia were also there. They said it was my fault all those people were dead."

"Did they say how it was your fault?"

"They said it was because I brought that spirit to the rave party where the fire happened."

"Are you talking about the fire at the old Swanson mill two nights ago?"

"Yeah."

"Were you there that night?"

She shook her head. "I don't know. I might have been. That was when I woke up in the forest and kept having these... flashbacks or something of the fire."

"But you don't know for certain if you were there?"

"No. It's only because of those flashbacks that I think maybe I was."

"I need to ask you a question, Cassie, and whatever you tell me is protected by patient confidentiality. It won't leave this room."

"Okay."

"Did you use drugs on that day? I know we had discussed this before, and you mentioned you had used ecstasy in the past. Did you on that day?"

She shook her head. "No. I haven't used anything since the crash."

"Good. It was just something I needed to clarify. Now your friends said you brought that spirit to the rave. Did they say how you did this?"

Cassie shook her head. "No. But I think it was inside me. It was inside me later that night when I went to that other party, and... you know... did all that stuff."

"What happens when this spirit is inside you?"

She thought about it. "Is it okay if I cuss?"

He smiled and nodded.

"It hurts like fuck. I mean really, really, really like

fuck. And it won't let me think, and I can't control what it makes me say or do. It's like I know it's happening, but it doesn't feel like it's me doing it."

"Is it inside you right now?"

She shook her head and almost laughed at the absurdity of the question. "You'll know when it's inside me. 'Cause it'll scare the shit out of you."

****

"She's still refusing to accept that it was a suicide attempt," Switzer said to Alison as they sat at a picnic table beneath a large oak on the Hillview grounds.

"But it was, wasn't it?" Alison asked. "I mean, she cut her arm open, for Christ's sake."

"Yes. Quite obviously it was a suicide attempt," Switzer said. "But Cassie's convinced herself that she did it to take her mind off a noise she felt in her head."

"What noise? Is this something new?"

"Apparently so. This is the first time she's mentioned it."

Alison shook her head in frustration and dismay. "Do you have any idea what's wrong with my daughter, doctor? I mean, have you figured out at least that much?"

Switzer took a breath. He could appreciate her frustration. "Possibly. Are you familiar with the term dissociative identity disorder?"

Alison shook her head. "No. What is that?"

"It's when two or more distinct personalities reside within the same person. Actual cases are quite rare, but I believe Cassie may be experiencing episodes of this.

Have you ever known her to experience memory loss?"

Alison thought about it and shook her head. "No. Not that I'm aware of. Is that happening to her now?"

Switzer nodded. "It would appear so. She's been experiencing these periods where she has no recollection of what happened, or where she believes this spirit has taken control of her."

"I know for a while before her accident, there were times I didn't even recognize her. But she's been better since then. I mean... well, she's been Cassie."

Again, Switzer nodded knowingly. "Those moments you mention were quite possibly times when this other personality had taken control."

"Is this something you can cure?"

Switzer sat back and seemed to be choosing his words carefully. "I'm always hesitant to use the term cure in the context of anything this complex, but I do believe we may be able to help her integrate these personalities into a whole."

"So, she wouldn't have these splits anymore?"

"That would be our goal."

Alison glanced around the dreary grounds, where several orderlies walked with patients. Then she took in the building itself, with its lifeless windows that seemed to watch her. It was a horrible place to look at. "I really hate to leave her here. Do you really feel it's necessary?"

He nodded. "It's for her own protection. At least until we're reasonably certain she's no longer a danger to herself."

Alison took a deep breath and nodded. "Just,

please, help her."

****

Cassie lay on the bed in her small room at Hillview. It was cold and drab, with gray cinder block walls and a small window that looked out on the hallway. Aside from the bed, there was also a chair, dresser, and adjoining bathroom with a shower. They also let her keep her laptop.

Conspicuously missing was anything a patient could use to harm themselves. That meant no knives, electric cords, or sharp objects.

Her mood at the moment was dour and frustrated. She hated this place and hated even more being locked up in it. If it looked scary in the daytime, she could only imagine how scary it was going to look at night.

And she knew there were real things that went bump in the night.

There was a knock at the door. Probably another nurse with more pills for her to choke down. "It's open."

The door eased open, and Justin poked his head in. His eyes made a quick scan of the room before they settled on her. "Hey," he said, opening the door a little wider. "Is it okay if I come in?"

She scooted up in bed and nodded. "Yeah... Hey."
How did he know I was here?

He walked over to her bed and set down his backpack. He pulled out some books from inside it and set them on her bed. "I picked up some of your assignments from school. I didn't know how long you'd be here, so I figured this way you could keep up."

"How did you know I was here?"

"I saw your mom at Mass on Sunday. She told me... you know... about what happened."

"That her crazy daughter tried to kill herself?"

"I don't think she used the word 'crazy.'"

"Psycho?"

Justin smiled and scooted a chair over to sit down.

"Maybe nutso," he added. And at that she actually smiled. But it didn't last long.

"So, is that why you came? My mom laid a guilt trip on you?"

"No," he said with a shake of his head. "I did enough of that to myself. I came because one of my oldest friends tried to kill herself, and it made me realize what a complete dick I've been to her." He paused a moment to swallow a lump that had built in his throat. "I'm so sorry, Cass."

In all the time she'd known him, she'd never seen him get choked up before. And it reached like a bridge across the loneliness and isolation she'd felt for so long.

"Thank you," she said softly as a lump built in her own throat. Then she looked him in the eye. "I didn't try to kill myself, Justin. I know that's what it looks like, but I didn't."

Now he looked puzzled. There was obviously a lot more to this than he had thought. "Do you want to talk about any of it?" he asked. "We don't have to, if you'd rather not."

"No. I do. It's just, every time I tell it to someone,

they don't believe me."

"Even your doctor?"

"It's not something a doctor can help me with."

"What is it?"

She hesitated a moment before finally saying it. "Demons."

****

Justin headed down the hallway after school. Most of the students had already left for the day, but he had someone he needed to talk to.

He had spent the entire afternoon with Cassie the day before, while she told him everything that had happened to her over the years since her dad died. And she had left out no grisly or profane detail. She needed him to know everything — from the séances and Black Mass to the extreme torment and compelled behavior when it was inside her. She told him about the *Shadow* that haunted her from the corner of her eye, and the *Presence* she felt when it was around. She told him about Rex, and her encounter with him, and the whispered threats she heard in her mind. She also told him about Kyle and his warnings about the *Shrill* — and its mind-shattering ferocity when it hit her that night. "I'm trying to use words to describe it," she had said, "but it's a level way beyond any words."

He had caught only the tail end of what had happened to her at the party, and that was after she had already regained much of her lucidity, but he had seen something in her eyes. And it had been more than simply confusion and humiliation — it had been the look of an innocent girl, pleading helplessly for her life as she was strapped down to the electric chair.

He had also heard talk for several months prior about the *Disturbances*, and while he had dismissed most of it at the time as exaggerations, in the context of what she was telling him it all made sense now.

He came away from their meeting convinced that everything she told him was real. Cassie had never been one for drama, and she had never sought people's pity, but he saw her utter hopelessness and despair as she described these torments.

Justin had been raised in a Catholic family, so the notion of demons didn't present the challenge it might for others. He more or less had always accepted the idea of their existence, just as he did the other spiritual beings that populated his religion. It wasn't that he was pious or anything; these were just things he had been raised to believe.

He also knew, as much from horror movies as he did from his religious education classes, that if Cassie was being plagued by a demon, then a doctor wouldn't be able to help her. But someone else might.

Justin found Father Sean in his classroom, where he was grading a stack of papers. He knocked on the inside of the doorway to get his attention. Sean looked up.

"Hey, Father," Justin said, "you got a second?"

"Sure, Justin. What's up?"

"I need to talk to you about Cassie Stevens."

****

"I've known Cassie since we were kids," Justin said, as he and Sean strolled down the breezeway, "and I've never seen her this scared."

"And she's had these visions ever since the accident?" Sean asked.

Justin nodded. "And they're always in the corner of her eye. You know, like that old saying."

Sean was familiar with it. "Evil hides in the periphery."

"Yeah. And it's not just the visions," Justin added, "it's all those other things too."

Sean gave a nod.

"So, you believe her, right?" Justin asked. "That all this stuff is really happening?"

"I'm sure something is happening with her, Justin," Sean said, approaching the topic gingerly, "but I think we owe it to her to let her doctor determine what that something is."

"But he doesn't believe in demons, or spirits, or any of that stuff. He thinks it's all in her head."

"In all likelihood, he's probably right."

The two stopped as they reached the end of the breezeway. Sean turned to Justin. "Look, Justin, I know you're just trying to help her, but everything you've told me can be explained by medical causes. There's split personalities, or bipolar disorder, or things along those lines. We don't need to go looking for demons."

"But what if it is demons? Then she's totally screwed."

Sean just shook his head. "I'm sorry, Justin, but I

have to side with her doctor. Let's just give him time to find the right treatment."

"She doesn't have time," Justin shot back. "This thing is getting worse, and he's not gonna be able to help her. But you could."

Justin stormed off down the breezeway in disgust. But halfway down he turned and fired a parting shot. "You know, being a priest is supposed to be more than just handing out food at soup kitchens. You're supposed to be there to help people like her, when science can't."

Then he stormed off. And a small itch scratched at the back of Sean's mind — it was the *resistance* he had felt before and that Jenkins had somehow sensed in him. Yet simultaneously with that came Jenkins' words of caution — *And you, my friend, are in the process of being disarmed.*

Was he?

CHAPTER TWENTY-SIX
Awakening

With the coming of night, Cassie's room at Hillview became bathed in moonlight from a narrow window in the back wall. It was inlaid with a screen mesh, so nothing could get in or out that way. At least nothing that doors and windows could keep out.

Cassie rose groggily from bed and walked over to the small bathroom across the room. She pulled a paper cup from the dispenser and filled it with water from the faucet. As she drank it, something dark dripped into the sink. It was followed by another drop... and then another. It looked like blood.

She saw that it was coming from her forearm, where the blood had soaked through her bandage. She must have torn her stitches in her sleep. She was reaching for a paper towel when her eyes caught something in the stainless steel mirror...

Something moved in the shower behind her.

A shadow drifted behind the filmy shower curtains. It was barely visible in the dim moonlight.

"He's coming for you, Cassie..." a low voice spoke from her right. Cassie looked over, and a dead teenage girl stood beside her. She was pale and emotionless, and her eyes stared like lifeless marbles. *"He won't stop..."*

"Give in, Cassie..." came a male voice from the shower. A gnarled hand slid aside the shower curtains, and behind them stood the dead heavy metal rocker she'd seen in the online obituary. Dark circles surrounded his glazed eyes, and like the girl, his expression and speech were emotionless. *"You can't fight him,"* the rocker said, *"he's already won."*

"He never stops," came a boy's voice, and the gray corpse of a teenage boy now stood beside the girl.

"He'll keep coming..." said the girl. *"He's always watching..."*

"Always there," said the boy.

"Till you die," croaked the rocker as he stepped from the shower and slid toward Cassie. *"And then he has you."*

"Like he has us..." said the girl, taking a step toward Cassie.

Cassie backed out the doorway and into her room. She kept her eyes on those figures as they slowly dissolved into darkness.

Then only silence remained... but she wasn't alone.

As she looked toward the window, a dozen dark figures stood there in the gloom.

Cassie awakened with a startled gasp. She felt herself in bed, just as she'd been several hours earlier when she'd fallen asleep, but it still took a moment to sink in that it had been a dream.

She finally sat up and wiped the sleep from her eyes. There was no way she was going back to sleep. Not in this place. It freaked her the hell out. And she had already noticed on her third night there that the building settled late at night with deep groans and creaks of its stone foundation. It wasn't doing it now, but she knew it could at any moment. And it gave this place a whole new layer of creepiness.

She grabbed the remote from her nightstand and clicked on the TV. Hillview only received a dozen TV channels, and they were all showing infomercials at the moment.

Freaking great.

She clicked off the TV and grabbed her laptop. It took a few seconds to boot, then she pulled up Kyle's blog, "Evil Hides in the Periphery." She looked over at the blog entries and saw a new one from earlier that night. She clicked the link, and her heart sank as she read the entry: "No sleep for 72 hours. It's getting worse. But I'll still stop it."

Cassie quickly scrolled down to the "Contact" button and clicked on it. A messenger window popped up, and she typed: "Kyle. It's Cassie. Are you online?"

His reply came in less than a minute: "How R U?"

"I'm in the hospital," she typed back. "It's close now."

"R U OK?" he replied back.

"Most of the time. But it's getting worse. I felt the Shrill."

"Shit!" came his response. "We need to meet. I think I know how to stop it."

Cassie reread this several times, making sure it said what she thought it said. She then messaged back: "I'll text you when I get out."

"When will that be?"

"Soon. I hope."

"Good. Just don't wait too long."

Shit. Shit, shit, shit. Now she really needed to get out of this place.

She had just started to type another message when a sound caused her to freeze —

Her door was creaking open.

Her eyes shot across the room to her door, which was now cracked open several inches. The doors in Hillview bolted on the outside "for patient protection," so someone would have needed to come by and physically unlock and open it.

"Hello?" she called in a hushed voice, then waited for a response...

A faint sound came from the hallway outside, so quiet she wasn't even sure if she had heard it. But it was enough to make her heart race.

It had sounded like a child's cry.

Then it came again. It was barely audible, but she was certain it was a child's cry.

She closed her laptop and walked over to the door.

It opened into a long hallway lined with doors to patients' rooms on each side. Its walls were built of cold gray stone and its floor of tiles. There were no lights, but windows at each end allowed in enough moonlight to see by.

There were three connecting hallways that ran perpendicular to Cassie's hallway, with one at each end and one in the center. The hallway at the end to Cassie's right ran to the hospital's containment wing, where they housed the more dangerous patients.

Someone was in the hallway.

She stood at the far end on Cassie's left, just a dark silhouette against the window. From the outline, she could see it was a woman in a long hospital gown.

"Cassie..." came a faint voice echoed along the walls. Cassie couldn't tell if the woman had said it but assumed she had.

"Yeah?" Cassie called back quietly. She didn't want to wake up the other patients.

"Come, Cassie..." came the hushed voice. *"Come... come with me... I have something to show you..."* The voice spoke slowly, and again it was hard to tell if the woman had said it. It was something about the way it carried through the air...

And how did she know my name?

"What is it?" Cassie called back to the woman.

The woman turned from the window and walked off down the connecting hallway. *"Come, Cassie... come..."*

Cassie hesitated a moment... this was stupid... she should just go back inside her room.

"Come, Cassie..."

Shit. Cassie took off after her. She jogged down to the connecting hallway, just as the steel fire door to the stairwell clanged shut. She went over to the door and opened it. Inside was a steel staircase that zigzagged down from the third floor she was on, all the way to the basement. Narrow windows along the outer wall gave enough moonlight to see by.

"Come, Cassie..." the hushed voice floated up the stairwell.

"Who are you?" Cassie called back, then heard the door clang shut one floor below her.

Cassie took a tentative step inside the stairwell... then another... She decided to just go down to the second floor and peek out the door. If anything looked suspicious, she was out of there.

She reached the second floor and cracked the door open just wide enough to see out. Nobody was there waiting to jump her, so she took a chance and stepped into the hallway. This was the floor Switzer's office was on, so she was already fairly familiar with it.

She eased the door closed behind her but kept it cracked in case she needed to get out of there fast. She was in one of the connecting hallways which had no windows at their ends, but enough ambient moonlight came from the main hallway to see by.

Something moved in the darkness down the hallway.

It had been standing there the whole time, but Cassie hadn't seen it until it moved.

"Come, Cassie... come and see..." came that strange

hushed voice again, and this time it seemed to come from all around her.

"Who are you?" Cassie asked.

A door creaked open, and the figure stepped into a room on the left. *"Come and see, Cassie... come and see..."*

Cassie took a deep breath. This was stupid, following this woman, but she was confidant she could outrun her if something happened. And she had to know who this woman was and what she knew.

Cassie walked down the hallway to the door. The room number was 226. Cassie knocked quietly, then stepped back as the doorknob turned on its own. The door creaked open... *and Cassie felt the cold air inside.*

Nobody was behind the door.

The hairs on her arms rose. She backed away from the door and caught something from the corner of her right eye...

The woman stood beside her.

Cassie nearly tripped as she stumbled back from the woman. Up close, she could see clearly now the unnaturally pale skin and the veins that coursed through her arms. The woman's head hung slightly, as if looking at the floor, then began to tilt up. First came the dark sunken eyes as the matted hair fell from around her face. Then the dark, drawn-in cheeks... and then the jagged gash that sliced her throat from one ear to the other.

The woman titled her head back till she was staring at the ceiling, and the gash on her throat split wide open. Thick blood poured from the gash and down her gown.

Cassie screamed and snapped from the shock that had held her frozen. She raced back to the stairwell and up the stairs, and didn't stop running till she reached her room. She ducked inside and quickly jammed a chair beneath the doorknob to hold it closed.

She leaned over to catch her breath.

Fuck! Shit! She needed to get out of here!

Then she felt a sudden tingling...

Something was in the room.

She spun around, and three figures stood in silhouette against the window. She screamed before realizing it was her goth friends. Then she was ready to kill them.

"The fuck, you guys? What're you doing here?"

"Liberating you, girl," said Trish, clearly amused at Cassie's reaction. "We haven't seen you since they locked you up."

"I'm not locked up," Cassie grumbled, still annoyed at the scare. "They're helping me."

"You should ask for a refund," cracked Seth, nodding to the chair jammed beneath the doorknob. "I don't think that help is working out so well."

"What spooked you out there, girl," Silvia asked. "Are you still seeing ghosts?"

Cassie nodded. "Yeah. And other things too."

"Like your dog," said Seth.

Cassie did a double take. "How did you know about Rex?"

Seth shrugged. "Didn't you tell us?"

Cassie shook her head. "I haven't seen you guys since you bailed on me after that séance."

"Just a lucky guess then."

"What does it matter, Cass?" said Trish. "So, we know. Big deal."

"It matters because I never told anyone. So how'd you guys know?"

"Someone needs to seriously chill out," said Seth. He dug into his pocket and pulled out a small bag of ecstasy pills. "Why don't you try this, instead of the meds they've got you on?"

He took a step toward her...

Cassie shook her head. "I'm not doing that stuff anymore."

"Why not, Cass?" said Silvia, and she and Trish also took a step towards Cassie.

"'Cause I don't want to," said Cassie, taking an uneasy step backward.

"Is that your shrink talking, or your mom?" said Seth, taking another step toward her.

Silvia and Trish also took another step toward her...

And the temperature in the room dropped.

Cassie took another uneasy step back and bumped against the wall. The goths watched.

"You're scared of us," said Silvia, taking another step closer. It was an acknowledgment — *she knew, that Cassie now knew...*

"No, I'm not," said Cassie. She was scared out of her mind, but couldn't let it show. She couldn't let them know that she *knew*. But they already did.

"Then prove it," said Trish. "Take a pill with us." She fished a pill from Seth's baggie and slid it under her tongue.

Cassie shook her head. "I don't want to." The fear was showing in her voice now.

"Since when?" asked Trish, as they took another step closer...

Cassie hesitated. "Since I died."

"We all died," said Trish, taking another step closer. "But you got to come back..."

"And we're still dead," said Silvia.

As Cassie watched, their faces rotted and decayed into the spectral corpses they were. Cracked gray skin clung like shriveled paper to their skulls, and dark empty eye sockets sneered at her with seething hatred.

Cassie screamed. She felt faint, and her legs went weak. She tugged the chair out from under the doorknob and flung open the door. She collapsed onto the floor and dragged herself out the door. She screamed into the hallway! And screamed!

From down the hallway came the pounding of feet. Two orderlies rounded the corner at the end of the hallway and sprinted her way.

Cassie glanced back into the room, where Seth, Trish, and Silvia slowly faded into the darkness.

"We'll see you soon, Cass," Seth sneered. And then they were gone.

And everything went dark as Cassie fainted.

****

Details from the night of her crash exploded back into Cassie's memory, and she could now recall everything.

She saw ambulance lights flashing in the night outside the shattered windshield.

Seth's car lay on its right side. She had sat behind Silvia and was now pinned against the back door. She couldn't move or breathe. She felt rain pelt down on her through the shattered side window above her.

Trish lay across her and crushed the breath from her lungs. She could see Trish was dead, with her neck twisted grotesquely and mouth forever frozen in its death scream.

Silvia lay twisted on the console between the two front seats. Her head had smashed into the windshield, and her skull was crushed like a melon.

Seth's head lay twisted on top of Silvia's. His head had shattered the windshield, and the jagged glass had torn the flesh from his face. Only one eye remained, staring lifelessly from his skull.

They were all dead and gone to wherever it is the dead go, and she would soon join them...

And then It was there. And she felt herself sink into darkness...

CHAPTER TWENTY-SEVEN
The Death of Hope

"You don't need to worry about me anymore," Cassie assured Switzer as she sat on his couch the day after her encounter with the goths. "I remember everything now."

Cassie had awakened shortly after the orderlies found her lying in her doorway. Her memories of the accident were back, and vivid, and she remembered it all now. And with it came the terrifying realization that the goths' appearances had been hauntings; and she knew they would return. But none of this was anything she could tell Switzer. More than ever, she needed to get out of this place, and to do that, she needed to convince Switzer that she was on her way to recovery and no longer posed a threat to herself. So she was going to tell him whatever it was he needed to hear.

"Is that what was happening when the attendants found you?" Switzer asked. "They said you were screaming."

Cassie nodded. "I was. I had a dream, and that's when it all came back to me. Seeing my friends dead like that, I guess I just freaked out."

"Quite understandable," Switzer nodded.

"So, yeah, I think I was having that thing you mentioned. Was it survivor's guilt?"

"Yes. That was one of my theories."

"And all the other stuff. You know, seeing ghosts and things. I think that was just the drugs leaving my system. It can do that, right? Cause hallucinations and stuff like that."

Switzer nodded. "It can."

"So, yeah. I think just knowing that will make me not freak out so much if it happens again. But I don't think it will, especially now that I know the truth."

She watched Switzer's reactions as he nodded along. Was he buying it — that she was getting better? Or did he think he was being played?

"So, now that I'm better, would it be okay if I went home?"

He sat back in his chair, and gave her a sympathetic smile. "Cassie, I know you're anxious to return home, and I do believe we've made a considerable amount of progress, but we need to be careful that we don't do it too soon."

Shit!

"But I'm better now. I know my friends are dead, and I think that was the big breakthrough for me."

"It was a considerable one, yes."

"Then can't we just go back to the way we used to do this, where I come in for appointments?"

Cassie saw that he looked hesitant. "Please. I think I would make better progress if I could adjust to normal life again while we still keep doing these sessions."

He considered this a moment. "I'm still concerned over these suicidal idealizations."

Cassie quickly cut in. "But that was never me. That was what I thought that thing wanted me to do. But now I know it was all tied to that guilt I was having over surviving when my friends and that girl were killed."

"And you no longer have those feelings of guilt?"

She sensed a trap.

"I still feel bad it happened, but I know it wasn't my fault. And it's all in the open now, where I can see it, and deal with it. My problem before was I didn't understand what was happening."

She could see him thinking.

"Please. I know I'll get better a lot faster if I'm back in my normal surroundings."

"And if we do this," he finally said, "do you promise you'll contact me if you feel any relapse?"

She gave him a big nod. "Oh yeah. Definitely. And I'll even keep your card with me in case it happens at school."

He thought for another moment, then finally nodded. "Very well then. I'll sign the paperwork for your discharge. But I want you to remember your promise."

"I will. Thank you!"

****

Cassie glanced out the passenger window at the passing countryside. Over the course of the afternoon, she had seen the terrain pass from the forested hills on her peninsula, to farmlands, and finally back to the rolling hills on the eastern side of the state.

It was the day after her discharge from Hillview, and she had asked Justin if he would come with her to see Kyle. She and Kyle shared a common foe, and she hoped he was right about knowing how to beat it, but, honestly, the guy still creeped her out. So she was grateful when Justin agreed to come with her. If anything positive had come from that night of the *Shrill*, and her second brush with death, it was having her old friend back in her life. It made her feel a little less alone.

"So, none of that stuff you told your doctor was true," Justin said.

"The part about Seth, Trish, and Silvia being dead was true."

"So, you lied about the rest of it."

"I just had to get out of there."

He grinned. "So, you lied."

She rolled her eyes. "I told him what he wanted to hear. And he didn't want to hear the truth."

"That you saw dead people in your room?"

"He'd have me in a straitjacket right now."

Justin laughed. And she did too. And it felt good to laugh again.

She turned to him. "Thanks for doing this for me, Justin. It really means a lot."

He looked at her, and despite her efforts to sound upbeat, her eyes betrayed the fear and sadness she felt. She really was all alone. He gave her hand a squeeze.

"Thank me by getting better."

****

The sun was setting over the foothills by the time they arrived. Kyle's town had been built around the coal mines in the early part of the last century and had flourished for decades, but with the closing of the mines, it had become all but a ghost town. Where once-thriving middle-class neighborhoods had enjoyed picnics and cookouts, there now sat graveyards of decayed, derelict houses, closed stores, and dead lawns.

Kyle's house was in one of the poorer sections of town. Rusted car bodies and unkempt yards littered the neighborhood, and Kyle's was the worst kept of the lot.

Justin's car pulled up out front and parked along the curb. He and Cassie glanced out the window at the overgrown grass and trash that had accumulated outside.

"This is it?" Justin asked, and it was clear from his tone he hoped it wasn't.

Cassie hoped it wasn't too, but a glance at the text on her phone showed it was. "Afraid so," she said with a cringe.

They climbed from the car and crossed through the tall grass to the front door. Cassie knocked, then gave it a moment for Kyle to answer.

He never did, so she knocked again.

"He knows we're coming today, right?" Justin asked.

"Yeah. And that's his car over there," she said, nodding to the run-down old car in the driveway.

She knocked again while Justin walked over to the large front window. He cupped his hands around his eyes to see in.

"I don't see anyone," he said.

Cassie knocked again, then tested the doorknob. It was unlocked. She glanced at Justin as he strolled back over.

"You're going in?" he asked.

"Might as well." She pushed the door open.

An overwhelming stench greeted them as they stepped inside. It was the smell of mold, and rot, and filth, and a look around the living room revealed the source. Throughout the room, flies swarmed over scattered dishes covered with half-eaten meals and spilled drinks. Mold grew from plates, and fast-food containers, and soiled clothes.

"Kyle?" Cassie called out, swatting aside a swarm of flies. She almost choked at the stench. "Kyle? It's Cassie. I brought a friend."

No response came.

"I don't think he's here," said Justin.

"Let's just check." She crossed the living room to a hallway and looked down it.

"Kyle? You here?"

A door was slightly ajar at the far end. She headed

down the hallway to it and tapped on it lightly.

"Kyle. You in there?"

When no answer came, she pushed it open and stepped inside. And froze...

It was Kyle's bedroom and reeked of soiled clothes and mildew, but what held Cassie frozen in shock were the drawings and photos covering every inch of the walls. They were a glimpse into the madness of a mind that had completely snapped. Each drawing and photo depicted a macabre scene of horror and death. There were decapitations and disembowelments; graves and corpses; maggots borrowing from rotted flesh; mass graves in Nazi death camps; hangings; eyes gorged out; amputations...

And drawings of the *Shadow* and the *Face*.

"Ho-ly shit," Justin exclaimed from behind her, and Cassie nearly jumped. She had been so focused on those images, she hadn't heard him approach. "What is all of that?"

"It's what he sees," she said, still unable to take her eyes off those images. This was the fate that awaited her.

"Do you see any of this?" he asked, and she felt him shudder as the depths of her horror slowly revealed itself to him.

"Just those two right there," she said, pointing to the drawings of the *Shadow* and the *Face*. "But he said I'd start seeing these other things too."

A slight breeze blew in from an open window somewhere in the house and carried with it a new stench more horrible than the others. It was the smell of death.

Cassie was too entranced to notice, but Justin did. He plugged his nose and followed the stench across the hallway. Moments later, he called to her.

Cassie walked from the bedroom and found Justin standing in the open doorway to a bathroom. He was staring across the room at the closed shower curtains, splattered with something dark. And he assumed it was blood.

Cassie stepped past him into the bathroom, drawn to those curtains like someone in a trance. "Maybe you shouldn't look," she barely heard him say, but she knew she had to.

As she approached the curtains, the only sounds were the pulse of blood in her ears and the steady drone of flies.

She took hold of the shower curtains and slowly slid them aside...

Kyle's dead body lay in the tub with a shotgun still clutched in his hands. The shot had taken off the entire top of his head, splattering brains and skull fragments over the walls and curtains.

She just stood there frozen, still gripping the shower curtains in her clenched fist. Unable to move or think. Kyle had been her hope, and this had been his fate.

And it would soon be her fate.

Justin set his hand on her shoulder, and she snapped from her daze. She sprang backward from the horror in that shower, and began screaming hysterically.

****

It took a little over fifteen minutes for the police to arrive, and maybe another hour for someone from the coroner's office.

Cassie sat on the lawn out front and just stared at the tall grass. Staring, but not seeing. Her mind was numb with the dreadful morose of a hope that had been raised and then shattered. This was what the death of hope felt like.

Justin spoke with the police on the nearby carport. Bits and pieces of their conversation floated Cassie's way. Why had they been there? Had they touched the body? Had they disturbed anything? Justin did his best to explain, and a quick search of Kyle's room revealed a severely disturbed mind. Foul play wasn't suspected. The officer handed Justin his card and nodded toward Cassie. "You should probably get her home."

They shook hands, then Justin walked over to Cassie and sat down beside her. He gently laid his arm across her shoulder.

"Hey," he said softly. "Let me take you home."

She trembled.

"Don't let that guy worry you, Cass. You're not him. You and I are gonna figure something out."

"It's not just him," she shivered and sniffed back a tear. "It's everyone that thing went after. They're all dead."

"Except you. You're not dead. And you're not gonna be dead. Not by that thing."

She turned to him, and her eyes were filled with hopelessness and fear. It was the desperate, horrific look of someone who had seen the doom that awaited her and was powerless to stop it. The anticipation of a slow descent into madness and agony, to be followed by a violent end.

She choked back a deep, agonized sob and just shook her head. "I don't know what to do anymore." It was the most pitiable, desperate plea for help a human soul could muster. So alone in her misery, and completely devoid of hope.

He wrapped his arms around her, and she sank her head into his chest. His mind raced through scenarios. He had seen what medical science had to offer, and it was a joke. More drugs? More therapy sessions? He saw one possibility for hope. It was a long shot; but it was a chance.

"I think I know someone who might."

CHAPTER TWENTY-EIGHT
Believe

Waves splashed against the serene New England shore. The air was crisp and fresh, and the cool salt spray tickled Sean's arms as he strolled along the water's edge.

Down the shore stood Amy, gazing out over the ocean. Golden sunlight painted softly across her hair as it tossed gently in the breeze, and the sight of her took his breath away. This was her. This was his Amy.

She turned to him with a smile as he approached.

"Remember this place?" she asked.

He looked around and nodded. A smile touched his lips. "Our first date. We were looking for crabs."

"And you saw that octopus in the tide pool."

His smile widened. "I remember that."

"It became my favorite place after that day," she said. "Like so many of the places we shared."

"They were mine too."

He was still smiling, but a sadness was taking over.

"I'm sorry I wasn't there for you, Amy."

Her eyes met with his, and she shook her head. "You were with me, Sean," she said in a voice that was soft and loving. "All those moments we shared together — every sunset, and mountain, and star — you were with me every time I thought of them."

A thick lump was filling his throat. "It was still a mistake becoming a priest. I should have stayed with you."

She again shook her head. "You had to, Sean. It's like those creeks we used to wade through, and how they would flow into streams then out to sea. That's how our lives are. We can't always control where the current is going to take us, but it takes us where we need to be. And everything you were, everything that's ever happened to you, all of it led you here. And this is where God needs you."

At the mention of God, Sean's face went slack. He let out a deep sigh. "I don't know if I believe that anymore."

Amy reached over and took his hand. Her skin was so soft and smooth, and her eyes sparkled warmly as they looked into his. "You need to let yourself believe, Sean." And then she turned toward the ocean. "Look out there."

He followed her gaze. "Now open your heart," she said, "and I want you to really see it." He did, and it was like he was seeing it for the first time — this sparkling marvel of beauty and mystery that flowed into eternity beyond the horizon. "Can you look at that, and still not believe?" she said and watched his hard look of bitterness and frustration slowly melt into serenity.

And she smiled. This was her Sean again. The boy she had fallen in love with that warm summer day so long ago.

"Cassie's going to need you, Sean," she said.

He turned to her. "She has her doctor."

Amy shook her head. "He can't help her. She's going to come to you soon, with no other hope, and you need to be the Sean I fell in love with."

She turned to him, and took his hands, and he could have melted in the warmth of her eyes.

"Believe, Sean."

Sean awoke with Amy's final words playing in his mind. It was morning, and colorful sunlight warmed the room through his curtains.

He lay there a moment and didn't want to let go of the dream. He had been there with her, and it had felt so real. The warmth of the sun and cool ocean spray. And the softness of her skin as she held his hand. He could even smell the...

Sean sat up. There was a subtle scent in his room that instantly triggered memories of afternoons in parks and strolls on the shore. It was the scent of Amy's perfume, Chanel No. 5. And it came from somewhere in his room.

He rose from bed and searched his room for the source of the fragrance. It was on his desk that he finally found it. Amid the books and ungraded test papers sat a sheet of paper he had never seen before. It had a single word written on it, and he knew that handwriting from so many letters he had read while in Afghanistan.

It was Amy's handwriting, and it said:

"Believe."

****

The church bells toned from the tower high above St. Matthew's Church. Beyond it lay a sky of dull gray clouds, and a thin mist hung close to the ground from the overnight rain.

Justin and Cassie sat in his car in the parking lot out front and watched Father Sean greet parishioners on the lawn outside the church.

She'd been hesitant to the idea of talking to Father Sean when Justin first suggested it, and as she watched the parishioners trail past, she wondered if any of them had the sordid stories to tell that she had. She was sure priests heard bizarre things during confession, but hers were beyond bizarre. And to make things worse, she would have to see him in class every week.

But if there was even a chance he could help her, and Justin thought there was, then screw her pride. She would tell him everything.

"You ready?" Justin asked from the driver's seat, watching her wring her hands into knots. She gave a hesitant nod.

"I think so."

"You'll do fine. Just make sure you tell him everything."

"I know. I know," she grumbled. "But he's going to think I'm a freak."

"No. He won't. Just trust me, okay." He gave her hand a squeeze.

"Okay."

They climbed from the car. As she started to step away, a tense vertigo struck her. She tumbled back against the car.

"Cass?" he rushed around to her side and helped steady her. "Are you okay?"

"Yeah. Just a little dizzy."

"Take as much time as you need."

She nodded, but a strange tension was building within her. It was more than the butterflies and nerves she had felt moments ago. Something dark and unsettling was coiling inside her like a giant serpent, prepared to strike at any intrusion to its lair.

"Cass?" she heard Justin say, and she opened her eyes. She hadn't realized they were shut till then. She clenched her teeth.

"Maybe we should do this another time," he said.

"No," she said. "It's not gonna let me come back." Her eyes met his. "It knows we're here, and it's pissed. We need to do this now."

"Okay. We'll do it."

"Will you hold my hand?" she asked.

"Of course." He took her hand, and they began walking toward the church.

"Whatever I say, don't let me leave. Okay?"

"Okay."

Together they headed up the sidewalk that cut across the lawn. With each step, she felt that tension inside her build.

As they neared the church, she glanced up at the cross mounted to its steeple. Suddenly that thing inside her snapped, and her mind filled with the blind fury of a rabid animal.

Justin felt her tremble. "Cass?"

She shook her head. "Just keep going."

She had to do this. Justin had been right. If that thing hated the church and a priest that much, then this is what she needed.

Maybe it would work... maybe it would work...

God help me, she muttered in a silent prayer.

Sean had just finished greeting a parishioner when he spotted Justin and Cassie approaching. It looked like something was wrong with her, as Justin kept helping her stand.

She's going to come to you, with no other hope...

Amy's words from the dream came suddenly. Was this the moment she meant?

Sean hurried down the sidewalk to meet them. He held out his hand and offered her a warm smile. "Hey. It's good to see you back. How are you feeling?"

She tried to smile as their hands touched... then instantly recoiled back. It had snapped, and a sheering pain shot through her. She staggered back as Justin caught her arm to steady her.

Sean's smile turned to concern. He looked at

Justin. "What's wrong with her?"

Justin shook his head. "We need to talk to you, Father. It's about what I told you last week."

Sean nodded. "Okay. Let me tell everyone that Mass will be starting late."

"Is your name Cassie Stevens?" a woman's voice called from across the lawn.

Justin and Sean turned to see Maggie Dunne storming over.

"It is you, isn't it?" she snarled as she stormed up. "I'm Maggie Dunne. It was my daughter Katie that you killed."

Justin stepped forward. "Woah. Miss Dunne. Take it easy. Okay?"

"No! It's not okay! That girl's a murderer."

Sean stepped between Maggie and Cassie and put his hand on Maggie's shoulders. "Maggie, please. I know you're upset. But now's not the time."

"Then you tell me when is the time. That girl killed my daughter!"

Cassie's bloodcurdling scream caused them all to stop. She dropped to the grass and writhed grotesquely like a worm in water. Sharp talons tore through her mind and body, as the *Shrill* struck more ferociously than ever.

She screamed and screamed till her throat was raw. Sean and Justin rushed over and knelt beside her.

"Make it stop!" she screamed in a voice torn with agony.

All around, parishioners had stopped and watched

in horror as this young girl twisted in torment across the lawn. Each felt something grip them at their most primal core, and they sensed what they couldn't see — a fellow human being, crushed by a monstrous brutality.

Then it faded, ever so slightly, and Cassie's eyes locked onto Sean's. It was the look of a drowning victim as she broke the surface in one last desperate cry for help.

"Help me," she gasped, and the stark terror in her eyes sent Sean reeling back. It was so far beyond any level of terror and agony he had thought possible that it shot tendrils of fear through his own mind.

Then the clarity in her eyes vanished, and she submerged back into that pit of excruciating agony.

Maggie's heart shattered to pieces as she watched Cassie writhe and convulse. Every trace of anger and bitterness was gone, and all she felt was profound sadness and empathy. She took a step forward to help, but something stopped her. A small voice had whispered to her and told her it wasn't the right time yet. But it would be soon.

Please help her, the voice had pleaded.

She dropped to her knees and wept deep bitter sobs. She knew the voice she had heard — it was her daughter, Katie.

****

Sean found Father Jenkins tending the small garden behind the rectory. He knelt down and joined him in removing some weeds that had spread amongst the squash. He tugged on one, and it snapped at the stem.

"Careful, Sean. You need to be sure to remove the entire root. Otherwise you'll return in several days and find it's regrown."

Sean grabbed the weed at its base this time and tugged out the entire root. He held it up. "Like this?"

Jenkins nodded. "Yes. Quite resilient things, these weeds."

Sean nodded. It was an interesting allegory for the reason he was there.

"I need to talk to you about Cassie Stevens," Sean said.

"Yes. Yes, I heard about the incident outside the church. Have there been any updates?"

Sean shook his head. "They have her under sedation at the hospital. She's scheduled to have some tests run tomorrow. That's all I know right now."

"God love her," Jenkins muttered. He had known Cassie since her family had moved to the small town and had watched her grow up over the years. He had also been friends with her dad before his death. "Let's pray it's nothing serious."

"Justin Mahoney spoke with me about her last week," Sean began after a brief pause to collect his thoughts. "He's worried her problems are more of a... spiritual nature."

Jenkins paused from his gardening to sit up. "How so?" he asked.

Sean hesitated a moment, then finally spoke those words he had dreaded to say out loud. "He thinks she's the victim of demonic attacks."

He had Jenkins' complete attention now. "What makes him think that?"

"It's a number of things," Sean said. "Her erratic behavior over the past couple months. I'm sure you've heard talk about what her teachers and the students call the 'disturbances.'"

Jenkins nodded. "I understood there hadn't been much talk of that lately. Not since her accident."

"It's been better, but it seems to have reoccurred the night she attempted suicide."

"I wasn't aware of that," Jenkins said. "Go on."

"She also claims to see a... some sort of entity from the corner of her eye and feel its presence at other times. She also believes it inhabits her at times, and those times seem to coincide with the disturbances."

Jenkins set his gardening tools down and sat back. "Does her doctor share this belief?"

Sean shook his head. "No. Apparently he feels she's suffering from dissociative identity disorder and dismissed the possibility of supernatural causes. That's why Justin wanted to talk to me."

"And what did you tell him?"

Sean took a breath. "I told him I agreed with the doctor."

"I see," muttered Jenkins. "As per the conversation you and I had."

Sean nodded. "It was several days after that when Justin and I spoke."

"And is that how you still feel?"

Sean shook his head. "I don't think so. Not anymore." He took another deep breath. "I saw something in her eyes outside the church that made me question a lot of my previous doubts. There was a brief moment when something like a veil came down from behind her eyes, and she looked at me for help, and she was filled with this terror I can't even begin to describe."

Sean physically shook at the memory. He looked at his arms, and the hairs stood on end. He showed it to Jenkins. "The whole time I was in the Marines, death was something we faced every day. And you'd see fear in the guys' faces sometimes. But this is the first time I've experienced just complete and utter terror."

He took a moment to shake off his arm then looked again at Jenkins. "I think I'm ready to believe again."

CHAPTER TWENTY-NINE
Redemption

Cassie lay asleep in her bed at Hillview, while Justin sat in a nearby chair attempting to read a book. He had been on the same page for over an hour. Every time she had shifted in bed or her breathing changed, he had checked to make sure she was okay.

They had rushed her straight to Hillview from the church. Switzer had met them at the entrance and prescribed a powerful sedative to help calm her. The *Shrill* had subsided by the time they arrived, but her nerves were shattered.

She had slept for over sixteen hours now. Alison had met them when they arrived and had stayed the entire night. She finally needed to leave an hour earlier, but Justin stayed on.

Justin glanced up from his book and was startled to see Cassie looking at him.

"Hey. You're awake," he said, closing his book and

setting it on the floor.

She nodded. "How long was I out?"

"Almost a day. How are you feeling?"

"Like hell," she muttered. "How bad was it?"

"You don't remember?"

She shook her head. "I remember walking up to the church and looking at the cross on top of it, and that thing got furious. I mean, it really, really hates God and pretty much everything. Then that woman started yelling, and that was it. That's all I remember."

"I think Father Sean's a believer now," Justin said.

"He saw it?"

"Everyone saw it."

Cassie cringed and squeezed her pillow. "He must think I'm a freak."

Justin shook his head. "No. He doesn't. He helped me get you to the car, and he said he was going to talk to Father Jenkins about you."

She rubbed her temples. "Now you see what that shrill does and how bad it is."

Justin nodded. "That's why Kyle killed himself, isn't it?"

"And why I almost killed myself trying to get it out of my head."

Justin reached over and took her hand. "Just promise me you'll hang in there till we find a way to fix this."

"What if there isn't a way?"

"There is."

"But what if there isn't? I don't know if I could

take that happening again."

"Just promise me you won't give up."

She nodded. "Thanks, Justin. For doing all of this."

"You'd be doing it for me." He started to say something else but was interrupted by a knock at the door.

Cassie looked over at the door. It was probably a nurse. "Yeah?"

It opened, but it wasn't a nurse — it was Maggie Dunne. She stared into the room a second, then hesitantly stepped in. Justin rose from his chair to block her, but she held out her hands in a reassuring gesture.

"Please," she said as she looked at Justin, then past him to Cassie. "I'm just here to apologize."

In her hand, she held a small cross on a thin chain.

****

Dr. Switzer skimmed through a medical report at the check-in counter in Hillview's lobby. A young technician, Charlene ("Charlie" for short), pointed to the signature line at the bottom. "They need you to sign it right there," she indicated.

Switzer scrawled his signature on the form and handed it to her. "You'll get me a copy."

She nodded. "I'll do it right now."

Across the lobby, the double doors at the entrance opened, and Father Jenkins strolled in carrying a small briefcase. He spotted Switzer across the lobby and walked over.

"Might you be Doctor Switzer?" Jenkins asked.

Switzer turned to the elderly man and immediately

noticed the white rectangle on his collar. "Yes," he replied. "Is there something I can help you with?"

Jenkins nodded, extending his hand. "I'm Father Jenkins. I left message for you earlier about a patient of yours, Cassie Stevens."

"Oh yes," Switzer said with a nod. "Her parish priest. What can I do for you, Father?"

Jenkins looked around the lobby. A few people sat there and seemed to be eavesdropping on their exchange. "Might we talk somewhere in private?"

"Of course."

Switzer led him down a short hallway to a small conference room and showed him in.

"So, what is it I can do for you, Father?" Switzer asked as he took a seat at the conference table. Jenkins slid into a nearby seat and placed his briefcase on the table.

"I'm concerned about Cassie," Jenkins said. "How do you feel she's responding to her treatment?"

Switzer leaned back. "Well, we haven't isolated the cause of her dementia yet, if that's what you're asking. I'm sure you can appreciate that much of this is a process of elimination."

Jenkins nodded. "Have you eliminated the possibility of supernatural causes?"

"Ghosts?" Switzer almost chuckled at the absurdity of the suggestion. He shook his head. "No, Father. I leave that area to men such as yourself. My focus is on the neurological causes."

"And what if there are none?"

"Then we look elsewhere."

"Does this elsewhere include the possibility of a demonic attack?" Jenkins asked.

Switzer was already tiring of the direction this conversation had taken. "Father, if I might be frank, I believe the church's obsession with demons and spirits is what may have planted the idea in Cassie's head to begin with."

Jenkins was unfazed by Switzer's tone. In a way, he pitied the man. "So, you don't believe in demons?"

"No, Father, I don't. And in twenty years of psychiatry, I've only had one patient suffering from a dementia similar to Cassie's who I wasn't able to successfully treat."

"And you're certain those other patients were cured?"

"I have no reason to believe they weren't."

"Then I'd ask that you consider the consequences," Jenkins said. "And that is, if I'm wrong about Cassie, she loses her sanity. But if you're wrong, she loses her soul."

Switzer felt it was time to end all this nonsense. "I'm well aware of the consequences, Father. And I assure you, Cassie Stevens will have the very best in medical care. Now, was there anything else?"

"No. That was it," Jenkins said, still appearing unfazed at Switzer's dismissal. "I appreciate your time."

"We're all concerned about her, Father," Switzer said.

Jenkins started to rise, then paused, as if

remembering. "By the way. What ever happened to that other patient of yours? The one who suffered from a malady similar to Cassie's."

The question caught Switzer off guard. He hesitated a moment but was fairly sure the priest already suspected the answer. "She died," he said. "As a matter of fact, it was right here in this hospital. She was found with her neck slit open."

Jenkins didn't appear surprised by this answer. "Self-inflicted, I assume."

Switzer nodded.

"I'm very sorry to hear that," Jenkins said in all sincerity.

Switzer acknowledged this with a nod.

Jenkins undid the latches on his briefcase and removed a book from inside it. He slid it across the table to Switzer. "I'd like to leave this with you, doctor. In case you run out of those... neurological causes. And I suspect you might." There was a slight note of sarcasm in his tone. He hadn't meant it, but he did see Switzer's closed-mindedness to even the possibility of supernatural causes as woefully ignorant.

Switzer picked up the book, and it was the same one Jenkins had previously given Sean: *A Case for Demonic Possession.*

****

Maggie sat in a chair beside Cassie's bed and ran her fingers across the small cross necklace. "Katie was only one when her dad died." Maggie thought back through her memories. "He and I had been married five years when it happened. And with him gone, Katie was all I had left."

"I'm so sorry, Mrs. Dunne," Cassie said from her bed while Justin watched from across the room.

"Please. Just let me finish," Maggie said and gently patted Cassie's hand.

Cassie nodded.

"This necklace belonged to Katie," Maggie resumed, again running the cross and chain through her fingers. "I got it for her for her first Communion this year. And after that, she just used to wear it everywhere. Even to bed." Maggie took a deep breath...

"She was wearing it the night she died."

A deep sob escaped Maggie's chest, and Cassie choked back her own tears.

"Oh God, Mrs. Dunne..." Cassie said.

Maggie quickly composed herself and looked up at Cassie. "I want you to have it, Cassie," she said, and, taking Cassie's hand, she laid it in her palm.

Cassie was speechless. She stared at the necklace a moment, then back at Maggie, before finding her voice.

"Oh, no, Mrs. Dunne. I can't. This was your daughter's."

Cassie reached out to give it back, but Maggie gently closed Cassie's hand around it.

"Please, Cassie. Just take it." Maggie took another deep breath. "I don't know how to explain how I know this, but Katie wants you to have it."

Cassie was again speechless. By now, her own eyes had filled with tears. She looked down at the small cross then back at Maggie. "Thank you," she said, and her voice broke. "I'm so sorry."

"I know you are, dear," Maggie said and leaned in to wrap Cassie in a warm hug. "And I forgive you."

She leaned back, and let her eyes meet Cassie's. "And I know Katie forgives you too."

****

It was late in the evening by the time Father Jenkins returned home to the rectory. He found Sean at his desk in his bedroom, reading the original copy of the book on demonic possession that Jenkins had given him.

Sean looked up as Jenkins entered the room. "How did it go with Cassie's doctor?"

"As you might expect," Jenkins said with a frustrated shake of his head. "What do you think of the book?"

Sean bookmarked the page and closed it. "Scary."

Jenkins nodded. "And keep in mind those are only words, Sean. Words used to describe something that's completely inexplicable."

"You mentioned that the other day," Sean said. "Something about feeling their threat."

Jenkins nodded. "And a part of me has never recovered from that encounter. Not even after all these years."

"Can you tell me about it?"

Jenkins sat down in a chair across the desk from Sean and seemed to stare at a distant memory. It was a place inside him that he didn't want to go, and yet he knew it was important to Sean that he did. "Are you familiar with the concept of summary evil, Sean?"

Sean shook his head. "No. I never heard the term."

"It's an evil that exists in and of itself as its permanent state. There's no motive or provocation behind it; it simply is, and always will be evil. And to encounter such a being is to encounter a vicious cruelty and intelligence that's vastly superior to you, and without a trace of mercy."

Jenkins sat back in his chair and again seemed to stare at those faraway memories. "My encounter happened shortly after I was assigned to my first parish in Los Angeles. There had been a series of particularly grisly killings in the city, and the police were tipped off that a group of high school kids were responsible. They traced these kids to an abandoned building, and what they found in the basement of that building would forever haunt even the most hardened of them."

Jenkins adjusted in his chair.

"I spoke with many of those officers later, and what they described was feeling a pronounced sense of presence as they descended into that basement. This evil surrounded them in the very air itself and filled each of them with an overwhelming sense of dread. But it was in a back room of the basement that this presence seemed most concentrated. As they entered that room, they felt a precipitous drop in temperature. The walls and floor were painted with satanic symbols, and as they explored farther into this rather large room, they began to find the remains of half-eaten bodies in pools of blood..."

Jenkins breathed back an unsettling discomfort before he resumed. "It was in the back of the room that they found the *girl*.

"Her name was Natalie Stark, and she was a junior at a nearby high school. But nobody who knew her would have recognized her that day. They described her as covered in blood and snarling at them with the wild, feral look of an animal. She had been eating the severed arm of one of the bodies, who were later identified as the other members of her coven. But it was what they saw in her eyes that would forever haunt them. Each of these veteran officers felt what they described as a threat to their very souls.

"It was because of the obvious satanic nature of the crimes that I was asked to come speak to the girl at the jail. But by the time I arrived, it was too late. She had chewed through her wrist during night and had already been dead for several hours. But there was a message for us on the wall that she had written in her own blood. It said 'Ave Satana,' which is Latin for 'Hail Satan.'

"But there was one more message for me, and it came as the jailer and I started to leave. It was something I heard in my mind, and I'll never forget it. It said, *'Soon, Father. We're coming for you soon.'*"

CHAPTER THIRTY
Katie

A chill night breeze whispered through the trees and tossed dry leaves across the long unkempt grass of the lonely playground.

Missing were the joyful sounds that typically accompany a playground: the giddy laughter of children, happily frolicking on swings and monkey bars; parents calling their kids to picnic tables for lunch; and fathers playing catch with their young boys.

But not this playground. It stunk of death and decay and was as quiet and desolate as a long-forgotten tomb. Cold moonlight filtered through skeletal branches of trees and bathed the playground in its ghostly tint.

But there remained dark untouched corners of it where even the moonlight feared to tread. It was from there that the eyes watched.

Cassie crossed the grass toward the far side, where

the playground's only other occupant sat on a swing. It was the *Little Girl*, and she was bathed in a warm radiant light. And those things of the shadows feared that light.

Cassie sat on the swing next to the girl and felt the darkness retreat to its corners. It was like the ocean tide, washing past her ankles as it flowed out to sea.

Cassie felt peace. She just sat there for a moment and basked in its gentle warmth. She never wanted it to leave.

She finally turned to the *Little Girl*. "You're Katie, aren't you."

Katie Dunne nodded while continuing to stare at a single white daisy she held in her hand.

"I'm Cassie."

"I know," Katie said in a soft melodic voice. It was tinged in sadness, and Cassie knew it wasn't sadness for herself; it was sadness for Cassie. For reasons known only to Katie and God, this beautiful young girl, whose life had been cut so tragically short had taken pity on Cassie.

"I'm so sorry, Katie," Cassie's voice broke. It was the most heartfelt sentiment she had ever expressed.

Katie looked at her, then reached over and handed Cassie the daisy.

Cassie's heart melted in tears. She held the daisy to her nose and smelled the sweet scent that had dispelled the darkness so many times.

Wiping her eyes, Cassie turned back to Katie, who was again looking at her hands folded in her lap.

"Thank you," she said, and her voice broke again.

Katie nodded, accepting Cassie's thanks. "He's wrong about the spirit," she said.

"Who's wrong?" Cassie asked.

"The doctor. He doesn't believe in it. But he will."

"So, you know about the spirit?" Cassie asked.

Katie nodded. "It's here. Right now."

In that instant, Cassie felt it — the unsettling chill of being watched.

Somewhere, beyond the ring of cold blue moonlight, the *Shadow* was watching. Turning ever so slowly, she caught it from the corner of her left eye as it drifted through the shadows.

Then it was gone.

"Only God can help you, Cassie," Katie's voice came like a soft echo.

Cassie turned back to Katie, but only the empty swing remained. Katie was gone, and Cassie found herself alone. All around her, the darkness began to creep in, and within that darkness stirred things of nightmare — things that had been kept distant by the warm light of Katie's presence. They were free.

And they were coming for her.

****

Cassie's eyes snapped open mere seconds before that darkness on the playground would have enveloped her. She sat up panting.

"Cassie!" came Switzer's voice from a nearby chair.

She looked around. She was in Switzer's office, lying on his couch. It was coming back to her now.

"That's it," he nodded. "You're in my office. You're safe."

She took a deep breath, trying to steady her nerves from the dream.

"You were crying, Cassie. Then you began screaming. Do you recall what you saw?"

It took her a second, but then she nodded. "It was the little girl. The one I've been seeing..." Cassie thought about it a second. There was more. She turned to Switzer. "I know who she is now. Her name's Katie. She's the girl who was killed in the other car."

Switzer sat back in his seat and nodded along with her. He'd long ago suspected a connection between this girl Cassie claimed to be seeing and what he felt was her guilt over her complicity in the girl's death. Cassie's recognition of this was a considerable step forward.

"This little girl, did she say anything to you?"

It always annoyed her when he patronized her like that. They both knew he didn't believe her, so why put up the act? But she played along anyway.

"Yeah, she did," Cassie said and turned to look him in the eyes. "She said you're wrong about the spirit. That you don't believe in it. But you will."

Switzer was taken aback by the boldness of that last part. *But you will.* He was quite certain that he wouldn't.

As Cassie watched his reaction, she realized there was something in her hand. Without even looking, she knew what it was by its feel. She held it up for Switzer to see — it was the daisy Katie had given her.

"And she gave me this."

****

Once you eliminate the impossible, whatever remains, no matter how improbable, must be the truth.

That line from Sir Arthur Conan Doyle resonated in Switzer's mind as he contemplated the daisy that sat in a small vase on his desk.

Also on his desk were two patient files. One of them was Cassie's file, and the other was for a female patient named Janet Sterling. A photo of each patient was paper clipped to the top left corner of each file.

Janet's photo was of the woman Cassie had encountered in the hallway, whose throat had been slit from ear to ear. She was the woman who, as Jenkins had surmised, had taken her own life.

Inside each file was a drawing that bore a strong similarity to each other. The drawing in Cassie's file was the printout she had found on Kyle's website. The similar image in Janet's file had been drawn by one of the nurses at Switzer's request.

Was this all just a coincidence? Switzer was beginning to question this as he again looked back at the daisy in its vase.

Switzer had no doubt that Cassie's hands had been empty when their session began. It was common practice to make sure they held nothing with which they might harm themselves.

And yet there it was.

Switzer was a man of science. You might even say it was his religion. He was medically trained and prided himself on his ability to find rational explanations for seemingly inexplicable behavior and phenomena.

And yet there it was.

In all of his years of practice, only one other patient's case had challenged Switzer to question his rigid adherence to scientific dogma. And that had been Janet's.

Like Cassie, she had claimed to see the specter depicted in the drawing from the corner of her eye, and nurses attending to her had reported various "disturbances," similar to those felt by those around Cassie. There had been a glass that had fallen, as if knocked from her dresser; lights that had flickered in her room, despite any electrical cause; and they had all reported an inexplicable cold they felt when in her presence. Before long, all of the nurses refused to attend to Janet.

Switzer had never personally witnessed any of these disturbances and tended to dismiss them as some sort of group hysteria; and yet they persisted. Several nurses had gone so far as to quit their jobs in order to avoid being in the hospital with her.

The disturbances apparently ended on the night Janet took her own life. But the staff continued to shun the room she had been kept in, so it remained unused to this day. It was the infamous second-floor room 226.

A knock at the door snapped Switzer from his musings. Charlie poked her head in and held up a large envelope. "Got the results on the MRI you ordered for Cassie Stevens."

"Please. Come in." He waved her over. "Let's have a look."

Charlie walked over and removed an MRI slide from the folder.

"Were there any abnormalities?" Switzer asked, taking the slide from her.

Charlie shook her head. "None the radiologist could find. He said it looked like a normal human skull."

Switzer held the slide up to the light, shifting it around as he examined it.

"What about the other slides?" Switzer asked. "Was anything there?"

Again, Charlie shook her head. "They're all pretty much the same."

Switzer decided to have a look anyway. He slid a second slide from the envelope and held it up to the light.

Charlie watched as he probed every detail for some sign of abnormality. But there simply weren't any. "If there's anything going on in there, it's sure not showing up on these tests," she remarked.

"No. Apparently not." Switzer put the slide back inside the envelope.

"Do you want to try again?" she asked. "Maybe recalibrate, and run some more tests?"

Switzer sat back in his chair, and his eyes drifted over to the daisy. "No," he said humbly, "that won't be necessary." He took his eyes off the flower long enough to give her a nod of thanks. "Thank you, Charlie."

"Not a problem. I'll see you tomorrow." She turned and headed off.

"Good-night," he said, but his thoughts had already drifted elsewhere. Once again he turned his eyes to the daisy. How curious, he thought, that something so small and delicate could unwind years of rigid scientific dogma.

Once you eliminate the impossible, whatever remains, no matter how improbable, must be the truth.

CHAPTER THIRTY-ONE
Fate

The rain had begun as a drizzle shortly before sundown and by nightfall had grown into a downpour. Distant flashes of lightning cracked the sky, and the deep rumble of thunder rolled in from the ocean.

Jenkins stood at his bedroom window on the second floor of the rectory. Below, he could see the school courtyard, with its wide marble fountain in the center and the arched breezeways that bordered it on four sides. Each breezeway had mercury vapor lamps mounted to its columns, and they cast the darkness in a yellow hue. It looked particularly foreboding that night.

The hour was late, and Jenkins needed sleep, but his thoughts were haunted by memories of that dead teenage girl he had encountered all those years ago.

Natalie Stark.

Jenkins and everyone involved in that case — police and jailer alike — had spent many sleepless nights after that encounter staring into the shadows and wondering what dark eyes were watching them. And with memories of that grisly encounter with evil stirred, Jenkins again felt those cold dead eyes watching him from the shadows. Each time he had closed his eyes to sleep that night, he felt the foul presence beside him and the sulfurous odor of its breath against his neck.

Soon, Father. We're coming for you soon

Two sharp knocks at the downstairs door startled him from his thoughts. He glanced at the clock on his nightstand, and it showed a little after midnight.

Who on earth could be out this late on a night like this? Had Sean maybe locked himself out? He waited a moment to see if the knocks persisted...

Two more knocks came. Jenkins threw on his coat, then headed down the hallway to the stairs and down them to the living room. The front door was directly across from the stairs, and the long window on the front wall gave him enough light to see his way over to it.

He pressed his eye to the peephole on the door — *someone stood outside.* The person was a dark silhouette against the night, but Jenkins could see from the outline it was a girl.

"The rectory is closed for the night," Jenkins spoke through the door. "We open again at nine in the morning."

There was a brief pause, then a girl's voice spoke from outside. *"I'm cold."*

Jenkins hesitated. She was probably one of the

homeless who often slept in the courtyard. There had never been a problem with any of them, and they always cleaned up after themselves in the morning. He knew the charitable thing would be to offer this girl shelter from the storm, and she could leave once it passed.

That would be the charitable thing.

Then why did he feel this strange sense of dread?

He hesitated a moment then asked through the door: "Is there anyone with you?"

There was another brief pause, then her voice came again in reply.

"I'm cold."

Jenkins pressed his eye back to the peephole. The girl appeared to be alone. But that icy fear was still there.

Run. Run away. Do not open that door.

He opened it anyway, and a gust of wind hit him. Beyond the shelter of the porch roof, the rain came down in sheets. But the girl was gone.

Jenkins stepped out onto the porch. He looked to his left toward the school and courtyard, and beyond that to the dark outline of the church.

"Hello?" he called out, but all he heard was the heavy drum of rain.

"Are you still there?" he called out again. There was still no reply.

He had waited too long, and she had gone off into storm. It didn't occur to him how she had vanished so quickly.

He started to return inside the rectory when a sudden flash of lightning lit the night — and in that brief flash, he saw the girl racing down the breezeway towards the courtyard. It was like seeing a ghost with the way her long white gown billowed swiftly in the wind.

Jenkins shook off that thought.

"Wait!" he hollered, but his voice failed to carry over the storm.

Jenkins pulled his coat snuggly around himself then pressed out into the downpour. It bit like stones, and within seconds he was drenched. He ran as quickly as he could over to the breezeway, then took shelter there while he scanned the courtyard for the girl.

"Hello? Are you here?" he called out. He cupped his hands to his eyes to help him see. The mercury vapor lamps, while providing sufficient light for the breezeways, did little to penetrate the darkness of the courtyard.

Lightning flashed and briefly lit the courtyard — the girl sat on the rim of the fountain in the courtyard's center.

"Young lady," Jenkins hollered to her. "Please, come in out of the storm. I can allow you to rest inside the rectory."

The brief flash of light was gone, but it didn't appear that she had moved. Maybe she hadn't heard him.

Jenkins stepped out from the breezeway and was again pelted by rain. It was cold and miserable, and yet the girl seemed oblivious to it.

"Please. Come in out of the storm. I apologize for my rudeness earlier."

He was close enough now to see her in the storm's dim light. Her head looked down, and her long dark hair concealed her eyes. She seemed to be staring at something near her bare feet.

As Jenkins stepped closer, he saw that her drenched white gown was tattered and stained with something dark.

Blood?

"Are you okay?" Jenkins asked, now less than ten feet from her. "Do you need me to call for an ambulance?"

It was only then that the girl seemed to notice him. She lifted her head, and while her eyes remained concealed behind wet tangles of long black hair, he knew she was watching was him.

And he knew that no human life existed behind those eyes.

"He sent me for you, Father," came her voice, croaking with a disturbing resonance that sent chills through Jenkins. She extended her arm from the long sleeve of her gown and rolled it over so that her palm faced upwards.

There was the deep gouge in her wrist where she had bitten through it decades ago in her jail cell.

The night she died.

Jenkins stumbled backward as he felt a steel vice grip his heart.

The dead teenage girl rose and took a lumbering step toward him... and then another...

Lighting crashed and struck the transformer on a nearby utility pole. It exploded into sparks. The mercury vapor lamps blinked off and plunged the courtyard, school, and church into darkness.

The girl took another step, and Jenkins could finally move. He stumbled backward to the breezeway, then raced down it to the back door of the church. He fumbled with his keys and finally got the door open. He took a quick look back down the breezeway, and saw her dark shape lumbering toward him.

Jenkins ducked in the door and quickly locked it. He was in the back room of the church, where shelves held weekly bulletins and reading materials. Behind him, tall double doors opened into the main sanctuary. Jenkins stepped through them into the church itself. Its vaulted ceiling rose high above, with a choir loft and rows of stained-glass windows lining the walls. What little light there was came through those windows, and was painted in ghostly hues.

He looked back at the room he had come from, and wondered how long she would stay out there? Till sunrise? Or later?

Was she still out there?

It was then that he felt the cold soulless eyes watching him.

She wasn't out there.

He turned in the direction of the altar at the far end of the church, and his blood turned to ice.

Like a grim harbinger of death, the dead girl floated in the air above the altar. Her blood-stained gown hung from skeletal shoulders, and her arms reached outward from her sides. It was an unholy mockery of the figure of Jesus on the large wooden cross behind her.

Jenkins took a step back, but invisible hands gripped him by the neck. He was raised five feet off the floor and slammed into the back wall.

Every muscle in his aged body tensed with frantic efforts to break free. But that grip held him like a vice.

The dead girl watched from beneath her long matted hair. Then she extended her arms forward and floated across the sanctuary toward him.

Jenkins could no longer move and could barely think; so great was the terror that froze him. He could only watch in horror as the phantom floated ever closer.

Stained-glass windows began shattering along the walls, spraying colored shards across the pews. Lights flickered on in the chandeliers, then burst in bright flashes. Heavy wooden pews broke from their floor bolts and crashed across the floor.

Then came a sudden, blinding flash. Lightning streaked through a shattered window and exploded on the large wooden cross. It shattered into splinters and shot large shards like missiles through the church.

One javelin-sized shard shot down the aisle past the girl and plunged through Jenkins' lower chest. So great was its force, that it planted in the brick wall behind him, pinning him to it.

That unseen force released its grip on his neck, and his torso fell forward onto the shard.

With his final thought, he whispered a prayer for Cassie's liberation.

****

Miles away, Switzer sat alone in his office at Hillview. He had committed to read at least a few chapters of Jenkins' book on demonic possession; and now, as the clock ticked well past midnight, he found himself completely absorbed in its well-documented chronicles of ordinary people who had fallen under possession.

As he read the case histories, each meticulously documented with footnotes and an extensive bibliography, he recorded notes to himself on a microcassette recorder he kept on his desk.

He reached the end of the latest chapter and traced his finger to a footnote at the bottom of the page. He pressed the record button on the small recorder and spoke into its microphone: "Page ninety-two. Have Cynthia locate the New York Journal article referenced in footnote sixty-three." He clicked it off.

Lightning flashed suddenly outside his window. There was a loud crash from somewhere, and the hospital's lights flickered out. It left his office cast in the storm's dim gray pall.

The timing couldn't have been worse. Switzer became suddenly aware of just how alone he was in that dark building. He had never been one for superstitions, but that had been before immersing himself in Jenkins' book.

It was, without a doubt, time to leave.

He fumbled for his briefcase in the dim light, when his ears picked up a strange sound. He held still for a moment and listened closely.

It came again, and he could swear it sounded like gurgling — like maybe somebody gargling water.

He had just sat back in his chair when he noticed someone standing in the doorway across the room. The person was only there for a moment, but it was long enough to see from its dark silhouette that it was a woman in a long hospital gown. Most likely one of the patients.

She had been watching him.

Switzer rose from his desk and walked over to the doorway. There was a noticeable chill in the hallway, and he couldn't recall feeling it before.

The faint gurgling sound came again.

It had come from down the hallway on his left, and as he looked in that direction, he saw the silhouette of the woman against the window at the far end.

She was again watching him.

Switzer's skin prickled with unease. He knew it was silly, and likely the effect of having read that book so late into the night, but he actually felt a sense of dread.

It had to be the book.

"Can I help you?" he called to the woman. But there was no response.

She stepped away from the window and drifted off down the connecting hallway.

Whoever this was, it was too late for patients to be out wandering the hospital. Someone had obviously neglected to lock her door.

Switzer headed off in that direction. He reached the connecting hallway, and without the windows at either end, it was considerably darker than the hallway he was in. He pulled his cell phone from his pocket and shined its flashlight down the hallway.

The hallway was empty, but as he swept its narrow beam across the walls and floor, he spotted a trail of blood leading across the floor. He knelt down for a closer look, and it was definitely blood. And it was fresh.

"Are you okay?" he called out, rising to his feet. He shined his light back at the floor and followed the trail of blood to where it stopped at a door. He shined his light on the room number... and felt icy fingers run along his spine. It was a room that hadn't been used for over a decade and was shunned by the staff as haunted.

It was room 226. Janet Sterling's room. His patient who had been haunted like Cassie. And had slit her own throat.

Every instinct told him to run; to leave this place and never return. But too many years of scientific dogma were working against him; he had to know.

He tested the doorknob, and as he had expected, it was unlocked.

It hadn't been unlocked in a decade.

Ignoring one final warning from his instincts, he opened the door and stepped into the room.

He was met by a foul rotted stench and such icy coldness that he could see his breath. Yet as he shined his flashlight through the room, he saw nothing that could have caused the stench or drop in temperature. There was only a bare mattress and an empty dresser and cabinet. It appeared exactly as it had a decade ago, when it was cleansed and sterilized after Janet's death.

He shined his flashlight back at the floor. The trail of blood picked up inside the door and led across the tiled floor to the bathroom on the far side of the room. If that woman was here, that's where she would be.

He proceeded over to the bathroom in slow cautious steps. It was only the irrational hope he clung to for a logical explanation that propelled him to step into that bathroom. How odd, he thought, that he now saw the logical explanation as being the irrational one.

The blood trail continued across the bathroom's tiled floor to the bathtub and shower where the curtains were drawn shut.

He startled back.

A bloody handprint was on the shower curtains.

He stood there for a moment, staring at those curtains and listening into the silence for any sounds. But even the storm's sounds were muffled by the thick concrete walls.

He had to know.

He gripped the curtains and drew them aside... the shower was empty. There were no words to describe his relief as he stared into that empty shower. He exhaled the breath he had been holding. All of that worry and tension had been for nothing.

He breathed a deep sigh of relief. He turned to leave the bathroom, and as he did, his eyes drifted past the stainless steel mirror above the sink...

Janet Sterling's ghost stood in the shower behind him.

It was grisly and decayed, with dark empty eyes that bore into his. Then that hideous gash in her neck opened, and blood oozed from it and down the front of her gown.

Switzer stumbled out the bathroom door. He slipped on the blood smear and fell to the floor. He quickly spun toward the bathroom, expecting to see Janet's ghost come through the door, but the doorway was empty.

He staggered to his feet and backed toward the hallway door, never taking his eyes off the bathroom door. As he reached the hallway door, that gurgling sound came again from the bathroom.

It was the sound of someone choking on their own blood.

Switzer raced from the room and down the hallway to his office. He grabbed his briefcase and keys and was soon gone from the building.

Dr. Benjamin Switzer, MD, would never return to Hillview.

****

"This is Doctor Benjamin Switzer, at the Hillview Hospital," Switzer said into his microcassette recorder as his car plowed through the storm. He was on a lonely stretch of forest road between Hillview and his home in the foothills of Capetown, and despite his wipers' efforts to slap the rain from the windshield, visibility was down to twenty yards.

This area had been developed around the coal boom in the middle of the last century, and the terrain was scarred with deep quarries that ran alongside the road. Most of the mines had closed over the years, but much of their machinery remained as rusted reminders of the region's past.

"If for any reason this tape is found," Switzer continued into his recorder, "it's imperative that it be delivered at once to Father Jenkins at Saint Matthew's Parish in Capetown, Maine.

"Father, I'm of the belief now that you're likely correct in your assessment of Cassie Stevens, and that her affliction is beyond the capabilities of medical science to cure. Please contact my office, and they can arrange to have her medical files delivered to you."

Here he took a brief pause to sort through his thoughts. Ever since climbing into his car back at the hospital, a sense of impending doom had pressed on him. He feared it was a premonition of his own death, and it wasn't something he could dispel. But if he was going to die, he needed to do everything left in his power to help Cassie. And that meant clearing the path for Jenkins to employ whatever remedies the Church had in its arsenal.

If there was a God, and Switzer had begun to think there might be, maybe it would give Him a reason to have mercy on this foolish old doctor's soul.

Finally, with a deep breath, he pressed the record button again. "I'm leaving this tape for you, Father, in the event that I don't make it home tonight. I encountered something inexplicable at the hospital tonight, and I'm of the belief that I will likely die." He took another brief pause to allow a rush of emotions to pass.

"Please help Cassie, Father. And don't let it be my arrogance that kills her." He took another moment to gather his thoughts before continuing. "This next message is for you, Cassie. It's critical that you trust Father Jenkins. I can't stress enough that your life depends on it. Please forgive my arrogance at having doubted you and the pain I know it caused. My intent was only to help you. And now my last hope is that Father is able to free you of this spirit. Please know that I tried, Cassie."

He swallowed a lump in his throat and set the recorder on the passenger seat. Hopefully he was wrong about that premonition, and he could meet with Jenkins tomorrow to discuss this in person.

The rain beat down harder now, and the wet pavement hid a minefield of potholes in its weathered surface. The car had already plunged into several of them, and each time he struggled to maintain his grip on the steering wheel.

His imagination had also run wild, and several times he thought he saw Janet Sterling's ghost standing alongside the road.

At least he hoped it had been his imagination.

But now, with less than an hour to go before reaching home, a new sensation stirred the hairs on his neck — the awareness that he wasn't alone.

She was in the backseat.

He forced his eyes to avoid the rearview mirror. He knew he would see her face in it if he looked. He just had to focus on the road and hope he made it home without anything happening.

A sound came from the backseat, and it was the sound he had both dreaded and expected — it was the deep gurgling sound that had come from the bathroom. His blood chilled.

He took his eyes off the road just long enough to look in the rearview mirror... and to his surprise, nothing was in the backseat. He turned back to the read...

Janet's ghost stood framed in the headlights.

Switzer slammed on the brakes. It was out of reflex, and a huge mistake. The tires locked, and the car spun out of control. It fishtailed sideways into the guardrail, crashed through it, then plunged down a steep embankment to the mine quarry below. It hit the bottom and bounded over rocks till it crashed into a large gravel mound. It stalled on impact.

The air bag exploded into Switzer's face and knocked his head back against the seat. It dazed him for several seconds before his mind cleared enough to function.

He wrestled with the airbag, and finally got it deflated and pushed aside. He could see again out the windshield, and saw that his headlights and taillights were still on. The car had power.

He tried starting it, but the engine wouldn't turn over. He checked his cell phone, but it wasn't getting a signal.

He now faced a dilemma — wait in the car till help arrived, whenever that might be, or walk back to the road and hope for a ride.

With Janet lurking out there.

As he pondered these equally unappealing choices, his eyes traveled across the windshield to the rearview mirror — and in the eerie red glow of the taillights...

Janet's ghost drifted across the quarry bed toward him.

Panic seized him. He reached for his seat belt and pressed the button... but the catch was jammed. He jiggled it and tried again, but it was still jammed. He took another glance at the rearview mirror...

The ghost was closer now.

A sudden bright flash streaked the sky, and lightning exploded on the heavy machinery at the top of the gravel mound above him. He looked through the windshield and saw a long metal rail snap off and plunge down toward his car. He leaned to the side, just seconds before it crashed through the windshield and planted its tip in the backseat.

It had missed him by inches, but now he was pinned against the driver's-side door.

He pressed the button on his seat belt again, but it still wouldn't unfasten. He would need to crawl out from beneath it.

A loud crash outside turned his attention again to the windshield. Several heavy pipes on top of the mound had shaken lose and had crashed down into his car.

His eyes then caught the rearview mirror, and renewed panic set in — the ghost was halfway across the quarry bed.

Switzer grabbed the door handle and forced the door open. He slipped the shoulder strap behind him and pulled as much slack as he could from the lap belt. He leaned out the door and worked at pulling his body out from beneath the lap belt.

His head was entirely out the door now, and he glanced back beneath the car at the quarry bed. In the red glow of the taillights, he saw the ghost's legs less than ten feet from the back of the car. Its feet were pointed downward, and floating several inches above the gravel.

He turned his attention back to the seat belt. He now had his legs halfway out from beneath the lap belt and continued to wiggle his way out inch by inch.

An avalanche of gravel from the mound caught his attention. A heavy pipe at the top of the mound teetered, while bits of gravel beneath it shook lose. With a heavy crunch of gravel, the pipe teetered forward and tumbled down the mound.

Switzer heard the sound and peered beneath the door to see what it was...

Within seconds, the heavy pipe crashed into the door like a battering ram and smashed it shut on

Switzer's neck. It tore through flesh and vertebrae till only bloody tendons remained; then they tore, and Switzer's severed head fell from his body onto the dirt.

On the passenger seat, the small LED light on the microcassette recorder glowed red as it continued recording.

CHAPTER THIRTY-TWO
The Tape

It was the morning after Jenkins' death, and the rain continued as a drizzle. Three police cars were parked outside St. Matthew's Church, and yellow crime scene tape hung across the church entrance.

The school's custodian had discovered Jenkins' body and the destruction to the church when he unlocked it for Mass early that morning. He had awakened Sean, who had called the police.

Sean had stood outside in the drizzle earlier to let parishioners know that there would be no more Masses in the church for the rest of the week; and quite possibly longer. They would try to arrange for use of the parish hall for the Sunday Masses, but for now he had no further information to give them.

He certainly wasn't prepared to tell them the circumstance of Jenkins' death.

It was approaching noon. The police had been

there since dawn, and were no closer to finding answers than when they arrived. Each discovery brought only more questions.

"Take a look at this, Father," said one of the officers to Sean. He knelt beside the spot where a pew had been torn from its mount on the floor. "You see this bolt?"

Sean knelt down and looked at the broken bolt he was pointing to. It was about the width of a man's finger.

"All of the bolts holding down those pews were broken in half," explained the officer. He nodded to the dozens of pews scattered around like firewood. "Not cut, broken. It would have taken a bulldozer to do all of this."

Sean could only nod. Obviously a bulldozer hadn't entered the church last night.

But something else had.

Sean walked to the back of the church where they had removed Jenkins' body two hours earlier. They had needed to cut the long shard at its base where it penetrated the wall, but a foot of it still remained inside the brick.

"Any idea how it happened?" Sean asked an officer, who stared in bewilderment at the butt end of the shard.

The officer shook his head. "Not a clue, Father." He pointed to the cut end of the shard where it protruded from the brick. "That wood goes about a foot back into the brick. And there's no indication anyone drilled a hole to shove it in."

"So, the wood just penetrated it?" Sean asked.

"Like a knife through butter. Plus, there's the whole question of how Father was five feet off the ground like that."

Across the church, the parish's elderly secretary entered through a side door. Her name was Patricia, and she had been a fixture at the church for as long as anyone could remember. Even longer than Jenkins, who she fondly remembered welcoming to the parish when he was a much younger priest.

She shook her head in dismay at the destruction to her beautiful church, then walked over to Sean.

"Someone from the police department dropped this off," she said, handing Sean a small envelope. Handwritten on its front was: "Father Jenkins, St. Matthew's Parish, Capetown."

"It was addressed to Father, but..." Her voice cut off. She looked around again at the devastation.

"You don't need to stick around, Pat," Sean said, giving her shoulder a gentle squeeze. "You should take the day off. Go see your grandkids."

She nodded her appreciation. "I've known him for over thirty years..." she reminisced for a moment before turning to the officer. "Do you know who could have done this?"

"We don't even know how they did this, ma'am," replied the officer. "I'm sorry for both of your loss."

Sean and Pat both nodded their thanks. Sean opened the small envelope Patricia gave him, and removed Switzer's microcassette recorder from inside it.

"Whatcha got there, Father?" the officer asked.

"A recorder," Sean said, flipping it over in his hand. The officer stepped over to take a look.

"Yeah. That's the one they found at the accident last night.

Sean looked at him. "What accident?"

"It was a psychiatrist at that old mental health hospital. He drove off the road into one of those mining quarries, and got decapitated when his door slammed shut on his neck."

Sean's eyes were wide open. He looked at the officer then back at the recorder.

"Was his name Switzer?" Sean asked. But it was only to confirm what he already knew.

"Something like that. You knew him?"

Sean nodded.

****

"This is Doctor Benjamin Switzer, at the Hillview Hospital..." came Switzer's voice on the tape as Sean played it for the third time in a row.

He sat at Jenkins' old desk in the parish office and stared numbly at the recorder. Switzer sounded terrified. He had seen something at the hospital, and again in the car, and whatever it was, it had caused his entire belief system to turn on its head. Where just days ago he had derided Father Jenkins for his beliefs, he had come to embrace them the night of his death. And he had recorded his testimony to ensure it survived what he saw as his impending death.

"And now my last hope is that Father is able to free you of this spirit. Please know that I tried, Cassie."

And that was where the message stopped. But Switzer had apparently left the tape recorder on as it continued to record the driving sounds and rain. Rather than rewind it again, Sean let it play out. It was obvious from the sounds when the accident had occurred, and then his car's collision with the gravel mound at the bottom of the quarry.

Sean jerked as the car door slammed, and he realized that was the moment when a life had ended. He felt nauseous — not only at Switzer's death, but at his own voyeurism in listening to that death play out on tape.

He reached over to turn off the recorder when he caught a new sound that was barely perceptible above the rain. It was a cacophony of whispers.

He pressed the rewind button, then played that part again. He leaned in closer, focused only on those sounds. He was certain they were voices, yet there was nothing human in their sound...

Sean suddenly startled back and quickly pressed the stop button. There had been a message spoken in that eerie array of sounds, and Sean instinctively understood it was meant for him —

"Here you die, priest."

****

"... And now my last hope is that Father is able to free you of this spirit. Please know that I tried, Cassie."

Sean clicked off the tape. He, Justin, Alison, and Cassie were in her room at Hillview. Sean had called Alison right after hearing the tape, and they had driven up to Hillview with Justin to see Cassie.

On the drive up, Sean briefed Justin and Alison on Jenkins' death and what the police had told him about Switzer's death. The hospital had already called Alison earlier that morning to inform her of Switzer's death, and that Cassie would be assigned a new doctor. But they had left out the gruesome details of Switzer's death.

Taken alone, Switzer's death was bizarre and macabre, but when combined with what she now knew about Jenkins' grisly death, it sent a wave of fear through her.

"What did he mean, about hoping Father could free her from the spirit?" Alison asked.

"Are you familiar with the term 'demonic possession'?" Sean asked her.

"Only from the movies."

"It's when a demon inhabits a person and takes possession of their faculties of thought, and mind, and even control."

"And that's what he thinks is happening to Cassie?"

"That's what it sounds like from the tape. And it's what Father Jenkins believed."

"Do you believe it?"

Sean took a breath. "I didn't at first, and Justin can vouch for that, but I do now."

"What changed your mind?" Justin asked.

"Things I've seen over the past couple weeks that there's no other way to explain. At least no way that wouldn't sound like a lie."

"So what do we do?" Alison asked. "Doctor Switzer said something about freeing her from this spirit."

"The Church has a ritual called Exorcism, and I think that's what we'll need to do."

"How soon can you do it?"

Sean shook his head. "I don't know. First I need to get approval from the bishop. I have a meeting with him this week to discuss her case."

"And you could do it after that?"

"It wouldn't be me doing it. They would bring in a priest who has experience with it."

"What if the bishop doesn't approve it?" Cassie asked.

Sean shook his head. "I don't know. I guess you would continue with your medical treatment."

"But it's not working," Cassie protested. "And it won't work. You saw my files; there's nothing medically wrong with me."

"Cassie..." Alison attempted to calm her.

"No," Cassie said, and panic filled her voice. "You can't let that happen. Please, promise me you won't let that happen."

"I'll do everything I can, Cassie," Sean said. "I

promise."

"But you need to make him believe. I'm serious. You saw what this thing does to me. And it keeps getting worse, and I'm getting weaker."

"I know, Cassie. I saw it. It's one of the reasons I believe now. But it requires the Church's sanction."

"But you're a priest. Aren't you supposed to be able to do this?"

"It still requires the Church."

Cassie's head sank. She took a deep breath then blurted out: "I was in hell."

Everyone stopped and turned to her.

"The whole time I was dead, I was in hell."

"You mean the actual place, hell?" Justin asked.

Cassie nodded. "Yeah."

"You never mentioned this before," Alison said.

"That's because I didn't want to admit it out loud, 'cause it scares the crap out of me. But you remember the first time you brought me here, and we were driving home, and you asked me if I wanted to kill myself?"

Alison nodded. "Yeah. And you said 'no.'"

"I said no, because what's waiting for me after death is way scarier than life. This is what I was talking about."

Alison sank back in her chair.

Cassie turned to Justin. "You know those nightmares I told you about, where there's that big place in the clearing?"

Justin nodded. "Yeah. The big manor."

"That's what that place symbolizes. It symbolizes

hell. And it keeps trying to pull me back into it."

She turned to Sean, who had leaned forward in his chair while listening. "Please don't let it get me again."

CHAPTER THIRTY-THREE
The Bishop

The diocesan offices for the Catholic diocese of Capetown were in a historic Colonial building just across the sound from the peninsula. It was there, on the second floor, that Bishop Monroe's office was located.

Like Father Jenkins, Monroe was of an older generation of Catholics that grew up in the days that predated the Church's reforms in Vatican II. He and Jenkins had been close friends, although Jenkins often chided him over what he saw as Monroe's caving in to the more extreme reforms. Monroe, he felt, had bent to the changing times much more easily than Jenkins would have liked. Although he was reluctant to admit it, Monroe didn't entirely disagree with Jenkins on this. It was part of the game of diplomacy Monroe had found himself in after his appointment to bishop. He was now part of a massive bureaucracy, with many factions to contend with, and Church politics was as much a part of his daily regimen as was the faith; and particularly so, in the wake of the horrific scandals that had recently rocked the Church.

Monroe had been crushed when he learned of his old friend's death, and had presided over Jenkins' funeral earlier that week. As part of his eulogy, he noted the passing of an era with Jenkins' death.

What had particularly horrified him, as much as the death itself, was the apparently ritualistic manner in which he was killed and the interior of his church desecrated. He had asked the police to keep him updated and readily offered the diocese's full support in their investigation. But so far they had turned up no leads.

Monroe had met Father Sean on two occasions — the first had been Sean's ordination and the second at a dinner Jenkins had invited him to at the parish's rectory. Sean had phoned Monroe's office the day after Jenkins' death to schedule a meeting regarding a student of his named Cassie Stevens. By all indications, there was a strong likelihood that Cassie was the target of demonic activity, and this was a belief that had been shared by Jenkins, as well as her physician. Sean also felt there was a connection between the paranormal activity surrounding Cassie, and Jenkins' bizarre death.

In his forty-three years as a priest, and then a bishop, Monroe had never encountered what was determined to be a credible case of demonic possession. He knew, however, that Jenkins had; and it had come with particular alarm when he had received a letter from Jenkins two weeks earlier, in which Jenkins expressed concern that a student at his school was likely under demonic attack. Something like this would obviously bring outside scrutiny down on the Church, so he cautioned Jenkins to be absolutely certain before they moved forward. Jenkins had responded in characteristic fashion, reminding his ever-political friend that the Church's function was to be a guardian against evil; and damn the politics if they didn't serve that function.

Monroe deeply missed his dear friend, and it was partially out of respect for him that Monroe had cleared his calendar to meet with Sean as soon as possible. Sean had arranged to have Cassie's medical records from Hillview messengered over several days earlier so that Monroe and his staff would have time to review them before their meeting that day.

Sean brought Switzer's tape with him to the meeting and had played it in its entirety for Monroe, beginning with the notes Switzer had made to himself while reading Jenkins' book, and continuing through the ominous warning that came at the very end.

Sean pressed the stop button. He looked up at Monroe, who was seated behind his desk in the stately office. Monroe looked ill.

"That voice at the end...?" Monroe asked.

Sean knew what he meant; he had also asked the same question of the police. "There was no one else in the car with him."

Monroe gave an uneasy nod and sat back in his chair. The sound of that voice was something he would never be able to erase from his mind.

"In the first part of the tape," Sean began, "you hear him leaving notes to himself to research footnotes. Those are in reference to a book on demonic possession Jenkins gave him a week earlier when they first met."

"How did that initial meeting go?" Monroe asked.

Sean almost chuckled. "Father indicated it went bad. Apparently Dr. Switzer was completely closed off to any possibility of supernatural causes."

"He seems to have had a change of heart."

Sean nodded. "He definitely did. I spoke with Cassie about it, and apparently the change began after one of her therapy sessions. One of the recurring visions Cassie's been experiencing is of a young girl, Katie Dunne, who was killed in the crash the night of Cassie's near-death experience. During this particular therapy session, her doctor had her under hypnosis, and when she came out of it, she had a flower that Katie had given her."

"And it hadn't been there before?"

Sean shook his head and motioned to Cassie's medical file on Monroe's desk. "No, Your Reverence. You'll see that her doctor even made a note of that in Cassie's medical records."

"I saw the comment but wasn't clear on what he meant. How long was this before his death?"

"He died the next day. The last person to see him

that night was the hospital's technician, who reviewed Cassie's MRI results with him. Those should also be in her file."

Monroe nodded. "They are."

"And I'm told they're free of abnormalities," Sean said.

"Our medical team wasn't able to find any."

Sean nodded. He was confident that would be the case.

"I understand you had your own change of heart on the matter," Monroe said. "Was it anything in particular?"

"It was several things. One of them was during the convulsion she had outside the church. There was this brief moment when it seemed like a veil pulled back from behind her eyes, and she had this terror in them that I can't even begin to describe."

Sean glanced at his arms, where the hairs had risen on them. He held his arm up for Monroe to see. "This should give you an idea of the fear I felt when I saw that look."

Monroe took note of this as he sat back in his chair and appeared to think about it for a moment. "You understand that if we were to proceed with an Exorcism, it wouldn't be you performing it."

"I didn't expect to, Your Reverence. But I would like to assist, if that's okay."

"That shouldn't be a problem."

"Do you know who'll be performing it?"

"I was referred to a priest in Kenya who's

performed several Exorcisms. I spoke with him last night, and he would be available next week, should we decide to proceed with this."

"Is there a reason why we wouldn't proceed?" Sean asked.

"Just precautions," Monroe replied. "We need to be certain that we've exhausted all medical causes, and I'm not sure we have yet."

"But that could take weeks. Or even months. With all respect, Your Reverence, I know this girl, and she doesn't have weeks. She has maybe days."

"My concern, Father, is that we might do more harm than good."

"That's not possible. I can tell you that right now. She will die without an Exorcism. And everyone will know it's because the Church failed to take action."

Monroe sat back again and rubbed the bridge of his nose. He saw more of Jenkins in Sean than Sean probably realized. And as had happened so many times when he had butted heads with his old friend, he felt a headache coming on.

"Are you prepared to take responsibility if anything goes wrong?" Monroe finally asked.

"Absolutely, Your Reverence. I take full responsibility."

Monroe considered this a moment longer and finally nodded. "Very well, then. I'll arrange for Father Enrico's flight from Kenya for early next week. But before you assist in the Exorcism, there's two things I need you to read."

Monroe rose from his desk and walked over to a bookcase across the room. He searched through the volumes till he found the two books he was looking for. He returned with them to his desk, where he handed them to Sean.

"The first book is The Rite of Exorcism, which is the ritual you'll be using. The other book is a diary kept by a young Exorcist who was about your age. It chronicles the devastation that an Exorcism inflicts on the priests themselves." He took a moment to look Sean in the eye and make sure he understood. "You need to be prepared for this, Father. Because what you're about to encounter will likely plague you for the rest of your life."

****

Rain beat down on the parking lot as Sean stepped from the diocesan building. The storm had rolled in during their meeting, and from the look of the dark clouds overhead, it wasn't going to let up anytime soon. He looked across the parking lot to his car on the far side. He had no choice but to make a dash for it.

Sean was drenched by the time he reached his car and climbed in. Thankfully, he had left his cell phone in the car and not in his pocket. The two books the bishop had given him weren't so lucky but had remained relatively dry beneath his shirt where he had tucked them.

Sean had three calls to make. The first was to Alison, and it went to her voice mail. He left a message for her to call him back and that the Exorcism had been sanctioned. It would happen sometime next week when the priest from Kenya arrived.

The next call was to Cassie, and it also went to her voice mail. He had seen her cell phone in her room at Hillview, so he knew sooner or later she would get the message. He again left the news that the Exorcism had been approved.

His third call was to Justin, who answered on the third ring.

"Justin. It's Father Sean. We have a green light for the Exorcism."

"When will it be?"

"Sometime next week. They're bringing in a priest from Kenya to handle it. I'll be assisting him and wanted to see if you'd be willing to assist us."

"Yeah. Definitely. I'm in."

"Good. You and I should meet to go over these books the bishop gave me." Sean slipped the books from his shirt and looked at them. "One is the actual ritual itself on the rite of Exorcism. The other is a diary an Exorcist kept. It might be good for you to read both of them."

"Okay. Want me to come by the rectory and pick them up?"

"Why don't we do it tomorrow. I'm on the mainland, and with traffic and the rain, it could take me a while to get back."

"Have you told Cassie yet?"

"It went to her voice mail, so I left her a message. Alison's also went to voice mail. Have you spoken to either of them?"

"Not today. Alison's at work, so hers would be off. But I've left Cassie several messages and haven't heard back."

"Let me know if you do —"

Sean suddenly froze. He had seen something in the rearview mirror. It had been so subtle, that he hadn't noticed it till it shifted. He spun around to look in the backseat, but it was completely empty. Then he saw the words, written into the condensation on the inside of the rear window: *"you die priest."*

"Father? You still there?" Justin's voice came over the phone.

Sean picked it back up. "Yeah. Yeah, I'm here." He paused a moment to glance again at the rear window. The words were still there but had begun to blur with fresh condensation.

"Be careful, Justin," Sean said. "They just gave me a warning."

****

Sean arrived home to the rectory several hours later, and the storm continued to rage on. It normally would have been an hour at most, but the drive had taken him down slick muddy roads and through several detours where the roads had washed out.

The rectory was dark as he stepped in from the rain. He flipped on the lights and looked around the living room. He was feeling its emptiness with Jenkins gone. Just this vast hollow shell that felt eerily silent and still.

And all the more so because he knew *They were watching.*

With that disturbing thought in mind, he considered for a moment heading down to one of the pubs or coffee shops at the wharf where there would be people around. But a look back out the door at the rain and he shook off that idea.

He closed the door and headed into the kitchen, where he fixed himself a cup of coffee. He hoped to get some reading done that night before going to bed. He took his coffee with him upstairs to his bedroom, turning on all the lights as he went. It would be the first time since he was a kid that he slept with all the lights on.

Sean sat down at his desk and slid the books from beneath his drenched shirt. It hadn't worked as well this time to keep them dry, so he fanned them for a moment to air them out.

The first book he read was The Rite of Exorcism, so he could familiarize himself with the ritual. He was surprised to find it rather short. It consisted of prayers to be recited and presented some guidelines for the Exorcist to follow, but for the most part, the procedure relied a great deal on the instincts of the Exorcist himself. He needed to know when to push, when to probe, when to back off, and what cautions to take — all things that came only with experience. Sean was grateful the diocese was bringing in someone with experience to handle it. All Sean needed to do was follow his lead.

Within two hours he had read the ritual book, then moved on to the diary. It turned out to be more of a journal the priest had kept and was written in a way to provide instruction to priests who followed in his grim footsteps.

It broke the Exorcism down into stages and provided indicators for the priest to be on the constant lookout for — anything that might show a change in the ever-shifting battle between the priest and the possessing demon.

It also warned of traps to be wary of that could quickly ensnare the priest in a prison from which he had little hope of escape.

But the most critical point of all, and the one it repeatedly emphasized, was that the priest must remember he is there only as a proxy for God. It's the source of his protection and authority, and without it, the priest would come under the full blast of the demon's fury, with little to no chance of ever recovering. So despite the vile personal slanders and emotional attacks the demon would hurl at the priest, the priest could never step out from behind that protection and engage on a personal level with the demon. This, the writer cautioned, was the deadliest trap of all, and it had lured many priests to their doom.

Despite the growing sense of dread, Sean was mentally exhausted, and within an hour he had fallen asleep at his desk.

CHAPTER THIRTY-FOUR
Something Wicked This Way Comes

"By the pricking of my thumbs
Something wicked this way comes.
Open, locks, whoever knocks."

— *Macbeth* by William Shakespeare

****

An ominous silence hung over the cold marble hallway. Cassie was alone in that dark crypt where she had once heard the dead stir from within their vaults. At each end, the hallway was lit by a silver candelabra that cast dancing shadows along its sphere of light.

Between those lights lay darkness, and it was from that darkness that eyes watched her.

She began walking toward a door at the end of the hallway, but she noticed that the farther she walked, the farther away it withdrew. She tried running, but this only made it recede away faster. No matter what she did, or how fast she ran, that door wasn't going to let her reach it.

She finally stopped to catch her breath.

Something was approaching her from behind.

Cassie turned, and from the darkness floated the ghost of a teenage girl. She made no sound as she glided inches above the floor. She raised her hand and pointed to a marble plaque on the front of a vault.

Cassie approached the plaque and leaned close enough to read its name in the dim light — "Cassie Stevens."

As she stared at the plaque, things emerged from the darkness behind her. She turned, and dozens of dark shapes now stood there. There were thirty-six of them — the number of her fellow partiers who had burned to death at the rave.

One by one, they broke out in flames till Cassie was surrounded by these walking human-shaped torches.

She squeezed past them, and raced as fast as she could toward that exit... only to see it retreat farther and farther away into an infinite distance.

And now the smoke from those burning partiers caught up to her, and her nostrils filled with the stench of burning flesh. She gasped for breath as she trudged forward, with no hope of ever reaching that elusive exit. She finally collapsed on the cold stone floor, and the smoke completely enveloped her. It filled her lungs till they burnt like fire. She could no longer breathe, and she squirmed as she suffocated in a slow agonizing death...

Only Cassie could no longer die — she was already dead.

She closed her eyes with the realization that this agony would never end. It would continue to grow worse and worse, and yet death could never offer her reprieve.

Just as all hope slipped from her grasp, a gentle warmth brushed her skin and cool fresh air filled her lungs... and with it came the scent of daisies.

Katie was here.

Cassie opened her eyes and saw Katie kneeling beside her. "He's coming, Cassie," she said. "You need to wake up."

****

Cassie startled awake in her bed at Hillview to the blaring wail of the emergency alarm in the hallway. It meant someone had escaped from the hospital's containment wing.

She looked over at her door and saw red emergency lights flickering through its narrow window. It meant the power had also gone out, and the hospital was running on its backup generator.

She went over to the door and pressed her ear against it, but could hear nothing over that alarm.

She opened the door and stepped into the hallway. The red lights mounted at each end of the hallway flickered like strobes, and in each flash she saw dozens of patients in their white hospital gowns shuffling aimlessly. As several of them shuffled past, she caught the glazed, unseeing stares in their eyes. They were like zombies.

She backed against the wall to avoid them, and that's when she saw two things crawling across the ceiling toward her. With each strobe, these things skittered closer. It was like watching two giant spiders till they were finally close enough to see their details — it was Trish and Silvia, with their limbs disjointed outward like insects.

Cassie screamed and retreated back into her room. She slammed the door shut and jammed the chair beneath the doorknob.

She raced over to her nightstand and grabbed her cell phone, then ducked behind her bed. She checked the display — there was only one bar, and it blinked in and out. She quickly typed "they're here" into her text app and sent it to Justin. And hoped it went through.

A skittering sound caused her to look up... and right into the dark eyes of Seth, Trish, and Silvia, who clung to the ceiling above her.

****

"Sean..."

Amy's voice called from the darkness, and Sean startled awake into his dark bedroom. His face was plastered to the priest's diary, where he had dozed off... how long ago had it been?

He slowly sat up and gave his mind a second to clear. He could swear he had heard Amy's voice and didn't recall having any dreams it could have come from.

The storm howled outside, and heavy rain pelted the window behind him. There was just enough ambient light from the window for him to see around.

Then it struck him — *why was it so dark?* He knew he had turned on all the lights because he had felt so silly doing it. Yet now the entire rectory was bathed in a cold gray gloom.

He went over to the window from which he could see the entire neighborhood, and the lights were out everywhere. Even the streetlights were out.

He headed from his bedroom and down the hallway, patting his way along the wall as he went. His hands finally came across a small cabinet, and inside it he found the flashlight he was looking for.

He flicked it on, then followed the hallway to the stairs. He shined his light down them to the living room and over to the front door.

It was open.

Sean knew he had closed and locked it before going upstairs.

He went down to the living and over to the door, passing the opening to the kitchen on his left. He looked out the door into the storm.

"Hello?" he called out, but he heard only the rain.

"Father?"

Justin's voice came from behind him and nearly startled Sean from his skin. He spun around and Justin stood there.

"Sorry," Justin said. "Your kitchen door was open."

Tom Lewis

"It's okay," Sean said, catching his breath. "What is it?"

"This." Justin showed him the text from Cassie on his phone — *"they're here."* "I think she's in trouble."

"Did you try calling her?"

Justin nodded. "It keeps going to her voice mail."

"What about the hospital?"

"I tried, but nobody's answering."

"There's no answering service?"

Justin shook his head. "There's supposed to be people on staff twenty-four hours a day. But I've tried five times now, and nothing."

Justin watched Sean as Sean seemed to debate what to do. "I'm going there right now, Father, and was seeing if you'd come with."

Sean nodded. "Yeah. Wait here while I grab some things."

Justin waited in the dark living room while Sean ran upstairs. He returned several minutes later with a backpack, in which he had packed the Exorcism missal, candles, two crucifixes, and two vials of holy water. He had also grabbed a second flashlight that he handed to Justin.

"You know this could go really bad for us," Sean cautioned. "I have no idea what I'm doing, so I'm just going off what's in the missal."

"But that has the ritual in it, right?" Justin asked.

Sean nodded. "Yeah."

"Then it should work."

"I hope so."

340

They turned to the open doorway, and in it stood the dark silhouette of a large dog. A low growl rumbled from its throat.

"Don't make any sudden moves," Sean cautioned.

"I think it's Cassie's dog," Justin said. She had told him about seeing Rex that night and the terror she had felt.

"Rex? Is that you, boy?" Justin said calmly.

The dog let out another deep rumbling growl.

"Back away slowly into the kitchen," Sean said. "We can go out that door."

Justin took a cautious step back, and then another... and as he did, the dog's head followed him.

Sean took a step toward the kitchen, and the dog's head snapped around to him.

He froze as another deep growl rumbled in Rex's chest.

Then Rex stepped in through the doorway. His head was low and ready to lunge at any moment.

Sean saw Justin disappear into the kitchen. "There's a broom in the closet," Sean said in a low steady voice. "Let me know when you have it."

Sean took a slow step toward the kitchen, and then another, while Rex steadily advanced. Sean heard the broom closet open...

"Got it," Justin's hushed voice said from the kitchen.

"Be ready," Sean said. "On three. One... two... three."

Sean leaped sideways through the kitchen opening

and quickly dodged past Justin.

Rex lunged in behind him. Justin swung the broom handle, and it cracked down on Rex's head. The dazed dog staggered back, then lunged again. Justin swung again, and Rex snatched it in his jaws. He bit down and snapped it in half like a toothpick.

Sean stepped past Justin holding a mop. He jabbed it at Rex.

"Get out the door," Sean said, "and be ready to close it behind me."

Justin dashed out the door, just as Rex bit down on the mop and tore it from Sean's hands.

Sean raced out, and Justin slammed the door shut. A second later, Rex crashed against it.

Justin and Sean raced across the lawn to the cars parked out back. "We'll take my car," Sean hollered.

They climbed in, just as Rex bounded out the front door and came at them across the lawn.

Rex leaped onto the hood as Sean started the car. Rex's head crashed into the windshield, and cracks spread across it.

"Shit! Go! Go!" Justin hollered as Rex pulled back and slammed his head into the windshield again.

Sean jammed the car in reverse and peeled out from his parking space into the alley. Rex lost his footing and tumbled off the hood, but was quickly back on his feet and chasing them.

Sean slammed it in drive, and the tires spun out on the wet pavement as the tires sought traction. They finally gripped, and the car fishtailed wildly as it barreled down the alley.

He spun a sharp turn onto the dark street at the end, and then they were speeding off into the storm.

To their meeting with a demon.

CHAPTER THIRTY-FIVE
What Rough Beast

*"And what rough beast, its hour come round at last,
Slouches towards Bethlehem to be born?"*

— *The Second Coming* by William Butler Yeats

****

The lone car plowed through the storm. Sean and Justin had been driving for an hour and had seen only a dozen other cars. They had watched through thick sheets of rain as the road climbed from the rugged coast into the sweeping foothills near Hillview. And the anticipation as they neared it was excruciating.

Sean had briefed Justin on what he thought they could expect and what each of their roles in the Exorcism would be. But all of that was based on what he had read only a few hours earlier. He admitted he was flying blind on this and was scared out of his mind.

The risk inherent in an Exorcism was more than its

failure to liberate the victim. It would be a clash of wills between the priest and the titanic will of the demon, and the journal had cautioned that the priest would come under ferocious attacks. And if he failed, the priest himself could fall into possession.

As the miles ticked by, Justin's initial courage had failed him as well. When they had discussed performing an Exorcism in Cassie's room that day, he had no idea of the terror he would feel when that moment arrived. And now, as they finally turned onto the winding drive that led to Hillview, Justin had his first doubts he would survive the night.

Lightning crashed through the sky as they wove through dense thickets of trees to the perimeter fence. And when they finally emerged from the trees, a cold fear gripped them.

Hillview was dead.

Hillview's massive structure loomed darkly beyond its perimeter fence. There were no lights anywhere — not on the grounds or in windows or even the lobby.

They pulled up to the main gate. It was open and the guard shack abandoned.

"Something bad happened," Justin muttered. "This gate's never open."

"Do we go in?" Sean asked. But it was as much to himself as it was to Justin.

"I think we have to."

Sean drove through the gate and up the drive that cut across the front grounds to the entrance. Justin stared out the passenger window at the dark grounds and noticed ghostlike shapes moving in the distance. A sudden flash of lightning lit the sky — and he saw that they were patients in their white hospital gowns. He turned to Sean.

"The patients are out."

Sean looked past Justin and saw them too. Several appeared to be heading their way. He sped the rest of the way to the entrance and skidded to a stop. He could see through the windshield that the lobby's front door was wide open and it was dark inside.

"Call the police," Sean said.

Justin pulled out his phone and looked at its screen. He shook his head.

"There's no signal."

Sean turned back to the dark lobby. Every instinct told him to get out of there. They were going to die.

Or worse.

"Do we do this?" Justin asked, watching the worried look on Sean's face.

Sean wanted to say no. He wanted to turn the car around and get out of there. But that word wouldn't come to his lips. It was too final. If they left, it would be over for Cassie.

She's going to come to you soon, with no other hope, and you need to be the Sean I fell in love with.

Amy's words from the dream came suddenly. Despite everything, she still believed in him. She knew he could do this. And that gave him the boost he needed.

"We need to," Sean said. "Just remember

everything I told you on the drive here."

They climbed from the car and were instantly drenched. Sean grabbed the backpack and flashlights from the backseat and they hurried over to the entrance.

It was eerily quiet and dark as they stepped inside the lobby. There were no more alarms or flashing emergency lights from earlier — only the hollow, empty feel of a tomb.

They flicked on their flashlights and shined them around the lobby. It was a wreck, with broken and overturned furniture, and papers scattered across the floor. There were also dark smears along the floor and walls that could be blood.

Then they caught the first sounds echoing from elsewhere in the hospital. They were demented sounds of screams and deranged laughter.

"Try your phone again," Sean said. "We need to get the police here."

Justin checked, but there was still no signal. He shook his head.

Sean swept his light over to the check-in desk. He hurried around behind it and checked the phone. There was no dial tone. He pressed several buttons and listened again but there was still nothing. He looked over to Justin. "We should check her room."

Sean led the way down the hallway behind the check-in counter. There was just enough light from the lobby's entrance to see by as they crept through the gloom.

They reached a door on their right marked "Stairs." Sean eased the door open and shined his light up the stairwell that wove up three flights.

They climbed the stairs to the third floor, moving as quietly as possible. Sean eased the door open and peered out into the gloomy hallway. Faint screams echoed from somewhere on the floor. He looked down the hallway to where it connected with the hallway Cassie's room was on. That hallway was better lit by the windows at each end.

"It looks clear," Sean whispered back to Justin. They eased from the stairwell and down the hallway to where it connected with Cassie's hallway. From somewhere on the floor came echoed fits of disturbed laughter. Sean gripped his flashlight tighter. He might need it as a weapon.

Sean peeked around the corner to Cassie's hallway. He could see all the way down to the far end and there was nobody on it. They crept down it to Cassie's door on the right-hand side. Sean tapped lightly.

"Cassie. It's Father Sean and Justin." He waited a moment, and when there was no reply, he tested the doorknob. It was unlocked.

Sean eased the door open and they crept inside. The room was icy cold and their breaths misted as they swept their flashlights around.

It was empty.

"Cassie?" Justin called out in a hushed voice. He peeked beneath her bed then checked the bathroom. He returned shaking his head.

"She's not here."

Then his phone buzzed.

It had been so quiet, they both startled at the noise. Justin looked at the display. "It's from Cassie," he said and opened its text app.

"Hallway," read the text.

He showed it to Sean.

"Are you getting a signal?" Sean asked.

Justin checked and shook his head. "Nope. Still nothing..." And then he realized, "I shouldn't be able to receive texts either."

Sean nodded. They exchanged an uneasy look, with neither of them wanting to say the unspoken question:

What if Cassie was no longer Cassie?

They stepped back into the hallway and looked both ways down it.

"Is this the hallway she meant?" Justin asked.

Sean shook his head. He didn't know either. "Just watch for anything."

Then a figure shifted in front of the window at the far end. It had been so still while watching them that neither of them had noticed it.

"Cassie?" Justin called to her, but it was too far away to tell if it was her.

The figure walked off down the connecting hallway, and from its dark outline they saw it was a girl.

"I think it's her," Justin said, but Sean stopped him.

"If it was Cassie, then why did she walk off?"

Justin hesitated. "Because that thing has her?"

Sean nodded. He removed a vial of holy water from his backpack and handed it to Justin.

"Holy water?" Justin asked.

Sean nodded. "It's supposed to give us some protection."

"I hope so."

They proceeded down the hallway to its end and shined their lights down the connecting hallway. It was empty.

"Should we check the rooms?" Justin asked, motioning to the rows of doors lining the hallway.

His phone buzzed again.

It was another text from Cassie. He showed it to Sean — *"basement."*

They searched the doors till they found one marked "Stairs." These ones were like the others, made of metal and weaving back and forth as they descended to the basement. They quietly took them down and were just passing the door on the second-floor landing when a hideous scream came from the other side of it.

Suddenly the door swung open and a crazed male patient stumbled through. He ran into Sean, who swung him around and held him against the wall. At first, the patient's eyes only stared with the glazed unseeing look of insanity. But then a clarity hit him and he stared at Sean like he knew him. He burst into an insane cackle.

"He's comin' ta get ya padre, he is... coming. Coming... comin'... ta get cha..."

Then the glaze returned to his eyes. Sean released him and the patient stumbled past them and up the stairs like he hadn't even seen them.

Sean's hands shook from the sudden adrenaline rush as he and Justin descended the final two flights to the basement. Sean cracked open the fire door and shined his flashlight through.

It was a pitch-dark concrete corridor lined with steel doors on either side and thick conduits and pipes running along the ceiling. It was so long, that the flashlight's narrow beam disappeared into the distant gloom.

Sean and Justin stepped into the corridor.

"Shit. What now?" Justin said, looking at the long line of doors.

"I think she'll let us know," Sean said.

And she did, as a new text buzzed on his phone — *"power plant."*

Justin read it and shook his head. "Even if I had reception outside, there's no way I would have it down here."

Sean nodded. He pulled a pair of crucifixes from his backpack and handed one to Justin.

"Will this work?" Justin asked.

Sean shrugged. "It can't hurt."

They proceeded down the corridor, sweeping their flashlights across the room names stenciled to the doors. They finally came to the one marked "Power Plant." It was unlocked and Sean pressed it open...

They stood in the doorway and swept their flashlights through the dark room. They could see that it was large as the narrow beams swept across generators and heavy equipment. Thick ducts and pipes ran along the ceiling and walls.

Justin cleared his throat. "Cassie?" he called out and his voice echoed back from the concrete walls, floor, and ceiling.

There was no response. They looked at each other, both knowing how insane what they were doing was. Then they stepped inside the room...

And that's when they felt the demon's *Presence*. And nothing could have prepared them for that horror.

It was the overwhelming sensation of something in the air all around them. And it was more than simply an atmosphere or aura — it was the pervasive sense of an *Other* with them — of a keen intelligence that was knowing, and waiting, and watching...

And completely and utterly evil.

Justin and Sean stood frozen. Any doubts to its reality were gone. It was there; it was felt; and it had no fear of them whatsoever.

"Fuck..." Justin muttered.

Sean stood to his right and gave a small nod in agreement. He had read about the *Presence* in the priest's journal but its reality was beyond words.

"It's the demon's presence you're feeling," Sean said.

Justin's fingers instinctively tightened on the crucifix.

Sean cleared his throat and called out: "Cassie?"

The temperature in the room dropped.

Seconds later, an eerie voice echoed back from the

walls: *"Cassie's not here."* The voice resembled Cassie's but with a hollowness and indifference in its tone that sent chills through them.

"Cassie. You need to resist it," Sean called out again.

"Resist?" the voice spat back with mockery. *"Is that what you did when you fucked Amy, priest?"*

A painful jolt shot through Sean's mind. His memory flashed to that night on the beach with Amy and the crushing guilt that followed.

And the demon knew this.

"That's it, priest. She trusted you, and you fucked her like a pathetic cur."

Sean fought off the memories as an instinct alerted him to a trap.

"Fuck, fuck, suck, fuck, priest," the taunts continued. *"You liked it, priest. You liked fucking, and suck—"*

"Amy's in Heaven, where you'll never be," Sean cut in. And it was with such contempt, that it startled Justin.

A furious growl rumbled through the room. The door slammed shut behind them and Cassie let out a horrified scream.

"She's back there!" Justin said, aiming his flashlight toward the far back corner. They hurried back that way.

They found Cassie in the back corner, curled on the floor and shaking. Justin rushed over.

"Cassie. Hey. Can you hear me?"

She looked up. "Justin?"

"Yeah. I'm with Father Sean. We're gonna get you

out of here."

Sean shook his head as he stared in horror at the room that seemed to have come alive around them. "It's not gonna let us take her out of here. We need to do it here."

Justin swallowed hard then turned back to Cassie. "It's the Exorcism, Cass. We're gonna do it here. You can do this."

She gave a terrified nod and pulled her knees to her chest.

Sean removed several candles from his backpack and handed them to Justin. "Light these and place them around her."

Justin did this while Sean emptied his backpack onto the floor. He picked up the missal from the pile and used his flashlight to skim through its pages.

"It says we're supposed to sprinkle holy water on ourselves," he said. He did this then turned back to the missal. But that was it for the preparations.

It was time to start the ritual.

"I need you to read for the assistant," Sean said to Justin. "Just follow my lead."

"Okay." Justin scooted close enough to read the missal.

Sean looked at Cassie. "Cassie. It's going to fight you, and you need to resist with everything you've got."

She nodded. "Okay." But she felt anything but strength.

Sean began with the *Sign of the Cross*. He traced his right hand from his forehead to his chest, then to his left shoulder, and finally his right shoulder, the whole while reciting the words: "In the name of the Father, and of the Son, and of the Holy Spirit..."

As he completed it, a deep groan rumbled through the room and shook the walls like a small tremor. They all felt a sudden shift in the *Presence* that surrounded them. It was preparing for battle and its enormity unfurled like a dragon's massive wings. They could have been ants staring helplessly from the ground at a foot hovering above them.

And knowing it could crush them at any time.

Sean felt a rush of panic. He was nowhere near ready for this; and it was only the recollection of something he had read in the priest's journal that gave him confidence — *Stay behind God; you're only there as His proxy.*

Be with me, God, Sean whispered silently then took a deep breath.

"Be merciful on us, O Lord, and spare us. Save this young girl, your servant..."

"Because she hopes in you, O Lord," Justin read his line.

Another groan circled through the walls and dust drifted down from the ceiling.

"Be a tower of strength for her, O Lord..." Sean resumed, "in the face of the enemy. Let the enemy have no power over her. And let the son of iniquity not succeed in injuring her."

A loud metal clang caused everyone to jump.

Sean took another deep breath then resumed.

"Lord hear my prayer."

"And let my cry reach you," Justin read his line.

Suddenly a pipe burst and sprayed steam from its crack. Another pipe pulled from the ceiling and swung down into the generator in a loud crash.

"God of mercy," Sean resumed, "come to the assistance of this child you created in your own image. And cast into the bottomless pit the spirit that torments her..."

"I'm so cold, Sean..." The eerie voice whispered in Sean's ears. It was the voice from his nightmare.

Sean looked up from the missal and saw Amy's ghoulish corpse in the flickering shadows beside Cassie.

"You fucked me, Sean... and then you left me."

Sean shook it off and turned back to the missal. "All-powerful God. Word of God, the Father. Christ Jesus. God and Lord of all creation. You gave power to your Apostles to pass through dangers unharmed. Among your commands to do wondrous things, you said: Drive out evil spirits. By your strength, Satan fell from Heaven. With fear and trembling, I pray and supplicate your holy name. Pardon all the sins of your unworthy servant. Give me constant faith and power; so that, armed with the power of your holy strength, I can attack this evil spirit in confidence and security..."

"God doesn't hear you, Sean..." Amy's corpse whispered in his ear. It was now beside him.

"You're not Amy," Sean muttered.

"Father!" Justin looked past Sean but nothing was there. "It's not real. Whatever you're seeing, it's not real."

Sean swallowed hard and shook his head. He turned back to the missal. "Through you, Jesus Christ, our Lord God, who will come to judge the living and the dead and the world by fire."

A low rumbling groan shook the room causing everyone to freeze. Deep cracks spread through the walls and concrete chips fell from the ceiling. A metal bracket tore from the ceiling and a heavy duct crashed down on the floor.

Sean picked up his crucifix. "Behold the Cross of the Lord. Depart, enemies!"

Then his eyes caught movement — just beyond the flickering glow of candlelight, things moved in the darkness. Dark, baleful spirits drifted like wisps and loathsome wails echoed from the walls.

Justin saw them too. "We need to keep going," he said. But his voice was shaking.

Sean turned again to the missal... "God the Father..."

Suddenly the *Presence* tore into Sean's mind and it filled with grotesque scenes of the demon's hatred and horror. It was in the starving infant, sucking futilely at the dry breast of its dead mother; it was in the starving child whose stomach burst open in a flurry of hatched flies; it was in the larvae that burrowed into the flesh of the homeless man passed out in the gutter; it was in the shriveled corpses piled into the mass graves of the Nazi concentration camps...

The demon reveled in the extremes of mankind's

wickedness and misery.

"Father...?" Justin's voice came to Sean from across dark gulfs of pain and despair. Sean clenched his teeth and continued —

"I exorcise you, unclean spirit, in the name of our Lord Jesus Christ — be uprooted and expelled from this creature of God..."

It tore into Sean again with a new viciousness. He was made to see, feel, hear and taste extremes of torment and the utterly grotesque. Open, puss filled wounds of lepers filled his mouth; maggots and worms burrowed from Sean's arms; acid stung his eyes like lava...

Sean yelled and keeled over sideways. He patted the floor blindly for the vial of holy water till his hands found it. He splashed it on his face... and the pain slowly eased.

Sean slowly opened his eyes and saw Justin crouched beside him. "Shit! What just happened?" Justin said.

Sean shook his head. "Don't let me stop, Justin. Whatever happens, we need to finish this."

Justin nodded and helped Sean sit up. But before he could resume, the room erupted in chaos. Furniture rattled and crashed into walls; steam hissed from burst pipes; red emergency lights flickered from the corners...

Cassie's scream spun Justin and Sean around. She toppled onto her side as the Shrill blasted into her mind with a ferocity beyond what she had suffered before. It was a million sirens and burning coals that pierced every nerve and cell. Her eyes rolled back in her head and she screamed!

Sean quickly grabbed the missal. "God, Creator and defender of the human race; You who made man in Your own image, repel and cast out the spirit that torments this young girl..."

A deep bellow rocked the walls. A sudden force ripped Sean and Justin from the floor and hurled them across the room like a canon. They slammed into the front wall and dropped to the floor unconscious.

The demon's fury let loose in the room. It quaked and shook. Concrete chips and dust fell from the ceiling and cracks spread across walls. Equipment tumbled over and thick ducts tore from their mounts and crashed down.

A deep crack spread across the floor. It ran the length of the room and separated Cassie from Sean and Justin. Its edges crumbled down into the earth and left a chasm five feet wide and seemingly bottomless.

Then flames roared up from the chasm and spread across the room in a wall of fire.

The *Shrill* receded enough for Cassie to open her eyes, and she saw the hell and mayhem that had erupted.

"Justin!" she screamed over the ruckus but she couldn't see past the fire to know if they were okay.

Then a strange new pressure filled her mind and forced it into silence. And from that silence came whispered taunts echoing up from the chasm.

"*Caaaaasssiiiieeeee....*" they hissed in Seth's voice.

Clawed hands reached up from the chasm and gripped its rough edge. Seth's decayed corpse pulled itself up from the flames and turned its hollow eyes on her. It began crawling towards her on skeletal arms that twisted from its sides at excruciating angles.

"Caaaasssssiiiieeee..." the hiss came from above, and this time in Silvia's and Trish's voices. Cassie looked up and saw their grisly corpses clinging to the wall like spiders. They began crawling down towards her.

"Take the knife Casssssiiiieee..." Seth hissed like a snake. He slid a large knife towards her.

"Do it Cassssiiiieeee..." Silvia hissed.

"It can all be over..." said Trish, reaching a skeletal hand down to stroke Cassie's shoulder.

"Do it!" Seth commanded.

"It can all be over..." Trish's voice came over Seth's.

"Join us, Cassiiiiieeee..." Silvia hissed over the others.

"Take the knife..." "it can all be over..." "do it..." Their whispered hisses played over each other in a dizzying torrent.

Then the *Shrill* hit again! Cassie's eyes squeezed shut. She screamed, and screamed, and squirmed in excruciating pain. And somewhere, somehow, from the deepest depths of her agony, her soul uttered one last desperate plea... *"help me, God..."*

And her plea was answered.

From deep within her agony, a warm glow touched her and she felt the harsh fury of the Shrill recede.

Then a soft hand brushed her cheek.

Cassie opened her eyes and saw Katie kneeling

beside her; and in those soft gentle eyes she saw peace.

Katie gently brushed back the hair that had fallen over Cassie's face in her convulsions. "Pray, Cassie," she spoke softly, and Cassie realized the background clamor had faded. "Don't stop praying. He hears you."

Cassie nodded. She pulled from her pocket the small silver cross Katie's mom had given her, then closing her eyes, she prayed...

"Please help me..."

"Sean..." Amy's soft voice spoke from somewhere in the darkness. And this time it was her voice. Sean opened his eyes and for a brief moment Amy stood before him. And it was the *real Amy*.

Within seconds she was gone and the room's clamor returned. But she had left him with something. It was *Hope*. Above the steam, and smoke, and stench, there lingered the subtle scent of her perfume. And it fueled him.

Sean sat up and looked at Justin who was struggling to sit up beside him.

"You okay?" Sean asked. Justin rubbed his bruised side and nodded. They both turned to the fire that separated them from Cassie.

"Cassie!" Justin hollered, rising to his feet. Sean struggled to his feet beside him.

"Justin?" Cassie's faint voice called back across the ruckus.

Sean stepped forward. "Cassie. We need to finish. Can you do this?"

"Yeah," she hollered back. "I can. I'm ready."

Sean nodded. He was ready too. He opened the missal. "We exorcise you, each unclean spirit, each power of Satan, each infestation of the enemy from Hell, each legion, each congregation, each Satanic sect..."

A ferocious growl thundered through the room and froze Sean mid-sentence.

"Don't stop, Father," Justin said. "Keep going."

Sean nodded. "In the name and by the power of our Lord Jesus Christ. Be uprooted and put to flight from this soul who was made in the image of God. And be cast into the infernal wasteland..."

Sean looked up from the missal and over to the flames. "Behold your fate, unclean spirits. The eternal fire that awaits you..."

A disturbing new sound now arose and filled the air. And this sound was the demon's sound, and terrifying beyond anything a sane mind could imagine. It came from nowhere and yet was everywhere all at once. It was neither high pitched, nor deep, and neither male nor female; it simply sounded — and disturbed — and was something no human ear was meant to hear.

And with it came a message, conveyed in its unnatural resonance — the message was of absolute dominance and superiority. It held no trace of kindness, or empathy, or mercy for these puny creatures that stood before it. It was brute uncaring force.

It was the sound of evil.

Sean swayed back on his feet at this realization. He

gripped his crucifix tighter and turned back to the missal.

"By the power of God. Depart now, unclean spirits!"

It launched itself at him again and tore deep into the core of his determination and person. He dropped to the floor like a wet rag as tentacles of filth poured through him like venom. It pillaged every nerve and cell and thought and left them corroded in its toxic bile. Memories of growing up as a kid and playing sports; of his family and brothers; pranks he had played with Conor; and the times he and Amy had shared — they were all painted over in a grotesque canvas of horror. Every hope and thought of love and joy was brought to unbearable despair, and he teetered on the edge of a deep gulf into which he would be forever lost...

Then he smelled it —

Amy's perfume.

His eyes opened and he staggered to his feet. "Depart!" he shouted, "and cease your torments of this child! It is God Himself who commands it!"

A large generator broke from its floor mount and skidded across the room into a wall.

"You, who were forever banished from paradise. You, who were defeated by Christ's victory..."

Another deep groan shook the room. But there had been another shift in the *Presence* that they all felt — it was weakening.

"Depart! And be gone! It is God who commands it!"

A long crack spread across the ceiling above Cassie and chunks began to fall. Justin was the first to see it.

"Cassie!"

Justin rushed forward and leaped through the flames. He landed on the far side and rolled across the floor to snuff out the fire from his clothes.

"Cassie! Move!" He grabbed her arm and tugged her back, just seconds before a large chunk crashed down where she had been.

"Are you okay?" Sean hollered from across the room. He couldn't see anything through the flames.

"Yeah," Justin shouted back. "Keep going. I think it's weakening."

"God of Heaven!" Sean shouted with a new forcefulness in his tone. "God of Earth! God of Angels! God of Archangels! God of Prophets! God of Apostles! God of Martyrs! God who has the power to give life after death and repose after labor: There is no god but You. Nor could there be a true god but You. Creator of Heaven and Earth. You are a true King. Your Kingdom is without end. Humbly, I supplicate Your majesty and Your glory: that You deign to free your servant Cassie from the unclean spirits. Through Christ our Lord."

And God heard his plea.

All at once they felt it — like a storm surge pulling back out to sea, everything evil was receding from around them. The noises, and whispers, and *Presence* — all of it receding into a point of darkness in a vast infinite distance.

The wall of fire simmered down to a tiny flame

then disappeared into the chasm.

And then it was gone. All of it. Every trace of supernatural horror was gone.

It was over.

Cassie looked around at the sudden calm that had descended on the room. It was gone. It was really gone.

"Oh, God. It's gone. It's really gone." She broke into deep sobs and threw her arms around Justin.

Across the room, Sean sank to his knees. His muscles and bones ached with a weariness he had never felt in all his years of sports. He scooted over to the wall and propped his back against it. He would be able to rest now. He buried his head in his hands and breathed deeply. Even the air felt fresh. The smells of decay and rot and smoke were gone...

Then he felt a sudden warmth and the sweetest smell he had ever known brushed his nose. He opened his eyes and there stood Amy, bathed in a radiance like the moon.

"Sean," she said with a warm smile, and for a moment he could only stare. She was so perfect. And pure. Like so many sunrises they had shared.

"Are you real?" he finally asked.

"What does your heart tell you?"

It told him yes. Somehow, in some way, God had sent him this gift for however brief it might be. A tear trickled down his cheek.

"And in my dream that night? And the letter on my desk? That was also you?"

She smiled and nodded.

"Is it over?" he asked, looking around the room.

Again she gave him a smile and nod. "It is, Sean. Cassie's clean. It won't be back."

Sean exhaled. "I couldn't have done this without you, Amy."

This time she shook her head. "No, Sean. I only reminded you of the boy I fell in love with. And who I fall more in love with each day. And who I'm so proud of."

He choked back a sob. "I miss you, Amy. God, I just miss you so much. And I'm so in love with you too."

He could see that radiant light beginning to fade, and Amy with it.

"I miss you too, Sean. But we'll be together again one day."

There was one final smile and then she was gone, fading into that golden light.

He sat there staring for a moment as the smell of her perfume slowly faded. He took a last final breath of it.

Then he looked across the room at Cassie and Justin. He wiped the tears from his eyes then walked over to join them.

Cassie's face broke into a smile as Sean approached. She pulled him into a hug with her and Justin and kissed his cheek.

"Thank you," she said, through eyes filled with tears. "Both of you guys. Thank you."

"It's over?" Justin asked Sean, but it was more to

reassure himself of what he already knew.

Sean smiled and gave him a nod. "It's over. It won't be back."

Cassie sniffed back a tear and wiped her eyes. But there was one last person she needed to thank.

Across the room stood Katie, who Cassie had spotted over Justin's shoulder. Cassie turned to her and whispered a heartfelt "thank you."

Katie returned a smile and then she too faded away as Amy had.

Sean and Justin both looked back in the direction Cassie was staring. "Who were you talking to?" Justin asked.

"A friend."

CHAPTER THIRTY-SIX
Ten Years Later

"Arise my beloved, my beautiful one, and come.
For behold, the winter has past, the rain is over and gone."

— *Song of Songs* 2:10

****

It was springtime in Capetown. The rain had ended shortly after dawn, and morning sunlight now glistened off grass and leaves. A fresh smell filled the air, combined with the sweet scent of pines and the songs of nature.

An SUV pulled up to a warm little cottage nestled in the woods. Justin climbed from the driver's side and went around to the passenger door to open it for Cassie. She climbed out, followed by a pretty little girl who had just turned four. Her name was Katherine, but they just called her Katie. She had her mother Cassie's soft brown hair and her father Justin's green eyes.

Following high school, Cassie and Justin had attended college together in Boston. He proposed to her their senior year and they married the summer after graduation. Katie was born just over a year later.

Justin had gone on to attend law school, and was now a new associate at a corporate law firm in Boston. Cassie was a full-time mom, and was working on her first novel.

Father Sean became a close friend of the couple over the years and had presided at their wedding and Katie's Baptism. They always got together for drinks or dinner or to catch a game whenever they were in town.

Alison peeked out the front window of the cottage and saw the kids heading up the walk with her granddaughter. She hurried to the front door, where she greeted them with a big smile.

Alison had remarried several years earlier to a restaurant owner named Ted. Although he could never be her dad, Cassie still welcomed him into the family and asked him to walk her down the aisle at her wedding. This had meant the world to her mom. Ted made her mom happy, and that made Cassie happy.

"Say hi to Grandma, honey," Cassie said, releasing Katie's hand. With a big smile, Katie raced over to Alison and grabbed her in a hug.

Alison, of course, smothered her in kisses. She

loved playing the role of grandmother more than she ever could have imagined.

Ted joined her in the doorway. "Cassie. Justin," he said with a welcoming smile, nodding to each of them in turn. Cassie returned the smile and clenched him in a hug.

"Hey, Ted," Justin smiled back as the two men shook hands.

"Well, come on in," Alison said, finally breaking from her granddaughter. "We were just fixing breakfast."

"You guys go ahead and start without me," Cassie said. "I just need to do something first."

"You want me to come with?" Justin asked, fishing the keys from his pocket and handing them to her.

"No. I'm good. But thanks."

They waved goodbye before heading inside, then Cassie drove off.

****

The SUV turned off Pioneer Road and onto the winding drive that curved through the cemetery. Cassie pulled over to the side of the road and parked. She climbed from the car and pulled a bouquet of daisies from the backseat. Then she headed off across the lawn.

She was always happy to see the grass freshly cut and the grounds well-tended. Two important people in her life had been laid to rest here.

"Hey," she said with a soulful smile as she strolled up to her dad's grave. She fished through her pocket and removed a wallet-sized photo of her daughter, Katie.

"So, I brought you this new picture of your granddaughter," she said as she knelt down and placed it at the base of the gravestone. "They were taking them of the kids at preschool, so I got an extra one for you."

Cassie took a look at the picture and shook her head with a smile. "She's growing up really fast."

She sat down in front of the gravestone and stared at it for a moment. Then she looked off at the trees and the sky.

"Mom seems like she's doing good. I know she'll always miss you, but I'm glad she has Ted around so she's not so lonely. We try to bring Katie up here to see her every chance we get. Let Mom do her grandmother thing." Cassie chuckled. "She's actually really good at it."

She turned back to the gravestone. "And Katie has you as this awesome grandfather, always watching over her from up there."

She wiped a tear from her eyes.

"Anyway. I just wanted to stop by and say hi. And let you know I'm doing good. And that I really miss you."

She climbed to her feet, then kissed her finger and touched it to the gravestone. "I love you, Dad. Don't stop looking out for me, okay?"

She picked up the daisies and walked across the lawn to another grave site beneath a tree. It was Katie's grave, and the epitaph on her gravestone read:

KATHERINE "KATIE" DUNNE. SLEEP WITH THE ANGELS, BABY GIRL

It gave Cassie a warm feeling in her heart every time she read that. She had no doubt Katie was with the angels. Along with her dad.

She set the daisies on top of the gravestone, then stepped back and just stared at the little grave. A lump filled her throat. It never failed. Every time she came here, she became so swept up in emotions that it was a struggle to find the words to express her enduring gratitude to that little girl. But she would try.

"I brought you some flowers, Katie," she finally said. "Daisies, of course. Your mom said they were your favorites, and they've become mine too. It's how I would know you were around — when I smelled them. And it let me know the darkness would go away."

She paused a moment to give her emotions time to settle.

"So, I have a daughter now. She's four. We named her after you. Someday when she's older, I want to tell her about you." She took a deep breath.

"I owe you so much, Katie. You didn't have to help me, but you did. And you showed me what forgiveness looks like." There was no stopping the tears now as she wiped them with her finger.

"I hope you think I was worth it."

And with that she kissed her fingers and touched them to the gravestone right above Katie's name.

"Goodbye, Katie," she whispered to her little angel.

The Author

Thank you so much for reading my book, and I hope you enjoyed the read. If you have a few minutes, please consider posting a review on Amazon. It's the only way people can find out about us indie authors. And always feel free to message or friend me on *Facebook* and *Goodreads*.

Thanks again!
Tom Lewis

Tom Lewis is an entertainment attorney and former Marine. He's a graduate of Arizona State University and the University of San Diego School of Law.

His first novel, "Aftermath," was published in 2015 as the first part of the "After the Fall" dystopian series.

"Hell: The Possession and Exorcism of Cassie Stevens" is his second novel.

He currently lives in Santa Monica with a bunch of squirrels that mooch off him for food.

29257748R00222

Printed in Great Britain
by Amazon